A Heavy

Give me the crown.

He felt his will fading. Give the

simple thing, after all. Elidor didn't need the crown. . . . What harm could it do? He reached for the metal band on his forehead.

"No!" The girl's voice, faint but frantic, pierced through his thoughts. "If you do, Elidor, you'll die."

Elidor stopped, his fingers pressed against the thin band. "Die?"

"The crown is keeping you alive." The girl's filthy hands twisted into her sodden rags. "If you take it off . . . you will die."

And if you don't, everything you love will suffer your fate.

THE NEW
ADVENTURES

ELIDOR TRILOGY

BY REE SOESBEE

Volume One
CROWN OF THIEVES

Volume Two
THE CRYSTAL CHALICE
(March 2006)

Volume Three
CITY OF FORTUNE
(July 2006)

THE NEW ADVENTURES

ELIDOR TRILOGY
VOLUME I

CROWN OF THIEVES

REE SOESBEE

COVER & INTERIOR ART
Vinod Rams

MIRROR STONE™

CROWN OF THIEVES

Distributed in the United States by Holtzbrinck Publishing. Distributed in Canada by Fenn Ltd.

Distributed to the hobby, toy, and comic trade in the United States and Canada by regional distributors.

Distributed worldwide by Wizards of the Coast, Inc. and regional distributors.

Printed in the U.S.A.

Art by Vinod Rams
First Printing: November 2005
Library of Congress Catalog Card Number: 2004116933

9 8 7 6 5 4 3 2 1

US ISBN: 0-7869-3833-1
ISBN-13: 978-0-7869-3833-9

605-95019740-001-EN

U.S., CANADA,
ASIA, PACIFIC, & LATIN AMERICA
Wizards of the Coast, Inc.
P.O. Box 707
Renton, WA 98057-0707
+1-800-324-6496

EUROPEAN HEADQUARTERS
Hasbro UK Ltd
Caswell Way
Newport, Gwent NP9 0YH
GREAT BRITAIN
Please keep this address for your records

Visit our web site at **www.mirrorstonebooks.com**

For a boy.

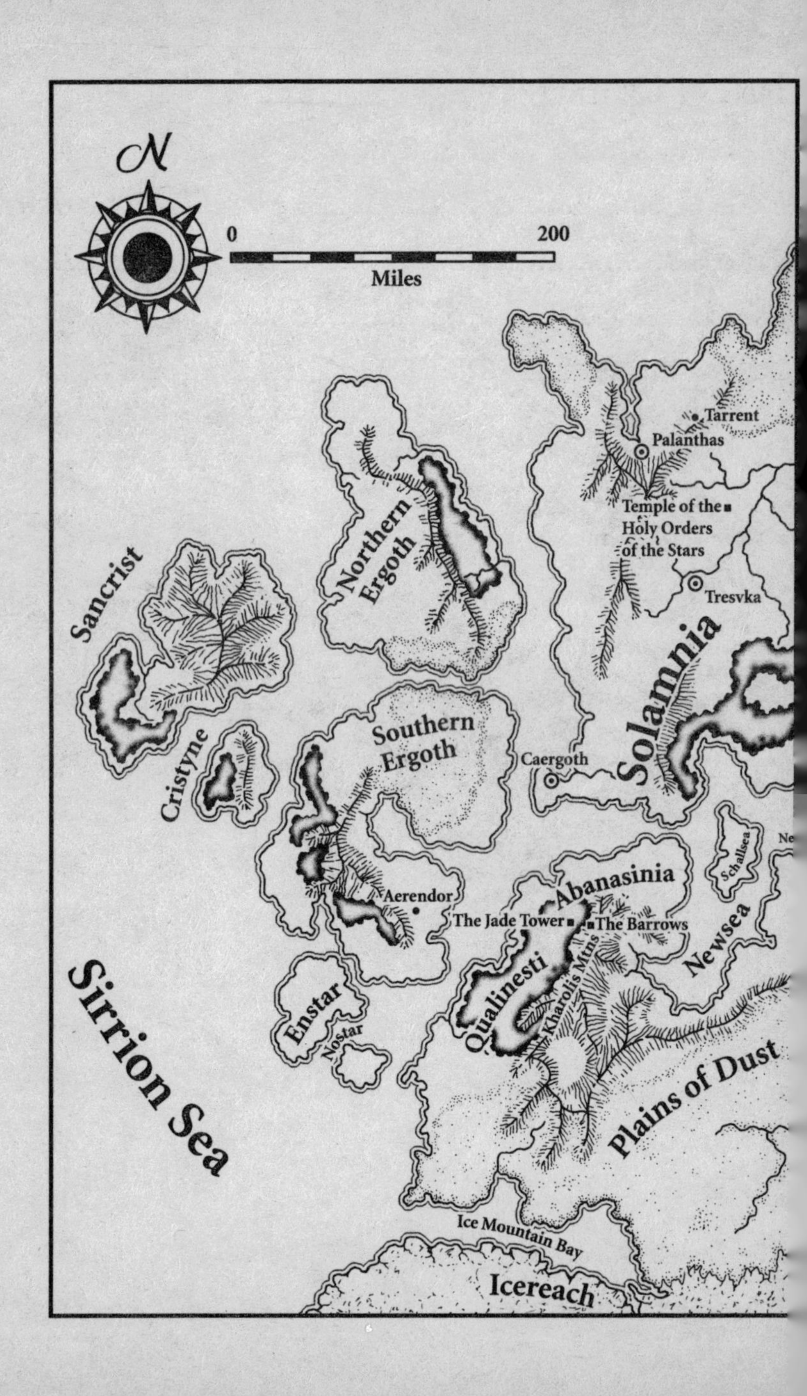
N
0
200
Miles
Tarrent
Palanthas
Temple of the
Holy Orders
of the Stars
Tresvka
Northern
Ergoth
Sancrist
Solamnia
Southern
Ergoth
Caergoth
Cristyne
Schallsea
Abanasinia
Aerendor
The Jade Tower
The Barrows
Newsea
Qualinesti
Kharolis Mtns
Enstar
Nostar
Sirrion Sea
Plains of Dust
Ice Mountain Bay
Icereach

Table of Contents

PROLOGUE

354 AC

Maddoc stood alone in the depths of Navarre, wounded and silent. His plan had worked. He had regained both his freedom and his power, but this was an unexpected complication.

Maddoc walked to the dais and stared for a moment at the twisted body of the elf. Elidor lay where Ophion had left him, the trickle of his blood lending a strange scarlet gleam to the base of Asvoria's throne.

It was a small thing, this little, broken life that fluttered in the pulse of the half-breed elf. No one would even miss him. No one would notice if Maddoc left him here among the dead echoes and buried secrets of Asvoria's tomb, forever entombed in stone and silence.

Maddoc frowned and stared, his hands folded within his sleeves. Then the wizard bent down and placed his hand upon Elidor's shoulder. His chants echoed in the empty tomb, and light sprang through the obsidian corridors, glinting in soft indigo and royal red hues. A rush of air engulfed both Maddoc and Elidor.

Then, they were gone.

"Gieden! Bring me the crown!" Maddoc's words echoed through the hallway of the Jade Tower as he strode into the laboratory with Elidor's body slung over his right shoulder.

Five granite slabs like funeral biers stood one in each corner of the pentagon-shaped room.

All were bare, save one. It was covered with a velvet cloth, the dark purple hiding a vaguely humanoid shape. The cloth fell in waves over the slab, reaching to the floor where powdered runes formed arcane patterns in a circle around it.

A young black-robed wizard hovered over the covered slab. As Maddoc entered the room, he looked up.

"How dare you walk in here unannounced, old man," the black-robed elf spat.

"Silence, apprentice." Maddoc gently laid Elidor on one of the bare stone slabs and then approached the younger wizard.

"I'm not your apprentice anymore." Haughtily, the elf lifted his chin. "Our bargain ended ten years ago when I passed the Test of High Sorcery and became a wizard. I am master of this tower, and I demand to know why you are here."

Maddoc raised a hand and light coalesced around the Gieden's throat. The younger wizard clutched at his neck, writhing in the sudden grasp of magical power. His eyes filled with hatred.

Maddoc leaned close to him and whispered into his former apprentice's ear, the words dark with threat. "I am here, Gieden, because everything has a price." He shook his hand and Gieden's body convulsed in his magical grasp. "Your tests in the Tower were nothing. What you learned under my tutelage . . . that was the true beginning of sorcery. And for that knowledge, you owe me."

Gieden nodded, his too-perfect face smoothing under rigid

control. After a moment, Maddoc released him and the elf fell back against the table.

"Now," Maddoc growled, "where is the crown?"

Gieden flipped his long black braid over his shoulder in an attitude of exasperation. "Why do you want it? It's useless."

Maddoc spun to face him with a growl. "If you have touched it, Gieden, I will—"

"Your trinket is safe." Gieden stormed to one of the bookcases, pulling down a wooden chest the size of a thick spellbook. "No one would want to steal it, old man, so you needn't worry."

He slammed the chest down on the table in front of Maddoc with a disdainful sniff. "I've studied it in your absence. It's a simple strip of metal, a worthless toy with no more magic than a smelted coin. Hardly an 'artifact' at all. I can't see why you bothered to return and take it back."

"I came for it because it is *mine*." Maddoc jerked the box away from Gieden and pulled it closer.

Gieden raised an eyebrow, watching quietly as Maddoc tapped the lock three times, ending the spell that held the box closed. He slowly raised the lid.

Inside lay a simple silver coronet. Maddoc removed it from the box and lifted the coronet into the light. There were no stones upon the crown, only a faint inlay of moonstone vines that traced their way around the band. Long ago, the crown may have been bright and shining, but now it was old and tarnished, the metal blackened with age.

Maddoc's gray eyes were lit with a strange fire. "Ornamentation does not make something powerful. Neither do fanciful words nor elegant robes." Maddoc lowered the coronet and walked back to the stone slab holding Elidor's body. "Listen, boy, and learn.

"This crown was created and enchanted by a master wizard, long before the Tower of Sorcery came to be. He was a member of

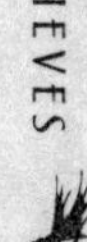

a race of elves whose blood no longer flows on Krynn. This artifact he created is capable of unimaginable power, the power to give life and much, much more. It will not work for any other race, and thus, no one has attempted to use it. No one . . . ," Maddoc stared at Elidor thoughtfully, "until now."

Gieden scuttled behind his former master, leaning forward to examine Elidor's features. He looked back at the older wizard. "Most unusual. A Silvanesti and Kagonesti half-breed? Those races of elves despise one another. Where did you get him?"

"An unexpected find. Really, as much as I dislike it, I have Asvoria to thank."

"Asvoria?" The apprentice spoke the ancient sorceress's name with disbelief. "The ancient sorceress? The one whose power you've been trying to claim?" Gieden laughed. "What has happened?"

"I freed Asvoria and brought her back to life. But in my attempt to acquire a living host for her spirit, the magic went awry. It was during my chase after her that I found him." Maddoc began adjusting Elidor's limp arms, crossing them over his chest. "I have little time to explain the intricacies of the matter. All that you need to know is that she is free, Gieden, and she is growing more powerful by the hour. I must do something to regain control."

"And why bother to test the crown on such a worthless creature? Have you gone soft?" Gieden's tone was almost pleasant. "Perhaps I can find some red robes in a closet somewhere, if you wish to change your clothes."

Maddoc dismissed Gieden's taunt with a shrug of his shoulders. "This elf's blood has a unique signature, perhaps unique enough—with enough traces of elven kind—to trick the crown out of its quiescence, to make it awaken and reveal its power."

Maddoc smoothed Elidor's blond hair across his forehead. Satisfied, the older wizard placed the tarnished silver coronet upon the brow of the dead elf. The crown was too large, slipping easily over the head and hanging loosely just above the ears.

A faint hum like the protest of hinges too long unused rang though the metal. The metal shivered, contracted, and within a breath, lay flat and snug against the brow.

The moonstone vine tracings shone for a moment as though trying to revive their luster, and then the glow faded and died once more.

The two wizards watched and waited.

Nothing.

Maddoc sighed, reaching again for the crown to remove it. His fingers jerked back.

A flicker of black and gold energy tumbled along the crown's length, circling the fallen elf's head with a sudden aura of broken arcs. Then, as quickly as it came, the energy vanished once more and the crown was quiet.

"Nothing." Maddoc's shoulders sagged faintly. "A pity. I had hoped . . . . Ah, well. The only way to remove the crown now is to destroy the wearer." The old wizard raised his hands, his black velvet sleeves falling back around his thin forearms as he began the preparations for a disintegration spell.

"Maddoc, wait." Gieden's hand snapped forward, catching his former mentor's wrist. "Look. He's breathing."

Both wizards froze and stared down at the body. The chest rose and fell ever so lightly, and between the parted lips, a faint hiss of air began to flow.

Maddoc gently pressed his fingers against Elidor's wrist. He shook his head. "It appears it will take days or weeks for the crown to fully awaken his body. I have no time to spare. Asvoria is still at large and I cannot wait." He sighed. "I hoped this experiment would provide me a better weapon to use against her. Unless it is immediately fruitful, then it is of no use to me."

"What will you do now?" Gieden's hungry eyes lingered on the crown.

"I have no choice. I must go to Palanthas and attempt to reforge the Aegis." Maddoc lifted a blue velvet cloth from the ground beside the slab and placed it over the crown and its bearer, covering Elidor from the laboratory's flickering light. "I shall trust you to study my specimen and relay any further improvements with the crown, apprentice." Three swift strides carried him to the door of the laboratory where he turned once more and stared back at Gieden with a steely gaze. "You are capable of that, of course?"

Gieden bowed, the long plait of black hair swinging below his shoulders. "Of course . . . "

Maddoc nodded briskly and continued back into the keep.

"*Master.*" The word was twisted and filled with loathing, too quietly spoken for Maddoc to hear as he walked away.

CHAPTER

1 STORM ON THE HORIZON

"Elidor! Wake up! This is no time for sleeping! The tower's collapsing!"

Sand clogged Elidor's eyes and dust choked his lungs. He coughed, struggling to roll onto his side, but his limbs were heavy and difficult to move.

Again, the shrill voice came. "Get up! Get up! I think we knocked the tower over. We didn't mean to, but there was a wizard and he was throwing spells at us, and then the wall collapsed, and then . . . oh, for Paladine's sake, Elidor! GET UP!"

A tremendous explosion somewhere nearby sent adrenaline rushing through Elidor's veins, and his eyes flew open.

Above Elidor hovered a small face that would have been cherubic had it not been for the panicked expression. "Elidor? Elidor!"

"Sindri?" Elidor murmured, and his voice cracked. The stone slab beneath him was cold and foreign. Elidor looked around, trying to take in his surroundings.

The first thing he noticed was that he was in a laboratory. The second thing he noticed was that it was falling apart, huge chunks of stone dropping from the ceiling. Around him were several bare stone slabs.

There was a small kender tugging on his sleeve—a kender whom he knew. "Sindri," he repeated as his memory returned. "Where are we?"

"It's a wizard's laboratory. It's called the Jade Tower, but it's not made of jade, and it's not going to be a tower much longer, and are you up yet?" The kender's black hair swung wildly over the shoulders of his purple robe as he tore the blue velvet cover off Elidor and tossed it to the ground. He guided Elidor to a sitting position. "We can't stay here. There's a fight going on."

Elidor heard a battle cry, and a feminine figure bearing sword and shield rushed past, through the shards of a table and over the chunks of fallen rubble.

On the other side of the room, he could just make out the figure of a man in black robes, darkness twisted around his fists like serpents. The black wizard brought his fists together, and a clap of thunder shook the keep. Elidor caught a glimpse behind the upraised hood—green-yellow fire where a man would have eyes. They burned with hate.

"Is that Maddoc?" Elidor asked. Something nagged at his memory, but he couldn't place it. The man in black robes didn't look familiar. He was thinner, lighter in build, and the robe clung tightly to his body like a wrapping of shroud over bone. The wizard's hands clawed at the air, summoning power to attack.

A sharp pain burst through Elidor's skull, and he raised his hands to grip his forehead. He felt cool metal there, a thin rim of smooth coldness against his skin.

The warrior raised her sword again and swung the blade toward the wizard's head. Something about her was familiar, but he couldn't place it. Numbly, Elidor watched as the sword shifted in mid flight and was pushed aside by a whirl of greenish-tinged wind. The wizard laughed, a bone-grinding sound.

"That's definitely not Maddoc," Elidor murmured, shaking his head to clear it.

Sindri chuckled. "Oh, no. Maddoc's on our side. Well, he was . . . is . . . sort of. Oh, Elidor! You've missed so much! I can't wait to tell you." The kender pulled on Elidor's vest, struggling to keep the elf in a seated position. "But right now we have to go. It's not safe here." Sindri leaped down, guiding Elidor's legs over the end of the table.

Another clap of thunder, and the keep shook once more. There was a brilliant flash of blue-green light.

The warrior let out a sharp cry. "He's gone! Teleported away, curse it!"

Elidor lowered his legs over the slab and gripped Sindri's shoulder. He leaned forward and was rewarded by a blistering fury of pinpricks through his legs. He toppled forward, right into the arms of the tall, red-haired warrior. He looked up through the faint smoky haze and finally recognized her face. "Catriona!"

"Are you all right?" she asked. "Can you travel?"

"Yes," Sindri answered for him. Catriona put one arm under the elf's slight shoulder, lifting him onto unsteady feet.

Elidor tried to stand, unable to tell if the shuddering was his legs or the unstable floor of the tower.

"Where's Davyn?" Elidor looked over his shoulder, trying to find the rest of his friends.

"He's not here," Sindri said. "Davyn couldn't come with us. It's just me and Catriona, and now you! Well, and the Knight of Solamnia. Oh, and his squire. There's so much to tell you!"

"Once we're outside," Catriona scolded. Elidor stumbled by her side, forcing his legs to work and to place one foot in front of the other.

As they reached the doorway, he glanced back into the collapsing laboratory.

Rubble crumbled from the ceiling and dust obscured his view. Stone slabs, many chipped by the falling roof, stood around the edges of the room.

All of the slabs were bare except one, its purple cover having fallen to the floor in a puddle of smoldering velvet. Elidor's eye caught a glimpse of something behind the stone near the fallen velvet.

Half-hidden by the slab's bulk, a girl looked at him, her eyes the color of summer grass. Brown hair, tangled and matted like an animal's fur, spilled over her shouders. She wore nothing but tattered gray-white rags. He saw no fear on her features, only pity.

Elidor yelled, pointing back into the laboratory, "There's somebody else in there! A girl!"

Startled, Cat looked back as Sindri dashed back into the crumbling room.

He circled the room once. "I don't see anyone!" he called. A rafter crashed to the floor beyond him. "Your eyes are fooling you, Elidor." Sindri raced back to the doorway. "But I guess that's to be expected, what with you having been dead, and all."

"Dead?" Elidor's eyes widened. "Wait . . . what?"

Sindri dodged aside as a hunk of stone crashed through the ceiling. It smashed into the wall just beyond the doorway, leaving a wide opening where it had gone.

"That's our cue," Catriona murmured, gripping Elidor's hand and pulling him through the hole. They fell from the tower, landing hard upon the mossy ground.

Elidor felt the breath whoosh out of his body, and his lungs burned for air. He rolled down a hillside next to Cat. Sindri laughed as he pelted down the hill behind them.

When Elidor came to a stop, he looked up at the remains of a tower, the sides crumpling to nothing but a smoking pile of green stone.

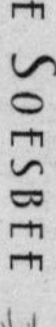

Two figures walked out of the smoke. Elidor felt Catriona's body stiffen, and for a moment he thought they were in danger again. But Sindri jumped up and rushed ahead eagerly.

"Corrigan! Rohawn!" the kender yelled in greeting. "Did you see the black wizard?"

"Saw him? By the Abyss, we've been fighting him down there! We couldn't capture him, blast it all," a man's voice replied, husky with smoke. "He had some sort of trick up his sleeve. That blasted elf!"

The older man walked toward Sindri. His body was thin and spidery, and his long delicate fingers ran constantly over a sparse goatee.

"You should have seen it, Catriona! A real battle of good versus evil!" The other figure, a youth built like a muscular oak tree, followed the older man. "Gieden was throwing fire and lightning and wind, and Corrigan pitched his shield at him to make the spell mess up, and wham! Oh, but he got away."

"No time for that. No time, my boy," the man's voice called out. "We need to get back on his trail. We'll catch him next time. It's as simple as tracking him, discovering his plans, and outmaneuvering them. He'll run out of tricks eventually, and then—by Huma!—we'll have him."

"Meet our new friends," Catriona muttered at Elidor's side, her voice low. "I'll tell you all about them later. Right now, let's just get away from this keep."

Elidor shivered despite the blankets that were packed around him. As Sindri helped Corrigan and Rohawn tend to the horses on the edge of camp, Catriona ladeled soup into a wooden bowl. Her red hair glowed like an ember, and the metal buckles and plates sewed onto her armor caught the weak light of the campfire.

She handed Elidor a bowl of soup. He leaned closer to her, pitching his voice low so that only she could hear him.

"Cat, where are we? What happened? Where are the others? Where's Davyn?"

"They've gone to Caergoth," Cat replied softly, "to help Nearra. We stayed behind . . . to find you."

"Find me?" Elidor frowned. "I was lost?"

"Not exactly." Cat dropped another piece of kindling on the small fire, and then sat beside him on the log. "What's the last thing you remember?"

Elidor tried to think, pushing away the haze of weariness that blurred his mind. "I remember . . . Tarrent. The village where I—" He cleared his throat. "The village in the mountains near Navarre."

"Do you remember the tomb?"

"Asvoria's tomb. Yes. It was underground. I remember visiting Tarrent and following Davyn through the caves and into the tomb. Davyn and I were hurrying to catch up to you. We found Nearra in the tomb—Nearra, Asvoria. The sorceress took over Nearra's body, and we were there to help her. Then I remember . . . pain . . . " He winced, closing his eyes. "And Maddoc!" Elidor's head snapped up. "Did he betray us?"

"No. No." Cat stared down, suddenly uncomfortable. "He helped us—Sindri especially. Even without his magic, the old man was useful. He knew how to defeat Asvoria, taught Sindri a few magic tricks, and . . . told us where to find you."

"What do you mean?"

"Asvoria's tomb was a disaster. The Aegis sword was destroyed, Nearra was lost, and you . . . " Cat looked down, scooping up a few more twigs and feeding them to the fire.

Elidor grabbed her arm. "I died. That's what you were going to say. I died, didn't I?"

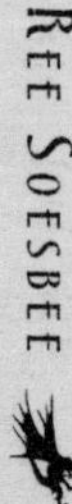

"Yes. No. Oh, Paladine. Elidor, I don't know." Tears lit Cat's green eyes. She knelt by his side, placing her hand on his knee. "Asvoria and her familiar killed you. We were badly injured, the Aegis was broken, and it seemed that all we had come to the tomb for was lost. We barely escaped with our lives. We spent the next several months—months, Elidor—helping Davyn and Nearra, stopping Asvoria, and rescuing Nearra from Asvoria's evil power."

Elidor clenched his fist. "So you did it? You saved her?"

Catriona nodded stiffly. "But we never forgot you. After we defeated Asvoria, Sindri and I decided to leave the others. We journeyed through Solamnia with Maddoc, and that's when he told us the truth about what had become of you. He said he was too old and tired to come with us, but he gave us precise directions, said we'd find you here—at the Jade Tower. I can't believe . . . ." Her voice broke slightly, and she looked down. "I can't believe you've been here all this time. I'm so sorry we couldn't come sooner."

"How long has it been?" Elidor asked quietly.

Catriona brushed her eyes roughly with the back of her hand, coughing away a sniffle. "Nearly a year."

Elidor's heart sank. Everyone he knew, everyone he cared about, had thought he was dead for a whole year.

"How are you feeling, Elidor?" Sindri bounced over from the edge of the campsite, bearing another horse blanket to tuck around Elidor. "I was hoping that wizard would have done all sorts of things to you! Like turn you into a dragon or make a magic sword out of you. He didn't do anything like that, did he? Anything interesting?"

Elidor sighed. The kender's idea of "interesting" was very different from his own. "I'm fine, Sindri."

"Better than fine! You're alive!" Cat reached out and squeezed Elidor's hand. "You really couldn't ask for much more 'fine' than that, could you?" She slapped her knee and stood up. "Now, who's hungry?"

While Catriona and Sindri served themselves soup from the pot over the fire, Elidor's eyes fell on the others in their company—the man and the boy he had just met.

The man—a knight—had moved closer to the fire. He sat on a stone, using a soft cloth to polish a bit of plate mail. He was a slender, weasely-looking man with blond hair that hung from a ponytail as though it couldn't muster the energy to escape. A thin mustache framed too-thin lips.

His squire was no more than a boy of fifteen, a burly youth with arms the size of tree trunks. He hefted a hatchet and chopped a fallen branch into pieces. He hummed as the axe rose and fell above his head in sturdy rhythm. "Corrigan, how much do we need?" the youth asked over his shoulder without breaking the rhythm of the axe.

"Only a bit more, squire," the thin man answered, looking up. "Although Catriona feels we need a larger blaze to keep her elf friend warm, I am rather opposed to burning the entire woods down in the endeavor." His voice was wispy and high-pitched, the words chosen with deliberate care.

"Where did you meet these people?" Elidor whispered to Sindri.

The kender smiled and jumped up. "Oh! In all the excitement, I completely forgot to introduce you." Sindri bowed, sweeping his hand past his knees with a flourish. "Elidor, this is Knight Corrigan Stormwatch and his squire, Rohawn. They're from the Knights of Solamnia. Isn't that wonderful?"

"And what is a Knight of Solamnia and his squire doing here in the far reaches of . . . " Elidor looked to Catriona.

"Abanasinia," she said.

"Well, we met your friends quite by accident on our way from Solamnia. We were headed to the Jade Tower as well." Corrigan cleared his throat. "The master of the tower, Gieden, is a black wizard. That sort of thing has to be put down, you know, lad."

"Put down?" Elidor repeated.

"Yes, well, not all the Knights of Solamnia feel as I do—that black wizards themselves are a plague on Krynn. But according to the law, I'm allowed to do battle only against those who actually perform evil acts . . . that can be proven . . . you know . . . " The knight's words faltered, and he waved the polishing cloth. "But there are always reasons, always reasons."

"We don't need much reason to go after Gieden, though." Rohawn dumped a load of wood beside the campfire that would fill a small cart.

The knight chuckled. "Indeed. Gieden's a bad nut, even among bad nuts. He puts the 'ack' in 'black'—wizardry, that is." Corrigan snorted at his own humor even though no one else laughed. He lowered his head, smoothing his mustache, and did not meet Elidor's eyes as he continued. "Gieden's wanted for crimes among the Solamnics. Bad business, he is."

"We'll catch him, Corrigan," Rohawn said seriously. "Don't worry, we'll—"

Before the boy could say anything else, Corrigan silenced him with a rough *heh-hem!* Rohawn ran off for another load of wood.

"Isn't it lucky that we bumped into these two on our way to find you?" Sindri climbed onto Elidor's log and perched beside him. "We knew you were in the tower, and they were going the same way, so we all went together! But then there was a fight and Gieden started throwing fireballs, and Rohawn had that big sword of his out and was swinging it all over the place, and I said to myself, 'Well, Elidor has to be here somewhere. Maddoc said so!' And I started exploring, and then I found you!

"You were on a slab, just lying there with the black wizard standing over you." Sindri jumped up, waving his arms slowly to pantomime the looming figure. "I think he had a knife! A knife,"

the kender rushed on, building the story inch by inch as he caught the attention of Corrigan, Rohawn, and Catriona. "I saw the wizard, ready to cut Elidor's head off with his sword—"

"Wasn't it a knife a minute ago?" Rohawn asked, holding another load of wood in his arms.

"Just go with it," Catriona whispered back.

Sindri stood up on the log, his arms waving madly in a sawing motion. "But before Gieden could strike, I jumped up on to the slab and . . . grabbed his hand!"

"No, you didn't." Rohawn's thick brows furrowed. "You were running around the slab like a mouse, screaming your head off. I saw you—" Catriona's stern look stopped Rohawn mid-sentence.

"And then, just . . . as . . . he . . . brought . . . the knife . . . down," Sindri's arm jerked back and forth with each word, mimicking a titanic struggle, "Catriona charged in the room with her sword at the ready to save you from the foe!"

"Sindri, old fellow, you've got something wrong," Corrigan chuckled. "Gieden wasn't up in the tower with you, he was down in the entrance hall fighting us! And I've the singe marks to prove it."

Elidor laughed along with the knight. "It's true, Sindri. How could Gieden be in two places at once?"

"I . . . I don't know. He probably teleported!" Sindri waved his arms about wildly, threatening to throw himself off the log in his excitement.

"Teleported?" Corrigan's face fell. He sighed, stirring the fire's bright coals with a long stick. "He couldn't do that . . . before."

"Don't worry, Master," Rohawn said cheerily. "We'll find him again, especially now that we have him." Rohawn pointed at Elidor.

Catriona stared at the squire. "What do you mean?"

Sindri looked up at Cat. "Oh! We were talking and I told Corrigan and Rohawn that we would help them get Gieden. Corrigan thinks that Gieden'll be looking for Elidor."

"Wait, wait," Catriona protested. "You're saying you want to use Elidor as bait?"

"Well, the wizard did fight pretty hard to keep him." Sindri made a gesture like a knife-fighter, pantomiming the battle from his wild tale. "I bet he wants him back. Or maybe just that funny-looking crown that Elidor's got on his head. And, anyway, I think that . . . "

While Sindri continued talking, Elidor reached out and pulled a sharp dagger from the sheath at his side. He stared into the reflective blade, catching his image in its shine. Indeed, there was a silver coronet upon his head. He'd nearly forgotten about it in all the excitement. His hand reached up uncertainly, and for the second time, he felt the metal twined about his brow. Elidor tugged at it, but it did not move. Strange. Yet, it caused no harm being there and seemed innocent enough.

"And what about that girl Elidor saw?" Sindri finished. "Gieden's probably keeping her prisoner. We should rescue her!"

"What girl?" Corrigan asked.

Rolling her eyes, Catriona answered. "Elidor said he saw a girl in the keep. I didn't see anyone when we entered the upstairs chambers, nor was there anyone on the stairs. Did someone go out past you in the hallway downstairs?'

"No, my lady," Corrigan said, smoothing his mustache thoughtfully. "There was no other way out of that laboratory, either."

"When I arrived to rescue her, Gieden probably teleported her away, too!" Sindri said. "Don't you want to help that girl, Cat?"

"Not if it means putting Elidor in harm's way again!" Catriona said.

Corrigan set his polished plate mail aside. "Nothing against your skills, my lady, but if you want to keep your friend safe, you'd

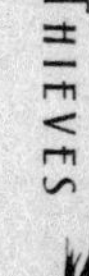

be better off traveling with us. If Gieden goes after him, you could use our steel in your midst. You'll need more than one warrior to fight the likes of a black wizard and it doesn't seem your friend there will be up to fighting anytime soon. I would be more than happy to offer our services." Corrigan half-bowed to Catriona, and she rolled her eyes.

Elidor put his hand on Catriona's arm. "He does have a point, Catriona. And I have a feeling that girl I saw was in danger. I want to help her. It's only right."

"Fine, it's your life." Catriona sighed and put her head in her hands.

As the others made plans around him, Elidor slipped down against the log, drawing his blanket up close against his chin. He tried to stay aware and listen to their words, but weariness had already begun to overtake him. The flickering of the flame drew his attention, and Elidor felt his body begin to relax.

When he felt a hand on his shoulder, Elidor smiled. "Cat," he murmured, opening one eye, "I'm trying to sleep here."

But Cat was already asleep, curled up with the others around the smoldering fire. Elidor shuddered and blinked, wondering what had awakened him.

Then he saw the figure standing alone just beyond the fire pit. The figure's black robes were drawn in close against its gaunt frame. Green-yellow eyes burned sharply beneath the hood.

It was the wizard from the tower.

"Cat!" Elidor tried to shout, but his voice caught in his throat.

The black figure stepped forward.

Elidor pushed himself to his feet, staggering backward as the arm of the robed figure reached for him. Elidor scrambled to find a weapon—a sword, a dagger, anything. Still, the black-robed shape advanced relentlessly. Its hand reached out, fingers pincered.

Elidor twisted, calling on his dulled reflexes to avoid the touch, but he was too sluggish. His movements were slowed by a year of sleep and fatigue.

Icy fingers clamped around Elidor's forearm and a searing pain shot through him.

He gripped one of the logs by the fire, attempting to swing it to block the figure's advance, but the log spun out of his hand as if torn away by some powerful magic.

The black-robed figure's other hand reached relentlessly toward Elidor's face, fingers brushing against the elf's skin with a clawed sting.

All the color left the world and everything changed—everything except the claws around his throat and the burning eyes within the hood.

Elidor found himself on top of a cliff overlooking a large elven city. The walls were gray like marble, veined through with age. Three tiers topped by palisades and spiral towers rose like contemplative trees above the city streets, and bridges arched between them, hundreds of feet above the ground. The city's gate was semicircular, shaped like the sun against the horizon and gilded with glittering metal. At the top of the gate shone a symbol—a crescent silver moon overwhelmed by a full black moon. It gleamed in the darkness, the black moon eating the brilliance of the silver one. The image struck Elidor, burning itself into his mind.

Carts littered the streets and the cries of city life echoed in his ears in a strange, unknown elven tongue. The black figure's hand was still clamped around Elidor's forearm, struggling to draw him close, and the world changed again.

"Who are you?" Elidor screamed as the terrain shifted around them. The city aged, blackened, and died. The towers crumbled, arches sagging into ruin. As they did, Elidor saw a figure, a woman in white robes with a stoic, regal demeanor standing within the crumbling city walls. She lifted bloodstained palms, touching the

stone of the city, smearing dark blotches on the gray and white marble. Then, just as suddenly, the white-robed figure crumbled from within, the form flickering into ash.

"What do you want?" Elidor tried to jerk his arm away from the black robed man, but the man's fingers were like iron bands.

The crown.

The voice seemed to come from both the figure and within Elidor's own mind.

"The crown?" Elidor's hand flew to his forehead, feeling the metal there, hot and strange against his skin. "Why? What is it? Why do you want it?"

Magic crackled around them both, leaping from the black-robed figure's hand. Fire rippled across Elidor's skin, but did not burn him. An enraged cry came from beneath the cloak, and the hand on Elidor's arm tightened painfully.

Sparks flickered, magic coiled and released around them, threatening to engulf them both. Ash from the city's decay flew about them, half-blinding Elidor, and he struck out blindly. His fist connected. With a sharp, sudden crack, colors trickled into the black and white world.

Images flooded Elidor's mind: a golden throne; a man in unadorned, plain black robes made of buttery leather; bloodstained floors and roadways lined with the dead; words in Elvish, but no form that he had ever known. The dialect was strange and difficult to understand, yet faintly familiar, like something Elidor had heard within a dream.

From the top of the cliff, he saw a cairn—a stack of boulders topped by a stone that was shaped like a knight on a rearing steed. Beneath it, screams floated up into the air, filling the night with the howls of trapped, tortured souls. Elidor could feel them, legions of eternally faithful soldiers willing to make others suffer in order to fulfill their oaths.

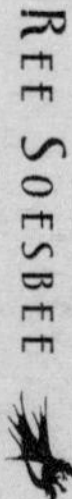

Suddenly, the thick sod beneath the cairn tore open. Spirits, their armor as white as bleached bone, rose from the grave. Their breath was as cold as frost.

Next came a vision of a silver crown bathed first in light, and then in blood. Elidor gasped when he saw it, recognized it as the metal that bound his forehead.

Give me the crown.

"I know who you are," Elidor growled and faced the hooded man. "Gieden. The black wizard. You did something to me when I was in your tower. You put this crown on my head and now you want it back. You can't have it. If the crown destroyed this city, then it is powerful, and I won't give it to you."

"Push him out, Elidor." The voice was a new one, soft and meek. Elidor turned and saw a girl kneeling beside him. It was the wretched-looking maiden he had seen in the laboratory. He recognized her tangled dark hair and her haunted eyes. "You can do it," she whispered. "Don't let him in. That's what he wants."

Elidor cried out, shutting his eyes. The icy cold claws sank deeper into his forearm. He felt his skin split and blood trickle down his arm.

Give me the crown.

He felt his will fading. Give the crown away? It seemed like a simple thing, after all. Elidor didn't need the crown. It was just something that he'd woken up with and hadn't bothered to investigate. What harm could it do? His other hand reached for the metal band on his forehead, fingers sliding against the metal.

"No!" The girl's voice, faint but frantic, pierced through his thoughts. "If you do, Elidor, you'll die."

Elidor stopped, his fingers pressed against the thin band. "Die?"

"The crown is keeping you alive." The girl's filthy hands twisted into her sodden rags. "If you take it off . . . you will die."

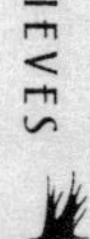

And if you don't, everything you love will suffer your fate.

A new set of shadowy images flitted through Elidor's vision—his parents, the village where he'd been raised, then Vael. Her white hair flowed down her back, and a laugh played on her curved lips. She was beautiful in his memories, with none of the sorrow that he had brought reflected in her eyes. Vael . . .

Elidor tore his arm out of the wizard's grasp and staggered backward into darkness.

Elidor sat up with a ragged, choking gasp. His hand flew to his forehead where ice-cold metal throbbed, bitter and cold against his flesh. The campsite was silent, sparks flying up from the fire as a log cracked and fell in two. He jerked back the sleeve of his tunic, staring in surprise at the raw and bloody marks upon his flesh.

A dream, but not entirely an illusion.

Elidor looked over at three sleeping forms huddled just within the firelight. He recognized Catriona, Sindri, and the knight Corrigan.

Another figure moved close, stepping from the trees at the edge of the clearing.

Elidor leaped to his feet, drawing a dagger faster than the eye could follow. But in an instant, he realized that the form was too broad and moved too clumsily to be that of the black wizard.

"Are you all right, Elidor?" It was Rohawn, Corrigan's squire.

The faint light from the fire clearly showed the worry on the young man's face. Elidor nodded, shaken. His dagger slipped once more into the sheath. "Fine. I'm all right."

But he knew that nothing was going to be right again for a very long time.

CHAPTER

2 Darkness

"Sure and certain, I did see something." On foot, Rohawn squinted at the dark, twisting path. Lunitari hung in the sky above them.

Rohawn had woken them all up when he'd returned to camp and urged them to follow him down the path into the forest.

"I'm glad the falling tower didn't scare away our horses!" Sindri smiled.

Corrigan looked at him. "Not that they had much choice, since we left them tied to a tree. We are fortunate they were close enough that we could get to them and still follow Gieden. We haven't lost any time at all."

"Look! Tracks." Rohawn pointed. "There's a sandal print there . . . and there."

Catriona kneeled in the dirt and raked a twig across the ground. "You're right. I'm no hunter, but they don't look to have been rained on or crossed over. They must be fresh."

"They're Gieden's, I bet." Sindri looked up at Catriona. "See, Cat, I was right! Gieden came looking for Elidor. He probably has the girl with him too."

"I think they're Gieden's prints. There's no sign of a girl's." Catriona brushed away the leaves that had fallen over the tracks.

"Maybe he's carrying the girl. Or floating her above the ground! Or . . . or maybe she's making herself float! She could be a sorceress too!"

"I doubt it." Elidor shifted uncomfortably in his saddle. "She seemed poor. Her clothing was torn, the edges ragged. She was far too dirty to be a sorceress."

"Then why did he have her there?" Sindri wondered aloud. "Who was she?"

"She could have been working for him," Corrigan mused, stroking his goatee.

Elidor shrugged. He had no answer to the questions. Why had he seen her in his dream last night? And what of Gieden? If he wanted the crown so badly, how long would it be before he came to take it for his own? "The girl can tell us herself when we find her."

"Well, if you're determined to rescue this girl, we should go this way—follow Gieden's sandal prints." Catriona brushed her hands on her leather pants and stood. "Or at least follow the path. I may not be the best tracker in the world, especially by moonlight, but this trail has to go somewhere."

"Lady Catriona is quite right." Corrigan spurred his gray gelding lightly and pointed the horse's head toward a space in the trees.

Cat sighed as she placed her foot in the stirrup and climbed aboard her own brown roan steed. "Corrigan, stop calling me that."

"What?"

"Lady." Drawing up the reins, she followed. "I'm not a knight, and I'm not interested in your pretty titles. Keep them, and your 'honor,' away from me." Bitterness oozed through her words, enough to make even Elidor wince.

"You are a lady born of the land of Solamnia, Catriona, and training or not, I shall treat you as one. Whether you disdain your heritage is not my concern. " Corrigan pressed his horse forward on the path. He didn't see the glare Catriona shot at him, but Elidor did.

Rohawn trotted up beside Cat's horse. "I'm sorry about him, miss. He's a bit set in his ways." He jogged beside Cat's stirrup, keeping up with the horse with seemingly little effort.

"Well, he'd better learn that those 'ways' won't serve him very well outside Solamnia, Rohawn," she retorted. "Solamnia is like an egg—pretty ideas all wrapped up in a fragile shell that no one ever talks about. One of these days it's going to break, and everyone who believes in that illusion is going to wake up to a very cold reality."

"Oh, Cat." Sindri clasped his arms around her waist. "You're so depressing."

"It's true, Sindri. You've seen it. All the 'honor' and 'duty' in the world don't mean anything to starving families, or lands ruled by tyranny, or people tortured by wizards like Gieden and Asvoria."

Elidor moved his horse close to Catriona's and murmured, "Cat. I know that you . . . that you're . . . I mean, you have your own history with the Solamnics. Aren't you afraid you're judging Corrigan based on that?"

"Yeah, Cat. Corrigan's just trying to be nice. And Rohawn's a squire like you were!" Sindri reached over and tousled the youth's dark hair.

"You were a squire too?" Rohawn's brown eyes were wide. "Really?"

Cat's nod was sharp. "Yes."

"But she and her knight were captured by bandits! The bandits killed her knight, and she couldn't stop them. So she got thrown out of the Order, and . . . oh, it's a terribly tragic story." Sindri chattered. "Shall I tell it?"

"I think you just did," she growled.

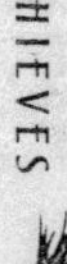

Elidor interrupted. "Why did you become a squire, Rohawn?"

"Why?" Rohawn shrugged, the hilt of his greatsword rising and falling over his shoulder. "I guess it's because I like knights. And I like Solamnia. My parents live there. None of my family have ever been knights, or noble, or anything. We live in a little town just outside Solanthus. My father is a farmer. He raises flax, which gets spun into linen. Me, though, I don't want to be a farmer, so I went to the knights and asked if I could help out. Corrigan made me his squire."

"I like Corrigan." Sindri bounced on the horse, trying to urge it ahead. "I think he's on some kind of a quest. Right, Rohawn?"

Rohawn blushed, suddenly uncomfortable. "He just wants to stop Gieden. That's all. It's not really a quest. I mean, it is, but—"

"It sounds like a quest to me—a fool's quest." Cat shook her head. "Gieden's long gone. We're all wasting our time."

"I think Gieden wants us to find him," Elidor said in a low, serious voice. "In fact, I know he does."

All eyes turned toward him.

"How do you know that?" Sindri asked eagerly.

"Because he wants this." Elidor's fingers roamed upward to the silver circlet on his brow. "I had a dream last night. I know it sounds foolish, but it was about Gieden. I think he was trying to convince me to give him the crown."

"Can I see it?" Sindri asked, reaching toward Elidor and leaning precariously over his horse's flanks.

"No," Elidor jerked away and his steed shuffled sideways. "I can't take it off."

"Might be you haven't tried hard enough," Sindri piped up. "I got my hand stuck in a jug once. Had to put grease on my fist just to get it out."

"You too?" Rohawn sighed.

Elidor shook his head. "No, you don't understand. I could take it off if I tried hard enough. But I think if I did that . . . ," the words sounded strange even to Elidor, "I'd die."

Catriona twisted around in her saddle, staring at Elidor. "What do you mean, 'die'?"

"I think the crown is keeping me alive." He met her gaze frankly. "You said I died, Catriona. You didn't say how I was brought back. Well, the only thing that's different about me is this crown on my head, and it's powerful enough that Gieden wants it."

"Which means, of course, that we can't let him have it, eh?" Corrigan interrupted. He had stopped his horse, allowing the group to catch up without them noticing. He ran a hand through his long, limp ponytail. Catriona and the knight exchanged uncomfortable glances, and then Corrigan continued. "Obviously, if you're right, Gieden will come a-looking for that bauble. But he knows he can't defeat us alone. One wizard? Against a Knight of Solamnia, a warrior, and . . . "

"A great wizard!" Sindri bounced proudly.

"Yes! Well." Corrigan nodded sagely. "Our little group here is certainly more than one wizard can handle. That's their great flaw, these black wizards. They don't make allies easily, and against a group well-prepared for them, they have a rough time getting the advantage without blowing their power out in one great bang. We'll have to stick close to you, lad. Very close, indeed." His thin eyebrows tightened together over beady eyes. "We can't let Gieden get away again. I won't allow it."

"Yes, sir," Rohawn said quickly. "Don't worry, sir."

They broke the crest of the forest then, staring out onto a great rocky plain tinted reddish in the light of Lunitari. The trees were withered and dead along the edge of the path, their branches browned and twisted by age. The plain was hilly, dipping and rising like an ocean's waves. Across the rolling grassland, the

path became a faint road of brown marked by tall stacks of boulders that jutted up here and there.

"More footprints." Cat peered down from horseback. "Crossing down into the plain. Clear enough that even in this moonlight I can pick them out. If Gieden came this way, he wasn't trying to hide his passage. I think he's more interested in traveling with speed."

"Then we've got him on the run," Corrigan said. "Let's go. He won't get away this time."

Catriona leaned back, shooting Elidor a glance before her horse leaped into a trot and followed Corrigan down the winding road. Elidor sighed, lifting his reins and tapping his steed lightly with his heels. With a snort, the horse followed, trailing its companions onto the plain.

"Elidor?" The voice took him by surprise and he pulled back on the reins swiftly enough to make his horse whinny and jerk to a stop.

Who could have called his name? It had come from behind him, the voice rusty sounding. He looked back over his shoulder in confusion.

The girl stood in the shadows under a tree, her gray dress hanging off her frame in long, trailing rags. For a moment, he thought she was an apparition.

"Elidor," she called again, more firmly this time. Her amber-green eyes, the color of the grasses on the plain, stared at him from beneath tangled masses of dark hair. She was not Kagonesti—a wild elf—which had been his first thought when he saw her kneeling beside the stone slab in the Jade Tower. Yet she was not human, either. The delicate pointed tips of her ears showed through the mass of dark, matted hair.

"Are you coming, Elidor?" Sindri yelled. "You're going to be left behind!"

Elidor glanced toward his friend. All of his companions were ahead of him, their horses pacing into the waving grasses of the plain.

He waved at Sindri. "Come here! The girl, she's—"

But as he looked back, he realized that the girl wasn't there at all. Sindri craned his neck, trying to see past Elidor as Catriona's horse carried them both away. "What is it?"

"The girl—she was just standing . . . " Elidor let his voice trail away. There were no footprints at the base of the tree, no marks standing out in the clear dirt where the oak's roots reached into the ground.

In fact, there was no sign that she had ever been there at all.

CHAPTER

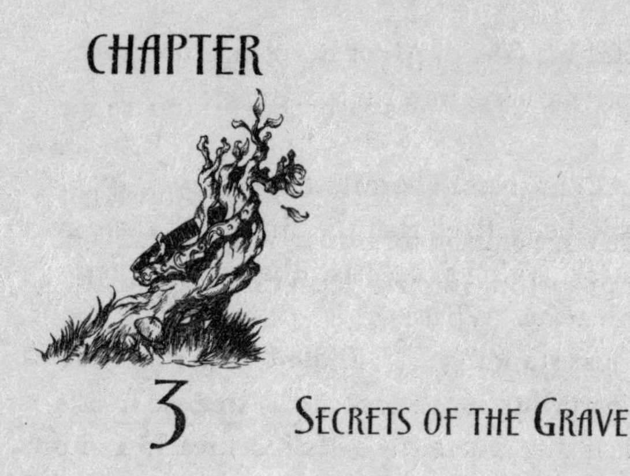

3 SECRETS OF THE GRAVE

A thin, whispering wind howled faintly across the plain, carrying the scent of decay. The tracks led up to a slight hill on the grassy plain, a rise that looked as if it had been created by human hands, not shaped by wind or earth. It was a grass-covered hill that stood two times the height of a man and as wide as a cottage, and the red light of Lunitari made it look even more eerie.

Many large stones had been placed on top, making the entire structure even taller. The lowest rocks of the formation were bigger than a man, and wide, leaning against one another with smaller rocks placed atop them. Once, the stones had been covered by inscriptions and symbols of protection, but the wind had worn those away to only faint rivulets in the granite. The topmost stones of the mound formed the vague silhouette of a horseman.

Elidor let out a quick breath. This was the cairn from his dream.

Sindri climbed atop the hill, peering in through cracks in the stones.

"There's something under here!" he cried eagerly.

"Of course there is," Corrigan said. "This is a barrow where people used to bury their dead. The hill is hollow, Sindri, and the pile of stones is called a cairn. The stones cover the entrance to the barrow room."

"Wow!" Sindri tried to push his way through the big stones, but none of the cracks were large enough for him to wriggle through. "You're right. I can see an opening in there. I just can't— oomph!— get to it."

"It's big." Rohawn whistled.

Catriona leaned against the stones, crossing her arms and staring out across the rolling territory. "Of course it is. Barrows house a great number of bodies. They weren't built just for one dead hero, but for groups of people—villages, destroyed by plague or fire; or heroes, left in a place where their deeds would be commemorated and remembered."

Corrigan pointed at two long marks in the grass. "Look at that! One of the boulders has been moved recently. It's likely the wizard's gone down into the barrow. Only a foul wizard would disturb a hero's resting place. The coward."

"So let's follow it!" Sindri said.

Corrigan stroked his goatee. "We could, though I think none of us will fit through any of the cracks here. How did that cursed wizard do it?"

Elidor knelt near Corrigan, his fingers tracing the edge of a crack. Dirt was pushed up around the edges, and a there was a faint line in the dusty ground. Through the crack, he could see an open space in the center of the rock pile and a patch of darkness that marked an opening in the floor of some kind of cave.

"Look." Elidor's fingers traced the mark. "This stone must move like a door. If it moved, then we could get to the opening beyond, the top of the hill. And I bet, from there, we could find steps down into the hollow part of the earth mound that we're standing on."

"Oh? Oh, yes! I see it now." Corrigan stared blankly at the

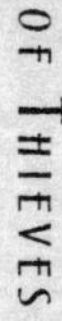

ground, and then stood quickly with a smile. "Well, if it opens, then we can force it."

Elidor stared for a moment at Corrigan's thin arms. "Oh, not me, no, no," Corrigan laughed. "Rohawn!"

The bull-like boy raised his head, looking up from the horses. "Yes, sir?"

"Come over here and take a look at this rock."

Rohawn crossed to his knight's side and squinted at the shadow between the stones. One of the boulders, the one Sindri had tried to wiggle past, was set apart from the others. The width between the big stones was just large enough that Rohawn could fit his ham fingers in the opening. Corrigan stroked his thin mustache. "Can you get that blasted rock out of the way?"

Catriona sighed, feet kicking up small dust clouds as she walked. "You'll never be able to move it. It's too big. There has to be a mechanism somewhere." Cat pushed experimentally at the block of stone, her weight shifting it not at all. "Maybe between the four of us, we might be able to force it enough to squeeze through." She leaned back, crossing her arms and sighing. "But it will take a while."

Rohawn jammed his fingers in farther, placing both hands in the opening. With brows furrowed, he bent himself to the task. Muscles on his arms bulged, straining like twin oxen yoked to a cart. He closed his eyes and leaned into the stone, face reddening.

"Rohawn, you can't possibly—" Catriona started, but Corrigan laid his hand upon her arm.

"Just watch."

Sindri's eyes got wider and wider as the crack in the stone began to pull apart. Rohawn redoubled his efforts, arching his back and pulling with all his might. The stone protested, screeching on ancient hinges, but it moved. It swung open like a door, and the smaller rocks on top of the pile of stone shifted, dropping dust and earth down on Rohawn's head, but the pile held steady. Cat gaped

as she watched Rohawn slowly swing the boulder away from the pile, inch by inch, until the space between two large boulders was wide enough for a man to squeeze through. Rohawn let go, sitting down on the ground with a solid thump.

"Strongest lad I've ever seen." Corrigan thumped Rohawn's shoulder with a weasely grin. "One of the reasons I took him on, don't you know?"

"I can't believe it," Catriona said. "Rohawn, how did you do it?"

Sheepishly, the youth grinned. "I just pulled."

The passage beyond was dark, and a cold wind blew up from the earth below. A small cave was inside the pile of tall stones, an empty hollow surrounded by the piled boulders. At the center of the tiny room was a square hole in the earth.

Sindri scampered into the small room, kneeling down and peering into the cavernous hole in the center. Elidor followed behind him. The smell of earth and old grass wafted up from below, floating on the wind now drifting in behind them.

"There are stairs here that go right down into the ground!" Sindri craned his head, staring down a long flight of stone steps. The dust on the stone was clearly disturbed, bearing three clear impressions of footprints.

"Oooh . . . and you were right," Sindri whispered, his voice echoing clearly inside the stone chamber. "Someone's been here."

"Get a torch," Elidor gestured to Catriona.

Catriona pulled one from her saddle pack and lit it.

Corrigan nodded to Rohawn as he drew a sword from its sheath at his side. "Might be fighting down there," the thin knight noted. "We'd best be prepared."

Sindri leaped down the stairs two at a time, pausing at the edge of the sunlight. "I'm ready. I have my magic spells all prepared. Don't worry, Corrigan. This will be easy!"

The stairs were steeply sloped, cut into the earth and stone by ancient hands. More carvings—these less worn—decorated the passage on both sides. Catriona stepped into the hole in the earth, holding her torch before her and staring at the stonework.

"These look like religious scenes," she said quietly, the faint echo of her words welling up from below. "See? That moon, above a city. Then here, farther down." She took another step into the passage. "The city's on fire and the moon looks as big as the sun."

Elidor followed her down slowly, his hands on his knives. He stopped when he saw the painting Catriona stood beside. It was a drawing of a gate topped by the symbol of a silver crescent moon being destroyed by a full black moon. "I know that symbol," he whispered. "I saw it in a dream."

Cat didn't hear him. "This passage is old. The language under these images seems elven. What do you make of it, Elidor?"

He shook himself out of the reverie, glad that Cat hadn't noticed. "It is Elvish—but only a few words make sense. It's a dialect I've never seen before, or some odd way of spelling words. I don't know." Gripping his sleeve in his fist, Elidor scrubbed at the wall to remove some of the grit. "This is 'sun.' And this is 'soldier.' Over here, looks like a phrase—'the crown shall . . . ' I can't tell. 'Save them'? 'Destroy them'? The word is very strange."

"Look down here." Sindri skipped ahead. Slowly, cautiously, the others followed.

Before them, the stairway twisted in a long, slow spiral. It ended in an archway covered in more of the strange symbols. The arch was not a traditional 'u' shape, but more of a circle, forcing Elidor and the others to step over the lip of the stone as they entered the room beyond.

It was a large room shaped much like a bubble in the deep stone, with sloping sides and a faintly arched ceiling. All along the walls were small alcoves, arched circles like the one they had stepped through, but only a fourth the size.

Cat, Rohawn, and Corrigan spread out to investigate the room. Elidor walked to one of the arches, peering into it.

"What are you looking at, Elidor?" Sindri bounced up and down near him, trying to see inside the alcove. Cat walked toward them, bringing the light so they could see.

A skeleton lay there, rotted and dry, scraps of flesh hanging from its bones like threads of a linen shirt. Its rotted hands clutched a rusted sword and a shield covered in spiderwebs and dust. The skeleton's jaw gaped open as if it were smiling at them, the empty eye sockets dark even in the light of Catriona's torch. Bright gold coins were strewn on the stone beside the dead man, where they had fallen from a pouch whose seams had long ago rotted away. The gold glinted in the torchlight and was the only thing inside the alcove that seemed to have any color at all.

"It's a corpse," Elidor said with faint disgust. He peered down into another of the alcoves that dotted the walls of the room. "And another. I think they're all corpses. This is a burial chamber."

"Neat." Sindri ran to one he could reach and stuck his head in. "It's only a skeleton. Oh, look, they buried him with all of his stuff! I think this one was a captain or something."

Elidor reached in, ignoring Catriona's wrinkled nose. "They're all wearing armor and a weapon of some sort. This looks like a soldier."

"They're all soldiers," Corrigan's voice called out from the middle of the chamber. Elidor and the others turned.

Corrigan knelt in the middle of the room, his squire beside him scrubbing at the floor with a bit of his cloak. "There's a plaque here. I can't read the language, but it's obviously some kind of military honor. There is heraldry—a silver crescent, like a moon, beneath a black orb. I don't recognize it. It's not Solamnic, that's for certain."

A bitter clanging sound jarred them, startling Elidor. The noise seemed to come from deep within the barrow.

"That sounds like a door opening," Elidor guessed.

"Or a knight falling over in his armor," Rohawn said. Everyone stared at him for a moment, and he ducked his head. His ears turned as red as Catriona's torch.

A moment of silence, and then the sound came again, louder than before. Corrigan pointed at the far side of the room, hidden in shadow. "It's coming from somewhere through there. We should—"

"Corrigan?" Rohawn's voice quavered. The noise came again, like the knell of a gong.

"Not now, squire." Corrigan stood, drawing his sword. "Gieden's in there. We must brave the danger, face the beast."

"But Corrigan," Catriona said, pulling her own weapon free of its sheath.

"Fear not, Lady Catriona." Corrigan straightened, his metal breastplate shining in the dim light. "The black wizard can't be far. Just down this passage. He's trapped, you see! And he has no allies to protect him. "

"Corrigan! Before you go charging off, I think we had better deal with that!" Elidor pointed at the alcoves.

Dark, choking smoke was pouring out from the recesses in the walls. The ashen mist shimmered faintly, then faces began to form. Skulls rolled and surfaced, only to sink back into the black tendrils of smoke.

"Looks like Gieden's found his allies," Rohawn said, lifting his greatsword over his shoulder.

One by one, figures began to form in the mist. Each took the form of a warrior, shining armor long ago tarnished and blackened, the faces little more than skulls within their ancient helms. Their bodies were shaped from black ash dripping and trickling down

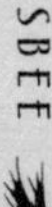

their arms and over their skull-like faces, barely covering the bone beneath. Their vacant eyes seemed to track the motion of the group as Elidor and the others gathered in the center of the room.

"We've got to get out of here." Elidor glanced toward the staircase, but their only exit was blocked by more of the thick, ash-like substance.

"Why leave?" Corrigan reached up and slapped the faceplate down on his helm. "With Gieden so close?"

Elidor stared at the thin knight. "You're insane."

"No." Corrigan grinned. "Just determined."

Around them, the undead began to pound their ghostly swords on spectral shields. And in one united movement, they advanced, blackness and dust trailing from their every motion.

Rohawn swung his greatsword over his head in a wide arc and pierced one of the ghostly warriors. The tip of his weapon sunk right through the ash, scattering black char around them. The warrior did not slow.

Catriona leaped forward, torch in one hand and short sword in the other. With a fierce cry, she plowed the creature in the face with the torch end. The creature twisted its head slightly. Flames lit its face, burning away some of the ash, but the undead soldier did not slow its advance.

Cat staggered back, dumbfounded. "A spell, Sindri," she hissed, regaining her stance.

Excited, the kender jumped forward and spread his hands as he'd been taught. His fingers wiggled strangely in the torchlight as he yelled, "*Ominatiati*!"

At first, nothing happened. Then Elidor noticed that one of the warriors had ceased to move, frozen by Sindri's will.

"Good job, wizard!" Corrigan laughed. "Do that to all of them and we'll have victory!"

"Uh . . . " Sindri backpedaled. "I'm not exactly sure, but I think

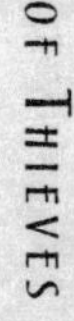

that particular spell only works on one or two at a time. I'm still learning!"

The undead clustered closer around them, bone fists clutching broken metal swords, preventing any means of escape.

"Ah, I see you've met my friends." The voice was soft, supple, arrogant.

In the far archway, a thin, willowy figure emerged, silhouetted by the crisp white glow of magical light. A long black plait hung down his back, and his emerald eyes shimmered with amusement.

"Gieden," Corrigan spat. For a moment, Elidor thought the knight would charge straight through the undead soldiers to battle the wizard.

"Corrigan, no," growled Elidor. "This isn't going to prove anything."

"Very astute, Elidor." Gieden smiled. He turned his green gaze back on Corrigan. "Has the knight told you why he hunts me?"

Elidor's eyes flickered over the soldiers in their armor of ash, hoping to find some weakness in their ranks. "You're a black wizard," he said. "That's enough."

"Oh, it may be enough for some, but not for Corrigan. Tell me, do you sleep well these nights, Corrigan? Is your bed warm and spacious, the fireside comforting? Do you think your son would approve, if he could see you now?"

Corrigan took a sharp step forward, halted only by Rohawn's hand.

"You will pay, black wizard," Rohawn said.

"Not today," Gieden purred. "Not today."

Meanwhile, Elidor stepped close to Sindri, leaning down to whisper in the kender's ear. "When I tell you, I want you to use that magic on those two soldiers—the ones by the stairway. Do you see them?"

"Yes, but—" the kender began.

Elidor cut him off. "Do you have any oil in your pouch?"

"Yes, but—"

"Give it to me." Elidor took three flasks of oil from the kender, palming them expertly so that Gieden wouldn't notice their presence.

He slowly backed up, stepping closer to the archway, all the while watching the black wizard. Catriona glanced at Elidor and he stared meaningfully down at the flasks of oil clutched in his hand, and then back at the torch in Catriona's hand. He nodded toward the soldier before her, the only one that had been burned by her torch.

Catriona smiled.

Swiftly, Elidor hurled the oil flasks. "Now, Sindri!"

The flasks crashed against the entrance to the stairway, splattering the stone with a thick, greasy liquid. Sindri spread his fingers and yelled again, and the two undead nearest the arch stopped, stiff and unmoving.

Seeing her opportunity, Catriona threw the torch. It spun in the air, casting stretched shadows across the shifting mist. With a burst of sparks, the torch struck the stone. In an instant, the heavy lamp oil caught fire and the archway was ablaze. The spirits around it flinched, turning for an instant to look at the conflagration that set their mists afire.

"Rohawn! Corrigan! We leave now!" Elidor charged toward the archway, heedless of the small inferno.

To Elidor's relief, the undead pushed aside, clearing the way for the others to follow. Sindri raced forward at his side, quickly outdistancing him. Catriona was right behind, shoulder-punching one of the more solid warriors.

So these creatures were only soldiers after all, and had some physical form. Elidor thanked E'li for small favors and leaped to the other side of the arch. The fire singed his hair and eyebrows.

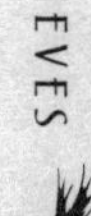

"Corrigan!" Elidor turned back, seeing the knight hesitate.

Rohawn took a few steps toward Elidor, his greatsword wavering in clenched fists. The squire looked back and forth between his knight and the doorway, but Corrigan did not move.

"Come on!" Elidor called.

Corrigan lowered his sword as though preparing to charge the black wizard. Only a fraction of an instant had passed, but already the fire was beginning to dim. Soon, it would go out and they would lose their advantage. There was no time to spare.

"I can't retreat!" Corrigan howled. "I am a Knight of Solamnia!"

"Corrigan!" Catriona's voice was angry, uncompromising. "Rohawn needs you. If you don't train him, no one will. He'll never make knight. Don't you dare let him down!"

This seemed to strike a blow, and Corrigan turned toward the fire. Rohawn stood at the bottom of the stairway, ready to charge into battle—and die beside his knight. The boy's face was white, his sword visibly shaking. Corrigan nodded, thrusting his sword into its sheath and leaping through the flames.

They hurtled up the stairs, with Sindri and Catriona taking the lead. They heard Gieden's voice behind them, ordering the still-forming warriors into action, but the flames at the mouth of the stairway slowed the undead.

Elidor burst outside to see Catriona swinging Sindri onto her horse. Corrigan's face turned red with anger and frustration, but he threw his leg over his gelding's gray flank without protest. Rohawn readied himself to run.

From the bellows of the earth came a terrible, low howl. It shook the earth, making soil flake from the ancient stone.

The horses, skittish already, panicked as black mist began to rise from within the alcoves. Elidor barely managed to climb aboard, hanging half out of the saddle as the steed broke into a run. The other horses quickly followed, Rohawn racing along on foot at their side with a grim, determined frown.

"Wow!" Sindri yelled, his voice carrying over the pounding rhythm of the horses' hooves. "They're riding ghosts too!"

Elidor looked back over his shoulder, desperately clinging to his saddle with one hand as he jolted on the back of his terrified animal.

"Horses" was the wrong word to describe the creatures that pursued them. Skeletal heads jostled atop long bony necks. Their feet were not hooved, but clawed, sharp bird-like talons digging into the ground. Black churning ash formed flesh over the creatures' thick bones. But it was their eyes—green, glowing with some hideous, otherworldly fire—that struck Elidor with a sense of malice.

The undead warriors rode the steeds, swords glinting in the moonlight. Their howls of glee sounded across the plain, making the rocky terraces that rose above the grasses echo with their hatred.

"We're not going to outrun them," Catriona called from the front of the group. "They're gaining on us."

"Then we're going to have to find a place to fight," Corrigan yelled.

A flash of white on the dark plain caught Elidor's attention.

The girl stood by one of the rocky terraces that ringed the plain, desperately waving her arms. Then he saw it. A faint black silhouette—a cave—darkened the stone wall behind her.

"There!" Elidor yelled.

Catriona nodded in agreement, turning her steed's head toward their new goal.

Together, they raced up a steep grassy slope and finally reached the cave's entrance. The hollow was deep, large enough to hold their steeds, with a long ledge of rock pointing out from its lip over the hill.

Corrigan pulled his horse's head back until the beast nearly fell, then leaped from his horse. Rohawn panted and gasped beside him, weary from the long run.

Elidor looked around for the girl, but saw no sign of her. Rohawn reached out to grab Cat's reins so that she and Sindri could dismount as well. The horses' hooves clattered on the stone as Corrigan drove them inside.

Then together, the group stood on the lip of rock, drawing their weapons and preparing for the undead to charge up the grassy hill toward them.

Corrigan stood beside Elidor, sword out, shield at the ready.

"You know we won't win," Elidor said.

"I know. But that doesn't mean we won't fight." Corrigan's sharp grin belied the obvious lack of strength in his arms. Elidor was struck for a moment at how small the knight seemed, how unwarlike, even in his shining breastplate and bright helmet. Catriona, her dragon claws before her, seemed ten times more comfortable in her stance than Corrigan seemed in his, and Rohawn's massive bulk dwarfed the knight's slender stature.

"Sindri, climb above, onto the ledge," Corrigan said. "Use your magic from there—it'll give you a better line of sight. Target the leaders first to disorient the troops." Corrigan commanded their attention easily, planning tactics as though he were born to the task. "Rohawn, Cat, and I, we'll form a wedge. Elidor stand behind, use your knives to cover us if they get too close. Everyone ready?"

It didn't matter if they were or not. The undead were upon them.

Swords flashed in the dim light. Howls quickly shifted into battle cries.

Catriona's swift, effective strikes were designed to cripple, targeting joints, weak places in the armor of her opponents. Corrigan fought almost hesitantly, taking advantage of the enemies' uncertainty or of openings within his opponents' style. When the undead lifted their slower weapons, he darted beneath their arms and attacked their joints. They turned to follow him and Corrigan thrust into their waists left unshielded by the movement. Although he was neither as fast as Catriona nor as strong as Rohawn, he seemed to know exactly when his enemy would create an opening through which he could attack. Yet even with all their ability and skill, only ash fell from the strikes of their weapons.

The undead fell back, but they were not harmed at all.

"We can't keep this up," Elidor panted, hurling another dagger. It struck against one of the warrior's helms, twisting the creature's head aside. He couldn't truly hurt them, but he could certainly inconvenience them. He dodged between Catriona and Rohawn, kicking viciously at an ill-placed foot. The warrior fell, toppling over from Elidor's blow. And yet, within a moment, it would rise again. Ten, twenty—and soon, those warriors who did not have steeds would arrive on foot—more than a hundred in all.

Elidor and his friends were overwhelmed, their weapons barely effective against the undead. Each touch from the warriors' bony fingers was as cold as ice.

The undeads' weapons drew blood far more freely than the humans' own, the evidence of the spectral soldiers' blows trailing down Rohawn and Catriona's skin with liberal color.

But just as Elidor began to give up hope, the sun touched the horizon, its first rays bringing an orange glow to the dark sky. The warriors moved back, their vicious steeds rearing at the brilliance of the dawn.

"They're afraid," Sindri cried. "They fear the sun!" He whooped, leaping up and down on his perch.

As if desperate to avoid the touch of the light, the undead scattered, most heading back toward the barrow while others sunk

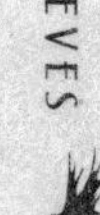

into cracks in the rocky terrace. They shimmered as they moved, the ash pouring through crevices in the stone, hiding them from the touch of the sun's light.

As his friends cheered their unexpected escape, a soft voice spoke in Elidor's ear. "They will return."

Elidor turned and saw the girl once more. She hid behind a rock now bathed in light.

"How do you know that?" Elidor asked, stepping toward her. He struggled to hear her over the clamor. Rohawn shouted and clapped Catriona's shoulder, nearly knocking her over. She coughed and grinned, and Corrigan laughed.

The girl in rags said nothing, staring at Elidor silently. She rose to her feet.

Sindri leaped down from the rocky face above. "Who were you talking to, Elidor?" he asked with an inquisitive tilt of his head.

"Her." Elidor pointed at the girl as she backed away into the cave.

CHAPTER

4 The First Touch of Evil

Elidor followed the girl past the opening and into the shallow cavern. It was about the size of a campsite, and Elidor could see signs of old fire markings in a depression near the front of the chamber. The girl stopped partway inside, where the low sunlight illuminated her torn robes.

Afraid to take his eyes off her in case she vanished again, Elidor circled her. "Who are you?" She shook her head, fear written on her features. He tried again. "Where did you come from?"

Her voice was strangely accented, the syllables elven but the lilt and pattern unfamiliar. "Far away. Long ago. And right here, right now. What does it matter?" She reached out as if trying to take his hand. "You are in danger."

"Elidor?" It was Sindri's voice in the doorway, nearly eclipsed by the laughter and celebration of the others outside. "Who are you talking to?"

Elidor waved a hand at him, still keeping his eyes on the mysterious girl. "What do you mean, 'danger'?"

She shook her head. "Danger. He will hunt you. He will not stop. You have . . . what he wants. You are there now, and he knows it."

"Gieden." Gritting his teeth, Elidor sank into a squat. In the shadow of the cave, the girl seemed like a fragment of his imagination, fading in and out of view. He struggled to understand her words.

"Gieden?" Sindri hurried into the cave, squinting around and tugging on Elidor's sleeve. "Now you have to tell me who you're talking to, Elidor, or I'm going to go get Catriona!"

Elidor leaned toward Sindri and whispered, "You don't see her?"

"See who?"

"The girl!" Exasperated, the elf pointed toward the figure that knelt at the center of the cave. "She's right there!"

"Oh, wow! You're seeing things?" Sindri crowed. "I'm very familiar with seeing things nobody else can see. I just wish I could see her too!" He rubbed his eyes, peering around in the cave's dim light. "Is she over here? Over here?" The kender put out his arms, waving them as he wandered around the cave. "Am I close?"

The girl looked up at Elidor, her eyes filled with pain and suffering. "You're in danger," she said. "Think. You've already seen the knife."

Elidor knitted his brow. "Gieden wants the crown."

"Did the girl say that?" Sindri asked. "Tell her we know that already. But—"

"And he'll do whatever it takes to get it," Elidor continued, ignoring his friend. "His undead soldiers can't travel during the day; the sun wounds them. We've seen that. It should be an easy matter to lose him if we travel during the day and cover our tracks. He has magic, yes, but if we head for a large city like Palanthas—"

"No." She shook her head. "You can outrun him, but he will destroy you nonetheless. You can't go to a safe place. You have to go toward danger. You have to go there. *There.*"

"Palanthas?" Sindri brightened. "She wants you to go to Palanthas? Wow, that's a long way! What a great journey, though. Will she come with us? Tell her to let me see her, Elidor. I'm a wizard now. I can help." Sindri flailed about a bit more, his arms coming dangerously close to smacking Elidor in the stomach. "Last time we were in Palanthas, everyone was so nice. I bet we could get Adyn to help! I'll go tell Cat!"

Elidor grabbed Sindri's wrist. "Sindri, I don't think we should tell Cat—or anyone."

"You're right. She'd probably want to see the girl too. And she's not even a wizard," Sindri sniffed haughtily, sitting down on a rock. "So now what?"

"You said we have to go toward danger?" Elidor addressed the girl again, trying to understand her words. "What do you mean?

The girl glanced toward the door in sudden fear and Elidor could sense that she was looking not toward his friends, but farther away, toward something he could not yet see. "Go home, Elidor."

He struggled to understand. "Home?"

Everything you love will suffer your fate.

The words echoed in Elidor's memory. "What do you mean?"

"Go home," she said more emphatically. Her gaze drifted up to the silver band that circled Elidor's brow. "He wants what you have, so he'll take everything else he can until the crown is all that you possess." Falling backward, she pressed her face to her knees in a position of abject terror. "And in the end, you'll beg him to take it from you."

Elidor's thoughts flew to his dream: his mother's face, the dark shade of an elven forest, his family.

Everything you love will suffer your fate.

Gieden had seem them all, watching like a vulture as Elidor dreamed about them.

"He was in my dream."

"Who? Gieden?" Sindri asked.

"Yes," she said. But her answer wasn't for Sindri.

"Yes," Elidor echoed the girl. "And I know where he's going next." He stood, still holding Sindri by the wrist. Looking down into the kender's wide, brown eyes, Elidor said more gently, "Sindri, we can't tell Catriona or the others about this. I don't know why you can't see the girl, and I don't know what she is, but I trust her." The words surprised even Elidor, but as he spoke them, he realized that he meant it. "We have to hurry."

He looked up again and was not surprised to see that the girl no longer sat upon the stone floor of the cave. She was gone.

"Where are we going?"

"Aerendor."

"Is that a person?" Sindri trotted behind Elidor.

"It's a place." Elidor stopped at the mouth of the cave, staring up at the rising sun. "It's . . . my home."

CHAPTER

5 The Fires of Home

The road to Aerendor led them through the thick forests of Southern Ergoth, where the shadows of the day nearly matched the darkness of nighttime.

It had taken them a journey aboard a ship to get there, across the rough waters of the Straits of Algoni. Every night, Sindri noticed Elidor watching behind them, sensing the approach of the undead soldiers. Their advantage lay in the fact that Gieden's legions could travel only by night. Once they'd reached the island of Southern Ergoth, Elidor pushed his friends hard to cover as much distance as they could, traveling all through the day and as far into the darkness as they could bear. Every night they took turns keeping watch. But Sindri wondered why they had bothered—Elidor barely slept.

"Stop." The voice startled Sindri. His hands clenched around Catriona's waist. Elidor's gelding was in the lead and the elf pulled his horse up sharply, eyes scanning the trees around them.

"Who goes there?" The words were heavily accented Common, not Elvish. Sindri craned his neck to see who was speaking and at last saw a pale-haired elven warrior in brown and green, squatting easily on a tree branch just above the path. Although the man's bow was lowered with no arrow against the string, Sindri felt certain that there were other arrows pointed directly at them.

Elidor moved his horse forward and raised a hand in greeting. "Elidor of Aerendor. Son of Elyana." A gust of wind blew his cloak back. Sindri gazed up at the sky. Gray clouds muddied the bright blue sky. A storm was coming.

The guard's eyes grew wide and he leaned forward to study Elidor's face. Sindri winced just from the look on the guard's face. Poor Elidor, he thought. So this is why he never goes home.

"Does she know you are here?" the guard asked.

"No," Elidor replied. "But I expect you'll tell her, Narath."

The guard sighed and gestured at the tree next to him. Sindri followed Narath's gaze and glimpsed a woodsman rising from a hiding place to go racing through the trees.

"Follow me," the guard ordered, "and do not stray from the path." He eyed Elidor again, barely hiding his loathing. "Things have changed here since you left, Elidor."

Elidor frowned. "Actually, I doubt that they have, Narath." He spurred his horse and followed the elven guard.

"What's wrong with him?" Rohawn whispered to Sindri and Catriona as they fell to the rear of the group. "Isn't he happy to be home again? These are his people, are they not?"

"They're Silvanesti—only half his people," Sindri answered. "Elidor's mother is Silvanesti, but his father is a Kagonesti."

"The two races despise one another." Catriona kept her voice low so Elidor wouldn't hear them. "The Silvanesti find the Kagonesti to be beneath them—including one who's only a half-breed. And none of them have ever let Elidor forget what he is. He was raised here in Aerendor by his mother, but I'm not sure he considers it a true home." There was no time to explain further, as the woodland opened into a city glade.

Aerendor was a small and modest town, even by elven standards. Three graceful towers stood in the center of a wheel-like spiral of streets. The towers' pale sides had no ornamentation other than slim windows that spiraled up their length, and the roofs of homes and other buildings clustered below them like grass beneath three tall orchids. Two guards, their brown and green livery blending into the forest around them, took the reins of the horses as Elidor, Catriona, Corrigan, and Sindri dismounted.

They walked through the central plaza of the little town, the flowers on every side glowing with brilliant yellows, blues, and reds. Catriona bent down to touch one, and the soft petals shifted beneath her fingers. The colors were almost iridescent, changing faintly in the sunlight.

The central fountain of the plaza was carved of simple stone, but with masterful artistry. The sculpture of a large oak tree carved in white marble stood in the center of the fountain. Water trickled down the roots of the mighty stone oak, cascading into the small pool. Surrounding the pool, carved of the same stone, was a series of marble statues. An ivory-colored deer bent down low, poised in the moment between drinking and flight. Stone birds fluttered among the tree's branches, held aloft by some miracle of artistry that Sindri couldn't comprehend. The effect was that of a grove frozen in a moment of time, shaped into a fountain that mimicked nature so precisely it almost seemed to move with the wind.

The roads were shaped with white grasses against the darker foliage of the forest glen. A young man dressed in a flowing robe of blue and green laughed while his maiden companion thwapped him lightly with a flower, a gentle teasing blow. An older woman with soft, graying blond hair sat near the fountain with a pad of paper and charcoal, drawing the two as they posed for her art. At the edge of the plaza, Sindri spotted a potter loading her kiln with dozens of clay forms.

The smell of wisteria blossoms drifted through the air, carried from large blossoms that swayed between several of the buildings.

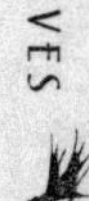

Sindri felt out of place here. Everything was slender, graceful, and delicate, and he felt if he touched anything, it would surely break.

Looking up, he saw Catriona run a hand through her wild red curls as if to tame them as she shifted uneasily in her armor. Rohawn's eyes were wide, staring openly at the elves and the buildings alike. Only Corrigan seemed at all at ease, bowing fluidly to the elves passing by despite their raised eyebrows.

Narath did not bother to look back at them, striding toward the tall towers with purpose. Elidor's face was grim. He pushed his hair behind his ears and let his distinctly Kagonesti features show. Sindri could tell more clearly now how different Elidor was from the Silvanesti inhabitants of Aerendor. His face was squarer, his movements like a hunting cat rather than a graceful willow. His hair, a dark ash blond among their silver and gold beauty, stood out like a torch among pale stars, and his body was thicker, more muscular and less elegant. Sindri saw looks of disdain, mockery, and even pity on the faces of the Aerendor citizens. Elidor didn't seem to notice, but it made Sindri angry.

He trotted up to his friend, tugging on Elidor's sleeve. "Where are we going?"

"To see the Council."

"The Council?" Sindri cocked an eyebrow.

Elidor nodded. "It's the ruling body of Aerendor."

"I thought we were here to see your mother," Sindri chirped as they reached the tallest of the three central towers.

"We are." Elidor didn't explain, and Sindri was forced to trot to keep up with him as they approached the tower.

Guards with silver helms and green livery saluted Narath, then opened the tall oak doors for the group. The doors were covered in carved knotwork and opened into a marble foyer. They passed through a short passage into a larger chamber.

Inside, the ceiling was held aloft on tall, arched silver railings. Six elves sat around a table shaped like a crescent moon. They were dressed in robes of linen and silk, their hair in elaborate braids with green ivy twined among long coils of color. There were four males and two females, their eyes taking in every detail of the group as it entered.

Sindri saw the woodsman who had been with Narath in the forest take a seat behind the table.

So the Council already knew they were coming. Sindri wasn't sure if that was a good thing or a bad thing. He glanced up at Catriona. She clenched her dirty hands behind her back, and Rohawn shuffled uncomfortably in his worn leathers.

One of the elves at the table rose. Her long golden hair, woven with silver threads and violet flowers, lay coiled upon her head in elaborate braids and twists. Her skin was a gentle ivory, and her eyes like midnight stars gazed serenely at the group. She placed her fists on the table, her long indigo sleeves falling down over her arms.

Elidor bowed stiffly, never taking his eyes off the woman's face. "Good evening, Mother."

"Elidor," she said, with no hint of compassion.

Elidor gestured toward his friends. "May I present my companions: Catriona, Sir Corrigan of Solamnia, and his squire Rohawn. And this, this is Sindri."

Sindri stepped forward. "Sindri Suncatcher, Wizard Extraordinaire. It is a pleasure, a real tremendous pleasure—"

Elyana cut him short. "It is overlong since a Knight of Solamnia has visited our humble community." She inclined her head toward Corrigan, and Sindri saw the knight flush with pleasure. "We are pleased to see Elidor has chosen some suitable company for his . . . travels." The last word was tinged with distaste, and one of the other elves at the table raised his sleeve to cover an obviously disdainful smile.

"My lady Elyana." Corrigan's bow of reverence was far courtlier than Elidor's or Sindri's, his smile one of pleasant courtesy. At his side, Rohawn fell to one knee, obviously unprepared to try the gymnastics of such a reverence. "We are pleased to meet thee. I ask thee to forgive our intrusion upon your son's happy homecoming. But there are grave tidings that must be given to thee and thy people."

"Yes, Mother," Elidor began. "We've come to tell you—"

"Sir Knight." Elyana spoke only to Corrigan. "You are saying there is trouble?"

"Yes, my lady." Corrigan looked uncomfortable, realizing that Elyana wasn't going to let her son speak. He glanced at Elidor, who had raised his hands in exasperation.

"Grave tidings?" A male elf behind the crescent table sneered. He was smaller than the other councilors, but something about the curve of his smile gave the impression that he considered himself in charge. "No insult to you, Master Knight, but we have heard wild stories before from . . . this one." A wave of his hand indicated Elidor. "Adventures, dangers untold, monsters in the woods. Oh, his childhood was filled with them. Your presence foretells trouble for Aerendor, indeed—but mostly because of his arrival. Elidor *is* trouble for this village. Tell me, Knight, do you trust this . . . man?"

"No one trusts Elidor," Elyana said haughtily. "No one would be such a fool. My son is many things, Fallerian, but he is—as we all know—a thief." The word was said with such dripping scorn that Sindri's jaw fell open. *This* was Elidor's *mother*?

"My lady," a portly councilor dressed in butter-yellow robes said as he leaned back in his chair. "I must admit that we are shocked and surprised that this boy has returned to Aerendor. I had thought that his last admonishment would have convinced him not to return."

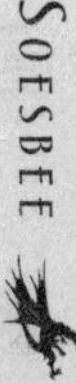

"In truth, Motek," Fallerian replied, "I do not understand why he has returned. Perhaps he wishes our artisans to build him a prison. It is where he's bound to end up anyway." A male elf in green robes laughed behind his hand at the statement, nodding in agreement across the crescent table as Fallerian smiled.

The other female councilor laughed softly. "Oh my, Elidor would never end up in prison. I doubt he's got the courage to be captured." She inclined her head, soft brown hair brushing against her shoulders. Her orange robes were shorter than the others. A bow leaned up against her chair. "Fallerian and Elyana are correct. No one would trust Elidor, of course, least of all the people of Aerendor who know him best." Her eyes were steely, though she continued to smile.

"Salaria, perhaps this time we should let you 'escort' Elidor out of Aerendor," Elyana said. "With your hounds at your side, of course."

The response behind the table was a mix of laughter and amused silence, and Sindri saw Elidor's face turning an angry shade of red.

Corrigan squared his shoulders. "I have fought beside Elidor, and I have seen his courage. Though we have not been companions long, he has shown that he is worthy of your time." The other elves at the table began to whisper, hiding their contempt behind masks of emotionless courtesy.

But Corrigan did not pause, rushing on with the same sober relentlessness that he showed during the battle within the crypt. "The tale he bears, the tale *we* carry," the knight's voice sank to a low warning, "is imperative, my lady."

Elyana raised a hand, and the other elves at the table fell silent, their whispers fading. "Very well. We will listen . . . to the knight." Elyana glanced scornfully at her son, then turned away as if dismissing Elidor's presence completely. "After all, it would be

intolerably rude of us to ignore you, Sir Corrigan." The other elves, her peers, slowly nodded.

"Oh, very well," Fallerian sighed. "If we must." He leaned back in his carved wooden chair.

"There is a wizard of the black robes, an elf named Gieden," Corrigan began. His voice carried within the arched chamber with great resonance. "I have hunted him for many years in order to bring him to justice for his crimes in Solamnia and beyond. Now he is headed for the city of Aerendor." More whispers rose from the councilors at the table, but a stern glance from Fallerian silenced them. Elyana said nothing.

"He brings with him a legion of undead, warriors with terrible and evil power," Corrigan continued. "Your city must prepare for their arrival or your people will suffer terribly."

"Are you certain he is coming here?" Fallerian asked. "Simply because there is danger in the land does not mean that Aerendor is in any jeopardy. We are a peaceful and often forgotten town."

Elidor shifted uncomfortably. "We are certain."

"How do you know?" Fallerian asked.

Sindri saw Elidor's discomfort. What was the elf going to say? That a ghostly girl in a cave said that Elidor's family might be in danger? Even to Sindri, that sounded ridiculous at best.

"I can't tell you how I know," Elidor said. "But it is the truth."

"The truth." Motek snorted. "A truth as Elidor tells it, which may be no truth at all."

Elyana spoke slowly. "Why would such an enemy come to our city? We are a small and gentle people, not a major city of the Silvanesti. We have no enemies and little need for warriors. Our people are artists, scholars, and historians. Aerendor was founded a mere eighty years ago, before the Silvanesti fled to this continent. Our people came here to be alone with our art, to leave behind wars and danger. We even spent time among the Kagonesti and tried to teach them the ways of civilized creatures, but they were not worthy of such beauty. Now we live alone, here in this town that we have built, this haven we have made our own. We are ill prepared to repel such an enemy."

Sindri's attention was drawn from the table for a moment as a slender elf maiden entered the room. This one was not dressed in formal robes, nor in the livery Narath and his guards wore. Her tunic was a simple golden yellow, her leather breeches tucked into high brown boots. Hanging from her neck was a long golden chain bearing a medallion shaped like a griffin's wing.

She knelt beside a very old elf at the edge of the council table and whispered into his ear. He nodded and she stepped away, meeting Sindri's curious stare. To his surprise, she winked.

The kender grinned at her and bowed. "Maybe they're not all bad," he whispered to the squire who knelt beside him.

"My lady Elyana," the older man rose from the table. His hair was graying, his skin faded like old parchment. "My granddaughter reminds me that I have promised to assist the Lady Oberalia set the fire in her kiln. She is my apprentice, you know, and she has no touch for the contraption." The old man smiled gently and patted the hand of the black-haired maiden beside him. "I ask the council's forgiveness, but I must depart. I leave Kaja here in my absence. She will relay to me any decisions that the Council makes."

"Very well, Hammon. Good eve to you," murmured Elyana.

The old man shuffled away from his seat at the table, his steps light and cautious. "They aren't taking us seriously," Elidor whispered to Corrigan.

Sindri nodded in agreement. "Tell them about the undead again, and their eyes! Ooh, and the ash, and the swords that cut through stone, and maybe tell them about the steeds that looked like they could eat me whole—"

"Sindri," Elidor hissed, and he realized that the room had again fallen silent.

"Oh." The kender's voice echoed in the chamber. "But it's true!" A red flush crept up from beneath Sindri's collar, yet he stomped his foot and continued. "We've fought these undead. They're very powerful. And with Gieden telling them what to do, they're smart. You're in danger."

Fallerian's stare pinned Sindri to the floor. "And exactly why are we in danger? For all your explanations that these undead are dangerous, you have yet to tell me why they are coming. Surely there is nothing in Aerendor that would tempt a black wizard."

"They come," Elidor broke in, "because my family is here."

"Your family?" Fallerian stood, his eyes flashing. "This dark wizard . . . he wants you, Elidor? You brought him here?" The dignified elf was nearly shouting, anger written in every barely contained movement.

"No. He would have come here whether I returned or not."

"But it is because of you, because of this shameful life you lead, roaming the countryside like some wild animal. No, Elyana, let me finish." Fallerian's fist clenched. "I told you he would bring disaster upon Aerendor. And now, it seems, he has. A legion of undead, Elidor? How long will it take them to destroy us? A few nights?"

"Less," Sindri muttered.

"Less." Fallerian's exceptional hearing picked up on the kender's whisper. "And when do we expect this black wizard and his soldiers to arrive?"

"Tomorrow night," Sindri said. Rohawn poked Sindri, but Sindri didn't stop. "You better hurry up and do something."

Fallerian stared fixedly at Elidor. "This Gieden wants Elidor, not Aerendor. Perhaps we should just stand back and let this undead legion do its work." He did not continue, but his meaning was clear. A sickening smugness colored his smile.

Corrigan placed himself between Fallerian and Elidor, meeting the older elf's gaze. "Good sir, you forget your place and your position. Such an obvious display of scorn is not appropriate in these chambers of policy, nor are open insults tendered to the son of the Lady Elyana. Whatever this council may feel about him, you must understand—your town and your people are in danger."

"Bah," Fallerian snorted. "There's no danger."

"No danger?" Elidor blanched, and then yelled, "Our people are going to die! Don't you see that? These undead can't be bargained with, or reasoned with. They're coming, and they're going to kill you all! Don't you hear what we're telling you?"

"Elidor!" Elyana rose from the table. "This is another of your tall tales, another wild story concocted to get the better of us. Oh, yes, we hear you. As we heard you when you lied to us, stole from us, and betrayed our trust. This village is filled with people who have heard you one too many times, Elidor, and have paid for it. Your stepfather was right about you, Elidor, and his soul would be spinning in his grave if he knew you'd come back to threaten our village again."

Elidor gritted his teeth, pointing at her. "I became a thief because I needed to survive. Aerendor never welcomed me. It taught me that I was second-rate, barely worth feeding and keeping alive. If I have disappointed you, *Mother,* then it's because you never cared in the first place."

"Care?" Fallerian didn't raise his voice, but the steel in it cut through Elidor's shout like a knife through butter. "Your mother—and the rest of Aerendor—stopped caring about you when you rejected our ways and left this village. That is, after you tried to steal from us, lied to us. What was it, Elidor? Beasts in the woods that came in and stole the jewels planned for an artist's work? Jewels found in your bedroll?"

"I was a child then. I wanted attention, nothing more."

Sindri heard Narath sneer from the entryway behind them, "You're still a child, Elidor, useless and meaningless as a babe."

"Don't you want your 'friends' to hear it, Elidor?" Fallerian said. "How you betrayed your people, took their possessions to finance your life of adventuring? A fine way to repay your mother for her care, to repay this village for accepting a mongrel like you. We should have known better, Elidor. But we know better now."

"Fine. May you all burn in a lake of fire, for all I care." Elidor turned on his heel, his eyes bright with anger. He said nothing, but strode out of the room with long, snapping strides.

Sindri stared after him, gaping in surprise.

"My lady," Corrigan bowed politely, signaling to Rohawn to do the same. The squire stumbled, ending up with a tilted stagger and a sheepish grin. "We are here to assist you. I hope that you will take our petition seriously and allow us to lend you and your people whatever aid we can." The knight's courtly gesture seemed to soothe tensions slightly.

Elyana stared out at the group from behind the table. She resumed her seat, hands shaking. When she spoke again, her voice was tightly controlled. "No, Sir Corrigan," she murmured. "I believe we have had quite enough 'assistance' for one day. Perhaps tomorrow we can speak of these matters, just you and the council. I can offer you no more." She made a gesture of dismissal and looked away. "Go."

"As you wish." The knight motioned for Rohawn and the others to follow. His heart sinking, Sindri bowed and trotted in Corrigan's wake. Narath led them to the entrance to the tower, opening the oak doors with a mocking smile.

"What do we do now?" Sindri whispered.

Catriona looked down at Sindri sadly. "We wait."

"Wait for what? Until they decide if they want to live?" Sindri trotted to keep up with Catriona's long steps as they passed

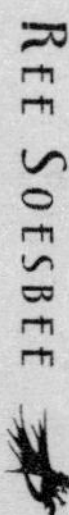

through the arched doorway and into the wooded street. The wind blew Sindri's black hair into his face, whipping it fiercely against his cheeks. He drew the edges of his cloak around him and stared morosely up at Cat.

"Oh, they want to live," a voice behind him said with forced cheer. "They just have to get comfortable with the 'how.' Aerendor doesn't like surprises. They're like a slow-moving river, but they'll come around in time."

Sindri turned around to see the girl who had winked at him in the council chamber leaning against the outside wall of the tower. But . . . no, it wasn't the same girl. The face and voice were similar, but this girl was dressed in a burgundy tunic with tight sleeves, much like an archer would wear to keep their clothing free of the bowstring. A bright red bandanna was tied around her forehead, keeping straight black hair out of her eyes. A lute hung at her side from a strap woven of brightly patterned material.

"Weren't you just inside?" Sindri asked.

"No, that was my sister Kaja. I'm Kelenthe." She held out her hand to Sindri with a broad smile. "And you are?"

"Sindri!" he answered. "Wow! You two really look alike! Are you twins? Elven twins—that's really rare, isn't it?" Sindri shook her hand. He gestured to Catriona. "This is my friend Catriona. Have you met Corrigan and Rohawn? And Elidor?" He looked back to see Corrigan and Rohawn arguing with Narath in the doorway of the tower. A faint echo of thunder rolled across the sky.

"I know Elidor," Kelenthe said. "We were in school together a long time ago, before Elidor left the town." Her tone held none of the hatred that Sindri heard from others in the council chamber. "I saw him running out of the tower a few moments ago. I take it things did not go well?"

"No, not well at all." Catriona scanned the area. "Did you happen to see where he went?"

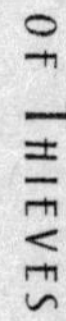

Kelenthe nodded and led them around the fountain to the far side of the plaza. Sindri trotted along beside Kelenthe, looking up at the bard eagerly. "Are you from here, too?"

"Yes." Kelenthe smiled, her grin filled with amusement. "Just like Elidor. But they don't like me here very much, either."

"Why not?" Sindri was mystified.

Kelenthe ran a hand through her black hair. "My sister and I grew up in this town. And like a lot of kids, we ask too many questions. Why do things one way, and not another—and finally, the town's all but tried to throw us out. You don't know how many times I've wanted to leave, but my sister always says we should give them another chance. So I make things different here in my own way."

"You look so different. I mean, you're . . ."

The bard laughed. "Not blond? Well, I was born with pale hair—just like my sister was. That's one of the things we changed, my sister and I. There's a dye made from walnuts, and we use it on our hair. Maybe it's not the greatest act of defiance in the world, but I like to think it shows the people of this town that we're going to be ourselves. Live the way we think is best. No matter what they say." Kelenthe sighed. "Elidor was right to leave. This town's too small, too narrow-minded. Even so small a change as the color of your hair makes people turn away from you." Kelenthe sighed. "I'm just lucky to have my sister. She dyed her hair, too, just so we'd still look identical. No matter what, I know she'll always be there for me."

She pushed aside a low branch that hid a small path. The grassy trail led into the woods that surrounded Aerendor on all sides. "When we were children, Elidor was often ostracized by the people of the village. He was different—we were kids. Anything different was bad."

"I know the feeling," Cat mused.

"Anyway, there's a willow tree down by the stream where Elidor would go whenever his stepfather yelled at him, which was almost all the time. We'd find him there a lot, I and my sister. If I had to bet, I'd say he's there now."

"I think I'll go see if I can find him there. I don't want him to be alone right now." Catriona strode down the path without waiting for Kelenthe's response.

CHAPTER

6 THUNDER

"Elidor?" Catriona called, pushing aside the branches of the willow. Elidor sat beside a bubbling stream, his leather breeches damp from the grass and the rain.

He looked up at her as she stepped closer. He nodded to her, and Catriona sat on a stone nearby.

"I'm sorry you had to see me like that," Elidor began. "My mother brings out the worst in me. My stepfather too, though he's gone and buried. It's this place, these people. I just can't stand them."

"I can imagine." Cat let one of the willow branches slide through her fingers, feeling the cool green leaves. "Elidor," she began, hesitantly. "Did you really do all those things they say you did?"

"Yes . . . I did a lot of things I'm not proud of, from stealing to vandalism. The original fountain in the central square had two deer. I smashed the other one with a hammer just before I left Aerendor. The last time I saw it, it was in pieces, scattered all around the fountain."

"Wow," said Cat. "No wonder they don't like you."

"It's not that. They don't like me because I'm half Kagonesti. The rest of it, well, they just consider it part of my nature. I'm a barbarian, uncivilized, less than them." Elidor hurled a rock into the stream. After an uncomfortable pause, he asked, "Where's everybody else?"

"I don't know. I think Corrigan's going back into the council chamber to talk to them about Gieden."

Elidor snorted. "Who would know I'd end up indebted to a Knight of Solamnia?"

"If he can do it," Cat added.

"Good luck to him. Fallerian and my mother hate me. Shalidrian is so much Fallerian's toady that he may as well be a finger on Fallerian's hand. Salaria and Hammon are usually neutral in any argument, listening to both sides. Motek . . . Motek is motivated only by his own belly. He'll stick close to Fallerian in this, if it gains him nothing else."

"Unless Corrigan can convince them." Catriona let out a long sigh. "I must admit, I have my doubts about that knight, Elidor. He's hiding something, and I don't trust him. Rohawn's nice enough, but Corrigan's trouble."

"Is that because you don't like him?" Elidor narrowed his blue eyes. "Or is it because you don't like the Knights of Solamnia?"

Catriona didn't answer immediately. "Both."

Elidor chuckled, the laugh forced and somehow sad. When Catriona spoke again, it was with a rueful tone in her voice. "Do you think your mother and the others will listen to him?"

"Oh, they'll listen. Fallerian loves when shiny, noble things are dangled in front of him. If he starts thinking that he'll get some kind of high-class rub off from Corrigan's background, or that he'll look like a hero, then he'll do it." The elf shook his head, picking up another smooth, flat rock from the grassy bank. As he dropped it into the running water, he continued. "Fallerian's been itching to make himself governor as long as I can remember, but he doesn't have the support. Aerendor is an artists' community. It's been ruled by a council for almost fifty years, since the last governor died in a hunting accident. There's never been anyone who could unify the council, so there's no governor."

"Well, if he can save Aerendor from Gieden's legion, then he'll be a hero for sure."

"Yeah," Elidor agreed morosely. "He will."

Cat reached into the cold water. "And that's bad?"

"No . . . " He fidgeted. "I want to see Aerendor safe. But Fallerian in charge—that's a heavy price."

"Less costly than the one Gieden will make them pay for their lives."

"I know."

Overhead, thunder crackled in the distance and fat raindrops pattered down on the willow limbs above them.

"My father—my real father—always said I had good hands." Elidor looked down, clenching and unclenching his fists. "I met him when I went to visit the Kagonesti after I left Aerendor. He taught me the hunting language of his people and how to walk silently even in a dry forest. He was a good man."

"Why didn't you stay there, among the Kagonesti?" Cat asked. "With your father?"

"My father was sick. And his people saw me not as a son, but as a Silvanesti. When my mother's people first came here, they had ambitions of Kagonesti. They almost started a war. The Kagonesti didn't appreciate being treated like barbarians, and they didn't want the Silvanesti here on their territory." Elidor sighed. "My father's village was no more a home to me than Aerendor. When he died, I left."

"I'm sorry, Elidor."

"It's all right," he shrugged.

"No, it's not." Catriona placed a hand on his arm. "Everyone deserves a home. Your heritage shouldn't keep you from having one. These people are stubborn, mule-headed idiots. Maybe we shouldn't have warned them and let them suffer their fate."

Elidor shook his head. "No, I grew up here. And whether it's my home or not, these people are innocent. Gieden will be here soon. I don't think he's far behind us. Tomorrow night, at dusk . . . " He let the words trail off. "I know how you feel about Corrigan and the Knights. It's the same way I feel about my mother and Aerendor. But all the same, I don't think either of us can just sit by and let them die."

"What can we do?" Cat whispered.

"We do what we can. That's all."

Catriona looked out over Aerendor's graceful buildings just a few hundred yards away. The towers looked like slender birch trees rising in the forest glen. She thought of it devastated, ruined, burned, and destroyed. "I guess that's all anyone can do, Elidor. We do what we can, and we hope that it's enough."

Footsteps approached just beyond the willow tree.

"Elidor?" Rohawn crashed through the willow branches, batting their long strands out of his way. "Hey, Cat! There you are. Corrigan was looking for you. Something about 'defensive plans.' You know how he is."

Elidor shook his head. "Did Corrigan get Elyana to listen?"

"What?" Rohawn blinked and smiled. "Oh—oh, yeah. He did."

"Good."

"Well, sort of."

"Sort of?" Elidor raised an eyebrow, and Catriona sighed.

Rohawn sheepishly continued. "They're willing to raise a guard to defend the city, but only once they have proof."

"Proof!" Catriona spat. "What kind of proof do they want?"

The squire shrugged. "They want to see with their own eyes. They've sent some of their scouts to go watch the edge of the forest tonight and get a view of the legion if they come across the mountain pass."

"Are they crazy?" Elidor lurched to his feet, fire in his eyes. "They're sending those scouts to their death. Gieden's legion can't be fought. They're too powerful. We know only that they fear fire—and not much at that. We need to defend the city, build firelines to surround the buildings, evacuate the children—"

"You sound a lot like Corrigan," Rohawn sighed.

"Well, maybe Corrigan's right about something for once." Elidor picked up his daggers and thrust them firmly back into their sheaths. "I'm going to talk to the Council. This is ridiculous." Elidor stood up, pushing aside the willow branches and stepping out onto the path toward Aerendor.

Rohawn trotted after him. "Oh, no. Don't bother, Elidor. The scouts have already left." A slow smile broke across Rohawn's face. "They wanted Narath to go, but no one could find him. Kaja and Kelenthe went instead. But don't worry. They'll be fine. They have a wizard with them."

Catriona stood at the edge of the tree, half hiding from the rain that was falling steadily from the dark gray sky. "What do you mean, Rohawn?" she hesitated to ask, but something in the squire's grin sent ice into her heart. "What wizard?"

Rohawn looked confused. "Sindri, of course."

CHAPTER

7 At the Edge of the Storm

"I always wanted to ride an elf's horse!" Sindri yelled, clinging to the back of Kelenthe's steed as they raced through the trees. The gray mare was smaller and faster than Catriona's sturdy steed. "Where's the road?"

"There is no road!" Kelenthe laughed, her dark hair flying in the wind. Her laughter echoed off the trees that flashed past, and she reached up to slap low-hanging branches as they rode by.

Up through the trees, Sindri could see the edge of the storm, a faint line of gold against advancing gray clouds. "How are we going to find the edge of the forest?"

Behind him, Kelenthe's twin, Kaja, answered. "The horses know the way." Her eyes were a darker gold than her sister's, filled with faint flecks of green—the only real difference between the two. It had taken Sindri hours to discover it, looking back and forth between them as they rode through the woods. It was amazing, really, to see them side by side.

"Look, there it is." Kaja pointed. Sindri turned to peer past Kelenthe, clinging to the back-buckles of her leather armor. And indeed, the forest ahead parted and showed mountains and plains beyond.

"Wow!" Sindri crowed. The horses slowed, their ears pointing forward and back with concern. Kaja's horse stepped sideways nervously, nibbling at a low-hanging branch. "That was half the time it took us to get here," he said.

Kelenthe threw her leg over the horse's flanks—narrowly avoiding Sindri, who had scooted back—and dropped lightly to the ground. She knelt for a moment, touching the earth lightly with her fingertips. "No one's been through here but the scouts. This is the most direct route to Aerendor. If this Gieden brings his legions, he'll come either through the road or by this route. If he can find the way, that is."

"Oh, his undead are made of mist and bone. Trees won't stop them." Sindri slid down the steed's tail. The horse whinnied with surprise.

"Sindri!" Kaja cried. "That's a tail, not a rope! You're lucky Yallen didn't give you a kick to the ribs for that."

Sindri only laughed, turning and bowing to the steed. "My apologies, noble Yallen, for my most rude behavior." He did his best impression of Corrigan's courtly bow, flourishing his purple robe wildly about with a sweep of his arms. To his surprise, the horse lowered itself stoically on one knee and bent its head nearly to the ground.

"Did you see that?" Sindri asked.

Kelenthe smiled, making another subtle gesture with her hand, and the horse obediently rose again.

"Kelenthe, Sindri—look," Kaja had dismounted and walked to the very edge of the trees. She pointed out over a low rise of land that led up to the forest. From here, Sindri could see a road exiting the forest somewhere to their right, cutting across the plain, and ducking behind a hill and out of view. "That's the road you took to get to Aerendor?"

"Yes," Sindri peered at it. "We followed it into the forest, twisted around a lot and then Narath found us."

The twins exchanged a look.

"What?" Sindri asked.

"Narath." Kaja pulled back her golden hood. "He has never liked Elidor. I can't imagine it was a pleasant homecoming. Not that it got better in council, of course."

"Why doesn't he like Elidor?" Sindri asked as he scrambled onto a tree stump, jumping up to grasp the branch of an old oak.

"A lot of people don't like Elidor. Take Fallerian, for example. Fallerian wants to rule Aerendor," Kelenthe said. "With Elyana's support, he could have himself appointed Royal Governor."

"He's even asked Elyana to marry him," Kaja added.

"But she won't," Kelenthe continued. "She says she doesn't want their council duties to suffer, but I think it's more than that. She was married once before."

"Elidor's father?" Sindri asked as he straddled the thick branch above him.

"No." Kelenthe laughed. "No, that would have been far too shocking. Her parents arranged a marriage for her to a Silvanesti named Rerdhen when she returned from her travels. She came back with a baby—it needed a family." She shrugged. "She and Rerdhen were lucky enough to fall in love thereafter. They had a daughter called Rina."

"I know her!" He grinned. "Elidor's sister!"

"Half-sister." Kelenthe's smile faded. "Her father's pet. Rerdhen didn't let Elidor and Rina near each other if he could help it. He thought Elidor would be a bad influence on his daughter. But he died in the war several years ago, and since then, Aerendor has changed. It is darker now than it has ever been before, and the people are uncertain."

Kaja straightened her cloak, drawing out from beneath it the symbol of a griffin's wing on a golden chain.

"Hey, what's that?" Sindri asked, staring down at her from his perch in the tree. "What's on your necklace?"

"My holy symbol," Kaja said, touching it lightly. "The sun is nearly down." She squinted at it, watching as the last sliver of the golden disk slid beneath the western mountains. "If you and your friends are right, Sindri, there will soon be undead coming down that road. They travel by dark, right?"

"Exactly. You'll know it's them because of all the ash and black mist. You won't be able to miss it. I mean, how many traveling black mists do you usually have in a forest? Not a lot, I'd imagine! Do you think your god can help with that? Will he help us fight them?"

"My goddess is Shinare, patron of wealth and freedom." Kaja took the symbol out and held it in her hand, fingers clasped tightly around the shimmering disk. "She's not a warrior. But Aerendor, with its workers of precious metals and jewelers, is dear to her. She will watch over us this night."

"We'll camp here," Kelenthe said. "No fire. No light. And if we see anything—"

"If we see anything," Kaja finished for her sister, "we ride."

They sat like that while the sun vanished away, all traces of light bleeding from the horizon. A chill wind swept across the tree branches, rubbing them together with soft sounds of woe. The moon Lunitari, red and glowing, peeked occasionally from between thick clouds, its face half-hidden in the gathering clouds.

It was Sindri's quick eye that saw them first. A thin trail of darkness shifted and moved across the plain. It was unlike any natural shadow, twisting in the moonlight, cast by nothing solid. He sat up on the oak branch, scanning again to see if he could pick out a shape. Another flicker, this time closer to them. "Kelenthe?" he whispered.

"I see it," she said.

The shadow drew steadily nearer. For a moment, they would

lose sight of it as it passed behind some rock or into some dip of the earth, but always it would return—closer than before.

"There," Sindri said at last, pointing a shaking finger into a patch of moonlight. "There."

A swirl of mist gathered on the road, and within it, they could see shining silver armor. Skull-like faces, half hidden by hood and helm, caught the moonlight with the reflections of white bone. Boots and claws echoed the pace of marching men. Over the hill they came—more than a hundred armed and armored.

"By Shinare," Kaja whispered. "It is true after all." Her face was pale. The moon ducked again behind the clouds, and for a long breath, they could not see the mist within the darkness. Thunder rumbled, and the sound of the strange steeds' claws was lost. "They're cold," she gripped the trunk of the old oak tree with one trembling hand. "I cannot see them at all. They have no life in them—only the chill of death. Elven vision can't see them."

"They're still there, and they're getting closer." Sindri leaped down from the tree. "We have to see if Gieden is with them."

"Where are you going?" Kelenthe scrambled to follow him.

"I'm getting closer." Sindri ran along the ridge of the forest, ducking from tree to tree. The twins followed, hoping that same darkness which covered their enemies would shield them from detection. They ran until they reached a sharp point in the ridge. Sindri threw himself down onto his stomach and crawled forward to see over the edge.

Below him, the road continued through a gully and into the forest's mouth. The dark, pitted earth showed signs of frequent use, standing out against the grass even in the faint light of the overcast night. There was another pass of thunder and the wet sound of rain falling on the leaves of the forest overhead. He huddled against the gnarled roots of a nearby tree and watched. Kaja and Kelenthe slithered up beside him.

"Isn't this exciting?" Sindri grinned.

"I wouldn't use that word, no," Kaja said.

"Actually," Kelenthe said, "I rather like it."

"That's the spirit!" Sindri laughed under his breath.

"No." Kelenthe pointed from beneath one of the roots. "There's the spirit."

The legion entered the gully from the far side. First two soldiers strode past, then a rank of seven more. Their armor was black and silver, just as Sindri remembered it, but now he could see the chain mail was pitted and stained with age. White bone showed beneath their misty tabards, and their hands clutched rusted swords. A pack of ghostly hounds bayed at their side, leashed with cords of spiderwebs.

Halberds and other polearms jutted up from within the ranks of the marching dead. Mists swirled around their boots. "More than seventy swordsmen," Kelenthe said. "I count twenty polearms and battle-axes. Thirty more on horseback, if you can call those demon-beasts horses."

"Shh!" Kaja warned. "Keep your voice down!"

"They move swiftly," Kelenthe whispered. "They will reach Aerendor if not tonight, then certainly at dusk tomorrow." She gazed at the torn and ancient banners, studying the unusual symbols blazoned on the rusted metal shields. Among them was one repeated charge—a silver crescent moon being swallowed by a full black moon. "That blazon is familiar, but I can't remember where I've seen it before."

"It's the same heraldry as on this coin I found." Sindri dug a small gold circle from his pocket, handing it to Kelenthe. "I kept it because—you know—gold coin, that's kind of rare. Not worth very much, but I thought it was interesting. And it wasn't as if it belonged to anyone, you know. It was just lying there in the barrow."

Kelenthe took it curiously, turning it over and over between her fingers. "There is writing on this. Have you tried to translate it?"

"There is?" Sindri looked at it eagerly. "Oh, no, I haven't tried. My magic doesn't help much with languages, you know."

"Keep it. It may come in handy later." Kelenthe handed it back to him and Sindri stuffed it into his pouch once more. He turned back to the gully to watch the army pass.

"Oh, look! There's Gieden." Sindri pointed at the black-robed figure. He rode easily on one of the spectral steeds, his velvet sleeves folded back to reveal pale white arms. His black plait hung against his shoulder. The figure at his side was also robed, but with a plain black hood pulled high over his features. He rode a half pace behind Gieden, his head lowered as if deep in thought.

"Who's that with him?" Kelenthe asked.

"Who knows?" Sindri cried. "Maybe it's a dark cleric!" His voice was excited and far too loud.

One of the hounds twisted in its harness, rotted ears flicking back and forth warily. It bayed, the sound of a broken horn crying out through the gulley, and other hounds turned. A second howl, then a third.

"Sindri!" Kelenthe grabbed him by his belt and tugged him back down, but it was too late. The hounds strained at their leashes, tugging their handlers toward the bank. "We've got to get out of here!"

As they struggled down the other side of the hill, a horn sounded. The bellows of the dogs increased and they heard scrabbling paws rushing up the other side of the gully, released to seek their prey.

"They're coming!" Kaja cried, a half step in front of her sister.

"And we're going!" Kelenthe retorted, increasing her speed.

The pack of hounds rushed over the edge of the hill at breakneck speed, their paws tearing up the sod. Fire swelled from their ghastly throats, singeing the grasses before them. As the three

reached their panicking horses, Sindri saw soldiers cresting the rise, drawing deadly swords from ancient and moldy sheaths.

Kelenthe dragged Sindri up her steed as quickly as she could. The horse reared and danced about, its eyes white and wide. With each second, the pack of hounds came closer.

"Go!" Kelenthe screamed, striking her horse's shoulder with the loose ends of her reins. "Go!"

The gray mare jumped into the woods, but Kaja held her steed in check. Her yellow cloak swirled in a gust of wind and she raised her hand above her head. A gold chain hung down from her fingers, and Sindri caught the faint sound of chanting. With a sudden, electric burst, yellow light flashed from the symbol. The hounds and the soldiers that followed them were bathed in it, screaming as they fell to their knees, shielding their eyes from the sun. For an instant, the dogs stumbled, their forward charge interrupted by the brilliant flash of light.

Then the light was gone.

Kaja spun her steed around to follow her sister into the woods. Sindri looked back over his shoulder. He could see the hounds spouting fire, the soldiers lifting their swords and gathering once more for the chase.

"They're on foot, we're not. We know these woods," Kelenthe shouted over the pounding of the horses' hooves. "We'll outrun the swordsmen."

"It's not the swordsmen I'm worried about." Kaja glanced back over her shoulder, and Sindri heard the cry of the hounds.

"The hounds will give up without their masters," Kelenthe said. "There's nothing to be afraid of!" She tore off her bandanna and waved it in the air, unafraid. "C'mon, you dogs! Try and catch us!"

They tore through the forest, branches and limbs slapping across their faces. Soon, the cries of the soldiers began to be lost in the echoes of the woods. Though the hounds were still close,

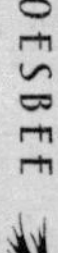

Sindri no longer heard the ring of steel. Whooping, he cried, "The soldiers are falling back!"

Kelenthe's steed raced at a full gallop through the tightly packed trees, but even as they gained more ground on their pursuers, Sindri felt something give. Beneath him, the saddle shuddered and the gray mare stumbled in its tracks. "Kelenthe, what's happening?"

The mare stumbled again, and this time, Sindri felt the saddle slide. "Hold on, Sindri!" she cried, desperately trying to keep her grasp on the mare's mane. There was a sickening snapping noise, and the girth of the saddle slid backward with a sudden jerk, hurling Sindri from the mare's back. He landed hard, the air whooshing out of his lungs. Kelenthe held on only a bit longer to the bucking mare. Sindri heard a sharp crack as her head struck a tree root and she lay still.

"Kelenthe!" Sindri screamed, pushing himself from the ground and crawling quickly toward Kelenthe. "Wake up." He shook her lightly, patting her cheeks with his hands and brushing the dirt from her hair. "We've got to get moving!"

Hoof beats broke through the trees and Kaja reined in her horse beside them. "What happened?"

"The saddle's girth snapped." Sindri shook Kelenthe once more.

"Snapped? But Kelenthe's always so careful!" Kaja leaped down from her own horse, slapping it on the flanks. "The horses will find their own way back to Aerendor. We'll have to stay here and fight."

"Get up, Kelenthe!" Sindri cried. "We're going to fight! You don't want to miss this!"

Kelenthe's eyes fluttered and she reached a tentative hand to the back of her head. "Wouldn't miss it for the world," she mumbled.

Kaja drew out her holy symbol once more, and from her belt she unfastened a club-like cudgel made of iron. Sindri stood beside her, fingers spread, trying to remember one of the spells Maddoc had taught him. Kelenthe slowly stood, reaching for a thin rapier that hung by her side. With her other hand, she drew a short dagger, the hilt curved to catch blades and block them while she fought. Kaja paused to give her sister a worried stare, but Kelenthe smiled, falling into a fighting stance without saying a word.

A bay sounded through the forest. The hounds had caught their scent.

Sindri thought he saw a flash of firelight, the dangerous breath of the beasts that pursued him. Another, like a candle flickering in the darkness of the woods, and then a third. "They're surrounding us," he whispered.

"Have any spells that could be useful, Kaja?" Kelenthe asked hopefully.

"Only one, but it will take a while to cast. If you can hold them off—" she was interrupted by another howl from a hound just outside their vision.

"I can hold them off. You just start praying." Kelenthe raised her sword and dagger together.

Just then the bushes were thrown aside and a dark form flung itself between them into the little clearing. The hound's breath caught the bushes on fire, lighting the scene with a fiendish glow. Kelenthe's sword cut into it as the beast leaped upon her, and black blood seared the ground where it fell.

A second hound, this one more cautious, growled from the shadow of the trees. Sindri spun to face it, his eyes wide with anticipation. "Good doggie?" he muttered as the hound opened gaping jaws, saliva dripping thick and dark from its fangs. It paced him, opening its mouth and breathing a ragged gout of fire. Sindri jumped aside quickly, but the hem of his cloak burst into flame. As he rolled to put it out, the dog threw itself at him.

Heavy jaws clamped around Sindri's arm. Sindri flailed, punching the hound in the nose with his free hand. The great dog shook him like a leaf. His fangs cut through the leather and into his flesh. Sindri punched again, this time connecting with the hound's eye. The beast yelped. It released him, hunching back in the darkness.

Sindri jumped to his feet and stared at the scene around him. Three hounds faced Kelenthe, each eager for the kill. One tried to race past her to attack Kaja, but Kelenthe stepped into the way, thrusting her shoulder into the beast just as it leaped. The hound spun out of control, landing hard on the roots of the elm tree that sheltered them. Kaja paid it no mind, cudgel in hand and a prayer on her lips.

The second hound snarled and ducked low, hoping to seize Kelenthe's leg in its quick jaws. She sidestepped, her blade striking the dog full in the head. The creature screamed, falling onto its side.

"We can hurt them!" Kelenthe shouted. She fell to one knee with a massive overhand thrust of her blade, sinking the thin sword between the creature's jutting ribs. There was a soft explosion. A gout of white fire sparked up through the puncture wound and the creature suddenly burst into flames. "And they can die!"

The third hound rushed her, its teeth tearing into her arm. Kelenthe yelled in pain, dropping her rapier in order to grasp the creature's jaws and wrench them apart. Her arm, bloodied and torn, came free of the bite.

Two more hounds crowded her, opening their mouths to emit bright waves of flame. Kelenthe grabbed the hanging branch of a tree near her and pulled herself up. Her cloak dragged behind her and burst into flames. She tore it away from her shoulders, letting it fall behind her to the ground.

Kaja swung her cudgel in time with her soft chants, keeping the area around her clear. The words were foreign, elven, but Sindri found them comforting.

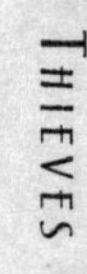

". . . iya allende, vivalende Shinare!" Kaja whispered, and a golden glow began to spread forth from her hands. Like an ever-expanding ball of sunlight, it enveloped them all. Sindri felt warmth spreading over his hands, his body tingling with the wave of summer's heat. In short moments, their shelter beneath the elm was filled with light, and the hounds shrank back into the shadows.

"What have you done?" Sindri stared in awe.

"It is not what I have done, but what Shinare has done for us. She has created a sanctuary where those beasts may not pass." Kaja smiled, lowering her holy symbol. "It will protect us until the sun rises. Then, we will be safe to return to Aerendor."

Kelenthe bound her wounded arm with a scrap of fabric, blood seeping beneath the tightly wound cloth. She reached down and lifted her fallen blade, then sheathed both weapons with a fluid motion. Walking to the ruins of her fallen saddle, Kelenthe lifted the girth strap from the ground and studied it closely. "There's nothing wrong with my tack. This was cut carefully so that it would not give immediately, but would break only when the horse was at a full run."

"Sabotage," Kaja murmured.

Kelenthe nodded warily. "Someone wanted us to leave—but not return."

"Who would do this?" Sindri knelt beside Kelenthe, taking the worn leather strap in his hands. Indeed, the marks of a knife were clear, quick and clean cuts in the girth that were designed to pull apart under pressure, when the horse was at a gallop.

"I can think of a few who might try it. People who don't believe the danger is real and want to take advantage of a false threat in order to focus their ambition. The Silvanesti are an arrogant lot. They don't like to be proven wrong." Kelenthe stared into the darkness as the last of the hounds slunk off into the night. "Or,

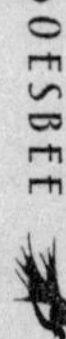

perhaps it is one who already knows there is truly danger and does not want us to warn Aerendor."

"Why would someone do that?"

Kaja answered for her sister. "I don't know, Sindri. But we're going to have to find out."

CHAPTER

8 An Unwelcome Dawn

"It's true."

Kelenthe and Kaja stood before the Council, the girls' clothes torn and stained from their journey though the forest. Kelenthe painted a terrifying picture of the legion marching through the dark forest, their steeds spectral in the moonlight. Sindri stood transfixed, leaning on the stone arch of the council room entry as Kelenthe told the tale. Her wound had been bound, but the stain of blood against the white wrappings on her arm spoke volumes.

When she was done, the room fell silent and several members of the council shifted in their seats. The afternoon sun shone down through the windows, golden and brilliant. In its warmth, the ghostly legion seemed almost a distant memory. Kaja stepped to Kelenthe's side and fell to one knee before the council.

"They were exactly as we have been told," she said, brushing a strand of black hair out of her eyes. "Aerendor can no longer ignore the danger."

Elyana steepled her hands above the crescent-shaped table, her eyes troubled. "No. " She turned her gaze to a glowering Fallerian. "We cannot. We must act—and swiftly. There are areas to the south—away from danger—where the children can find shelter. The river will give them flowing water and they can carry enough supplies to remain for some few days while we defend the city. But they must leave now, while the sun is in the sky."

"Really, Elyana, I must protest." Fallerian rose from his chair. "This is all mere panic. This black wizard has a goal. We have simply to meet it."

"Yes," Motek agreed. "We can bargain, offer a price. Aerendor is a wealthy town; we're not without resources."

Fallerian's eyes were cold as they rested on Elidor. "Exactly. And we have at least one thing here that we're very certain this Gieden wants."

Elyana spoke sharply, cutting off Fallerian's protest. "Offer up my son as a sacrifice for the city's safety?"

The room fell silent, elves turning away their eyes in embarrassment. Only Fallerian met Elyana's gaze. "It is a far better fate than handing the lives of this city into the hands of the undead."

Kelenthe could see Elyana waver, and her heart went out to the stateswoman. So much pain Elyana had suffered—everyone in Aerendor knew it. First the wild elf, of whom Elyana never spoke. Then Rerdhen, her Silvanesti husband, the archer whose death Elyana mourned to this day. These two men had marked her in ways that few elves could understand. Kelenthe exchanged a knowing look with her sister, and Kaja nodded. They could only hope Elyana had enough strength left to lead them.

"There might be another way." Salaria, the huntswoman, pursed her lips. "These creatures are only undead, after all, mindless and driven by the lust to kill. They could be easily enough stopped in their tracks, broken apart like so many bones." She tapped her fingers on the table, perhaps measuring such a battle in her mind.

Kelenthe approached the table, placing her fists on its edge and leaning in to the assemblage. "These undead will not stop with

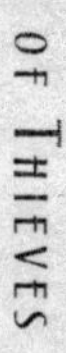

one man, Fallerian. And no, Salaria, they are not mindless, simple creatures. Further, their leader is a man of great power. Giving them Elidor will solve nothing. They will come to Aerendor and they will destroy it out of spite, if nothing else. Perhaps we should give them your sons instead? Or Shalidrian's? Or Kellemvor's? Or myself and my sister?" The other councilors behind the table shifted uncomfortably, and Hammon, Kelenthe's grandfather, frowned.

Kelenthe went on. "Placing our children—however ignobly born—into the mouths of lions will not solve the problem. Elidor may have brought this threat upon us, but he cannot lift it from our heads. I have seen the hatred in their eyes—these creatures live for the kill. If Elidor left this place or gave himself to the black wizard, they would still destroy us."

Fallerian growled, anger spreading over his face, but a new voice spoke before he could seize the moment.

"You won't give them my brother!"

Heads turned. Elyana sank into her seat with a quiet sigh. At the doorway to the council chambers, a lithe figure removed its cloak and walked with surety into the room.

"Rinalasha." Elyana shook her head. "You should not be here."

The elven girl was small, her youth apparent in her delicate features. Barely old enough to be allowed to speak in council, Rina was considered a teenager among the elves. "I should not? When Aerendor is in trouble, I should be elsewhere?" Her fists clenched in anger. "When you sent me to scout to the south yesterday, I did not think anything of it. Several days in the forest along the forest border—a routine trip, nothing more. I trusted you, Mother. As soon as Narath told you Elidor was coming, you sent me away. I want to know why." Rina fisted her hands against her hips.

Sindri waved. "Hi, Rina!" The elf girl didn't notice, storming up to her mother.

"What are you saying?" Elyana shook her head. "I never gave any such order."

"Someone did."

"Rina." Breaking the sudden uncomfortable silence, Kelenthe reached out and took Rina's hand. "I'm glad you're here. How did you know to return?"

"I saw the marks of a battle in the woods. There were many dead hounds, black blood all over the roots of our ancient trees. And I found this." From within her cloak, Rina drew out a broken war horn, its fragile ivory shell covered in dust and ancient writing. It was the horn of one of Gieden's minions. Rina threw it on the council table, letting it fall from her fingers with a sharp and solid thud. "Is it true, Mother? Is Aerendor going to be attacked?"

"Yes, it is," Fallerian answered for Elyana, rising from his seat at the council table. "And it was I who sent you away, for your mother's sake. I will not deny it; it was the correct choice, and now that you have returned, things will be the more difficult for both Aerendor and for her."

"How can you say that?" Kelenthe gasped. "Rina has as much right to defend Aerendor as any of the rest of us."

"How was I to know Elidor's 'threat of danger' was true? Rina's half-blood brother was returning. His mother was certain to be upset. And I am even more correct in placing her out of danger, now that we know the threat is real," Fallerian smoothly countered.

"What you mean is that Rina might talk some sense into Elyana and convince you to listen to Elidor." Kelenthe was angry now. "She's old enough to attend her mother on the council, the same way Kaja and I do for our grandfather. She has a right—"

"Elidor lies." Fallerian's bitter reply cut off Kelenthe's argument. Several of the soldiers in the chamber stepped forward, their hands instinctively reaching to the shafts of their bows. "He has lied to us in the past. He will lie to us again." Rina reddened, hands balled

into fists at her sides, copper eyes gleaming with anger and unshed tears. "We cannot trust the word of a half-breed thief."

"He is not lying now," Kelenthe breathed, anger tracing through her cultured tone.

"Please." With the single word, Elyana brought the entire council room to silence. She rose and walked away from the council table to the center of the room. "I have lost many whom I loved. My parents and my husband fought for Aerendor until the end of their days. Who am I to tell my children that they should not also believe in this city and in its future?" She turned toward Fallerian and those members still standing behind the council table. "I will fight for this city. My children, if they choose, will fight. Aerendor will fight, and we will survive even this." She lifted her chin. "Go, if you wish, Fallerian. Run to safety in the woods. But I call upon all those who are loyal to this land, to this city, and to its dreams, to stand beside me in the darkest night, to show these enemies that we will not give up even the lowest of our people to their will. We shall not surrender anything to evil when it knocks upon our doors. Those were the dreams of the elves who built this tower in which we stand.

"And now I ask you: who is with me?" Elyana turned, not to the council, but to the guards that stood beside the walls of the chamber. Her eyes caught those of the twins, of her daughter, and of each elf in turn who listened to her words.

Rina stepped forward and took her mother's hand. "I am." Though she was young, her face was serious, on it the cold and certain look of one who has already known much of war.

"We are," Kelenthe said gratefully, her sister nodding silently at her side.

One by one, the guards of Aerendor stepped forward, some nodding their agreement, others falling to one knee in respect. The whispers in the room swelled with relief, becoming cries of pride in their city, and even three of the five council members behind the table strode around to meet Elyana in the center of the room.

"You are correct," Hammon said. Kelenthe swelled with pride as she saw her grandfather place his wizened hand on Elyana's shoulder. "We will not give up a single elf without a fight."

Fallerian and Shalidrian remained in their seats, watching the spectacle. With a seething dignity, Fallerian rose from the chair. "We will, of course, do as the city bids us, for we are ever the servants of Aerendor's will." The long-faced elf bowed regally, his blue sleeves sweeping the ground as he turned and strode from the room. Shalidrian followed silently.

"Kelenthe, Kaja," Elyana's quiet voice commanded their attention.

"Yes, my lady?"

"I will need you to give our guards as much information about these undead as you can. Kelenthe, can you search your trove of ancient lore to identify them more accurately? Any information we can garner gives us a better chance to defeat them."

"I saw their banners, my lady." Kelenthe described them briefly. "If I can take some time with my scrolls, I may be able to find their heraldry—or at least some mention of it. And Sindri, the kender, had an item he took from their burial site. He had some kind of golden coin with that symbol on one side, and writing in a foreign tongue on the other. I may be able to uncover more information if I can study it in greater detail."

Kaja raised one reserved eyebrow. As the quieter of the sisters, she did not often speak before the council. Elyana listened as Kaja spoke. "I can tell the guards what they need to know, everything we learned while spying on Gieden's troops and fighting his hounds. My sister's study of this coin and the undeads' banners is critical."

"Very well," Elyana tried to hide her surprise at Kaja's offer. "It will be done. But I implore both of you to make haste. The sun is at its highest point, and during every moment after this one, it will be fading in the sky. We have little time."

The twins bowed as Elyana strode toward the door to the council chamber. "We will make preparations for the evacuation of those who cannot fight, while you prepare those who can. Come," she gestured to the councilors to follow her. "We have much to do."

CHAPTER

9 A Story Long Forgotten

The city of Taeloc, alone among its elven companions, turned its back on the gods of old. It stood in the wilderness, solitary as a star in the evening sky. Its golden gates were closed, and above the spires of its tallest tower flew a banner of black and silver, of dark Nuitari blotting out the light of the silver moon forever.

"That's it!" Sindri shouted, interrupting Kelenthe. "That's the banner we saw!"

"Sssh," she said, continuing to read from the scroll.

But the people of Taeloc were frightened, and though they trusted in their king, they feared that the isolation had driven him to madness. His famed mercenaries, the White Blades, kept the city in order, using their powers and their legendary training to maintain order even at the cost of lives. Yet the Defiler was not content even with his army of assassins, his city of thieves. The immortality of the elves was not enough for him, and he sought more. He crafted a silver coronet into which he placed the power of both the night sky and the earth below, and within it was his most precious gem, a sacrifice beyond counting.

"But, I've seen the crown and there's no gem on it, is there, Elidor?" Sindri craned his head toward Elidor, who listened silently in the corner of the room. "This story doesn't make any sense."

"Sindri," Cat sighed. "If you don't stop interrupting, Kelenthe will never finish telling us the tale."

Elidor and Rina glanced at one another across the small room of the elven cottage, their reunion cut short by Kelenthe's eager recital. She strode back and forth across the room, scroll in hand, waving her other arm in sharp, excited bursts. Rohawnenjoyed the story while lying on the low bed, staring curiously.

"Go on, Kelenthe," Elidor said. The plain silver circlet glinted on his forehead in a shaft of afternoon sunlight.

The Defiler, king above kings, Lord of Shadows, Master of Taeloc and the secrets of the ancient lands, fueled his creation with the power of a thousand souls. This, then, was his greatest work of all: the Crown of Thieves. Those who denied him were condemned to pain and eternal suffering; those who obeyed him were rewarded with eternal life. His soldiers, men of steel and war, lay down beside their arms, swearing to rise again when called by the Defiler's power.

"So this Defiler was the guy who made the crown, right?" Rohawn blurted out. "Elidor's crown?"

"Why is it called the Crown of Thieves?" Sindri piped up.

"I don't know. It doesn't say, but that's what it's called in the story." Kelenthe scanned over the story once more. "It says here that the Defiler put a great deal of his power into the crown. He gave it power over the undead, over the souls of others, over something called the 'shadow,' but I don't know what that means. 'Souls of others'? Huh. No wonder this black wizard Gieden wants it so badly."

Sindri looked at Elidor. "Can you control my soul? That's great! Make me do something!" He trotted over to Elidor's side. "Come on, Elidor. Make me dance like a chicken!"

"Sindri, cut it out." Cat grabbed Sindri by the shoulders and shoved him to a seat on a nearby stool. "Even if the crown does have any such power, Elidor doesn't know how to use it. Do you, Elidor?"

"No." Elidor shook his head. "Nor would I want to."

"But Gieden would. Black wizards know all sorts of things." Sindri rubbed his shoulder with a hateful look at Cat. "That must be why he wants it so badly."

Kelenthe scanned the scroll further, trying to piece together the snippets of fact from within paragraph after paragraph of myth and rambling description. "The sage who wrote this should have been locked away. He spends five paragraphs on how magnificent Taeloc's wine was and almost nothing on the Defiler, the crown, or what happened to the city." She frowned. "Here's something else. It says that the Defiler was insanely protective of his crown. He built into it certain safeguards such as . . . " Kelenthe glanced up, her face white. "Oh, Elidor."

"I already know," he said. "Tell them."

"Anyone who wears the crown binds their soul to it. Without it . . . if they take it off . . . they die. Uh . . . oh, this sounds bad. Their soul is trapped in the crown forever, as part of the Defiler's revenge." Kelenthe's voice fell. She cleared her throat, shuffling the papers around on the desk. "There's got to be a way around that."

"Maybe so." Elidor took the scroll from her, scanning the text. "But we don't have time to find it now." Elidor's rough hands, more used to a dagger's hilt than the thin paper of ancient scrolls, fumbled with the parchment. "What's this part? Here, where they've drawn the banner?"

Kelenthe looked over his shoulder. "Let's see." Muttering in Elvish, she busied herself with the scroll's translation. "Oh, yes, here, after the 'death' bit." Kelenthe continued.

The city of Taeloc turned away from all of the things that belong to the sun and was plunged into eternal shadow. The Defiler himself, a creature of spiteful desire, found too soon that he was both powerful and alone. For many decades, all that he saw, he commanded. With magic beyond modern understanding he ruled a land of darkness. Yet in the end, he was not powerful enough to command the crown, and it drove him to his doom. Madness overtook him, light overcame him, and he retreated forever into the shadow of his soul. As for the crown, it was lost in darkness, cursed and forgotten by all but the oldest sages.

"I don't think it's going to be of any more help." Kelenthe sighed. "The rest of this is mostly gibberish. I assume that Gieden's going to try to do what the Defiler did—use the crown to gain immortality and great power."

"It doesn't sound like a very good risk," Rohawn said. "If the crown can drive you mad, then why would anyone be stupid enough to wear it? Oh . . . " He sheepishly lowered his bull-like head. "Sorry, Elidor."

Elidor sighed. "It wasn't by choice, Rohawn. I was a white mouse in their experiment."

"And now you're risking madness if you keep it on, or death if you take it off." Cat stomped around the edges of the room.

"We can't worry about that now, Cat." Rina had been standing close to Rohawn, but she quickly stepped away when all eyes turned to her. "From what you've told me about the crown, it's not something we can deal with at the moment. Right now, we have to protect Aerendor. Corrigan and Kaja are doing their best to get the troops ready for battle against Gieden's legions. Whatever this black wizard's long-term plans are, we have to contend with *today*."

"Rina," Cat tugged on the other girl's golden curls. "Your impatience is going to get us all in trouble. We have to think this through."

"Cat, you know me. We've been through a lot together. Don't tell me that this is nothing or that I should calm down." Rina's eyes flashed.

The red-haired warrior nodded. "I won't. I'm really glad you're here, Rina. I just don't like the thought of you risking your life."

"Again?" She eyed Catriona seriously. "It's nothing I didn't do for Elidor when we thought he was dead, and I certainly won't stop just because he's alive."

"I know," Cat answered. "But just have a little patience. If we're lucky, we can find a way out of this so nobody has to get hurt."

"All right, Cat," Rina said at last. "I trust you." She leaned back against the wall and sighed. Beside her, Rohawn sighed at exactly the same time. The two looked at each other and flushed abruptly.

Ignoring them, Kelenthe said, "I can translate the rest of this, but it will take hours." The bard rerolled the scroll carefully and placed it in a long wooden tube.

"You've already helped us a great deal," Elidor said. "The scroll mentions that the crown is tied to powers of madness and darkness. Maybe light can be our weapon. Catriona, remember how fire hurt that one soldier when we were fighting them in the barrow?"

"Not much," she replied grumpily. "But better than my sword."

"The hounds backed away from Kaja's light spell too." Sindri bounced down from the stool. Outside, they could hear the sounds of hammering and horses neighing as Aerendor prepared for battle.

"Then we fight them with fire and light." Elidor turned to Rohawn, "Go tell Corrigan to stock the garrison with oil, torches—anything that burns."

"Hey now!" Rina reached out and grabbed Rohawn's hand, stopping the boy before the squire could charge out the door. "You people are mad. You do realize that we're standing in a forest? If you lose control of the fire, we could have an inferno on our

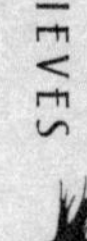

hands—and us standing in the center of it. We'd be saving ourselves from one death just to deliver Aerendor into another."

"It's a risk we'll have to take. I'm with Corrigan," Rohawn said sheepishly, making no attempt to remove his hand from Rina's grip.

"I'm glad you are," a deeper voice came from the door, and they turned to see the knight standing there. He held a map covered in red marks in his hands. "I came to show you the battle plans. What's the problem here?"

"Kelenthe's translated a scroll, and we've got to burn them—light—fire," Sindri garbled the words excitedly.

"Sir, I think we have to use fire against them. It's our best hope," Rohawn spoke over Sindri. "Kelenthe's found a scroll about these undead and their history."

"Well, good, but no more time for history lessons." Corrigan pushed past Rina and Catriona, spreading the map of Aerendor onto the bed. "Here are Aerendor's borders. Here, here, and over by this stream, we've built garrisons and blockades to force their invasion down certain channels—these streets, north and east of the central towers. Fire, you say?" He lifted a hand to stroke his mustache thoughtfully. "We can stock these houses with oil . . . hmm." Corrigan ignored Cat's glare.

Rina pointed down at the map. "Kelenthe, this is the school here, near the center of town?"

Kelenthe peered over Rohawn's broad shoulder. "Yes. It's one of the biggest buildings outside of the meeting hall in the towers."

"It's perfect. Flanked by wide streets, the stream and city water supply are close at hand," Corrigan mused. "We move this blockade, shift this so that they must turn left down this passageway. We might end up with less cover fire for the archers, unless they have the range to shoot over this high rooftop, but that's acceptable. With a swift group leading the undead, we might be able to do it."

"Do what?" Elidor stared at the map, a confusing jumble of streets, arrows, and boxes marking building locations.

"Herd Gieden and his foul troops into this building."

"And then what?" asked Sindri curiously, running his fingers over the leather map.

Corrigan's smile was brittle. "And then we set the whole thing afire."

Muted and orange, the last curve of the sun's disk sank beneath the horizon. Aerendor rested in silence, its twinkling lights stilled, the once-familiar sounds of singing or laughter lost amid a thick swell of fear.

Elidor and Rina walked through the forest at the edge of the village, their footsteps muffled by decaying leaves. Darkness pressed around them, and they strained to hear movement in the forest. Their steps followed the same pattern, their movements obviously trained by the same source. When they reached their objective—a large oak just at the edge of the city clearing—Elidor touched the bark lightly.

"Some homecoming," Elidor whispered.

"Oh, Elidor!" Rina reached out to take his shoulder, squeezing her half-brother's arm warmly. "Stop that. Not everyone here's angry. As for me, I'm so glad to see you again. I still can't believe you're really alive. When they told me you were . . . told me . . . " Tears welled up in her eyes. "You're here. It's a miracle."

"You should be with the others in the village. I'm going to have to get Gieden's attention. It'll be dangerous."

Rina snorted. "What, and miss all the fun? Elidor, I'm not afraid of danger. I practically died back in Solamnia fighting that shapeshifter. I wasn't going to let him get away with killing you." She shuddered at the memory. "I missed you, brother. I'm so glad you're back again."

He smiled. "Don't worry. I won't go get myself killed again. And neither should you. I want you to go back—"

"No," she interrupted him. "I know this city better than you do. I'll be fine."

He sighed then, softly. "Fine. You'd follow me anyway. I might as well be able to keep an eye on you."

"My eye's on you, too, brother." Rina squeezed his hand. "Don't you forget that."

Elidor smiled, a pale shadow of his usual confident grin. In the shadow of the oncoming night, he was a ghost behind the tree they had chosen for cover, hiding where he could not be seen from the road. "Thanks."

Rina stayed near him as though afraid to let Elidor out of her sight. She pressed herself to another oak. Over her shoulder was a quiver of white-fletched elven arrows, their stubs sticking up over her back like porcupine's quills. She drew a long elven war bow from her side and swiftly strung it, testing the tension of the bowstring with a soft but solid pull. In the silence that settled about them, Elidor drew his daggers, kneeling to place two on the ground and holding two more in each of his hands.

As the twilight sank into complete darkness, Elidor's eyes began to pick up stray forms in the village. The movement, scuttling along the road that led into the heart of the village, reassured him that the town was not sleeping, but preparing just as he was for the enemy that was soon to arrive.

Elidor was reminded of the days of his youth, the few times walking in the woods with Rina when her father—his stepfather—didn't know. Her father had been a respected archer, a huntsman, but he had never been kind to Elidor. They were never allowed to be together when Rerdhen was watching. Elidor was lucky to know his sister at all, due to the hatred that her father bore for his half-Silvanesti stepson. Still, somehow none of Rerdhen's bigotry seemed to exist in his

daughter. She was the only real family Elidor ever knew, though he didn't know her well. He would have to fix that someday.

Rina smiled at Elidor, turning to meet his gaze with a quizzical expression, and he realized he had been staring at her. A faint sound in the bush interrupted Elidor's reverie. Rina lifted her head as well, tilting it toward the subtle motion of brush and branch. Something inside Elidor hoped that it was a deer, that he had been wrong and that Sindri and his friends had not seen Gieden in the woods.

But the low growl of a hound and the soft, red light of fiery breath destroyed that last hope. Two beasts padded out of the bushes. One of the dogs howled a warning. Elidor felt a sharp chill go down his spine as the howl was echoed by a hunting horn. He heard the sounds of claws shuffling on the hard-packed road.

In less than a fraction of a heartbeat, he saw them.

They rode on the jet-black steeds that he remembered from the plain. Skull grins stared out beneath steel visors, white and silver in the night. The soldiers carried long spears, gripped by iron gauntlets that surrounded fists of bone and ash. Their helms shone in the moonlight. A pack of hounds raced beside the spectral steeds. And behind the riders, the legion marched. The ash that swirled around them turned the forest pitch-black.

Elidor saw Rina flinch at the sight, and he remembered the gut-wrenching feeling of his first encounter with these undead. She swallowed, her hand shaking on the bowstring, then lifted the arrow carefully to her shoulder. The string stretched, arching the bow into a perfect curve, and she glanced at him. Her eyes spoke the word that she could not whisper—*ready.*

Elidor paused only a second longer, then lifted his daggers and threw.

They knew undead soldiers were immune to normal weapons, so they fired upon the hounds. Elidor's daggers bit deeply into one creature's shoulder, drawing a surprised yelp from the beast. The

arrow launched from Rina's bow sank through another hound's leg, and the creature tumbled forward in a ball of fire.

The first rider turned, the skull within the helmet grinning in a stray shaft of moonlight. Then ash swirled around the rider's head, and the moonlight was snuffed out.

The rider pointed his long spear toward Elidor and sounded his horn once more. Elidor felt fear, its cold touch grasping his heart, but he shook it aside. There was no time for fear—not if Aerendor was to be saved.

"That's right, you hideous creatures," he shouted, pitching two more daggers at the riders. "I'm the one you're looking for!"

"What are you doing?" Rina hissed, stringing another arrow onto her bow.

"I'm getting their attention, like Corrigan wanted."

"Their attention is one thing," she cried, loosing two more shots as the ghostly horses charged. "Suicide is another!"

"Come on!" he yelled, reaching to grab Rina by the arm and pull her to her feet.

The undead legion raced behind them, hounds baying and horns sounding. Elidor smiled. Everyone in Aerendor would hear them coming.

Though they were slower than the oncoming rush of cavalry, Elidor and Rina were able to use the terrain to their advantage. They rushed down steep inclines and through tightly packed stands of trees in order to force the cavalry to slow.

As they reached the city, archers volleyed flaming arrows down onto the legion, but the attacks barely slowed the soldiers. Doors taken from their hinges leaned against wooden troughs to form rough blockades through the village streets. Rina and Elidor darted behind the first blockade they came to. While the soldiers on their ghostly steeds had to turn aside, the hounds were not as easily fooled.

One of the dogs squeezed through a hole in the planking. It launched itself at them, sinking its teeth into Rina's leg. She shook it off with a yell and it fell aside, ripping Rina's leather pants. Elidor saw Rina clutch at her leg as blood rose to stain her leathers.

The hound leaped again, forcing Elidor to sidestep between them. He gripped it by the throat, wrestling it aside so its charge would not take advantage of Rina's sudden stagger. It roared, flames rising to its mouth, but Elidor tilted the head away and the fire blazed harmlessly overhead. Claws scraping on the road ahead warned him that there wasn't much time. He gripped the dog's hindquarters with his other hand and hurled the creature back toward the blockade. It clattered against the wooden planks and lay still.

Rina leaned against the arched doorway of a nearby house, gripping her wounded calf and taking stock of the injury.

"Can you walk?" Elidor asked.

Rina nodded, but shakily. "Go on. I'll be fine."

"By E'li, I won't." Elidor dragged her arm around his shoulders. The sound of scratching claws ricocheted from the other side of the blockade, and he watched, horrified, as one of the spectral steeds leaped over the wooden planking. Fire sparked from the tips of its claws as it landed, and ash roared in its wake. The warrior upon the ghostly mount lifted his massive spear and prepared to plunge it into Elidor's chest.

Gripping Rina at his side, Elidor spun and burst open the thin wooden door behind them. He dragged his sister inside just as the warrior's spear splintered against the outer wall of the house.

They raced through the front room, scattering a table filled with delicate paintings. Behind them, the soldier cried out in fury. The rider and his steed plunged through the front door of the house.

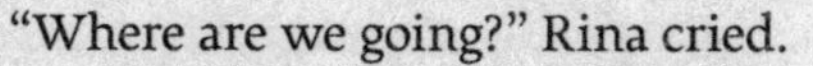
"Where are we going?" Rina cried.

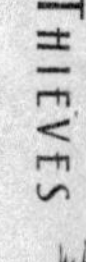

"Up!" Elidor took the stairs at the center of the small house two at a time, half carrying and half dragging his sister behind him.

But the horseman was not deterred. Where an ordinary horse might have balked at the close quarters, the undead steed rushed onward. Elidor could hear the sound of its terrible advance shattering furniture and burning through the floor with the heat of ashen claws.

Elidor swung open the small door at the top of the stairway. The cottage's second floor, little more than a garden patio, spread before them. Elidor paused, considering their options. There was no obvious way down from the roof, no walls to hide behind, no buildings close enough for Rina to leap to with her injured leg.

They were trapped.

The undead steed broke through the doorway at the top of the stairs. The warrior's bone grin sadistically took in Rina's bloody leg. In a sharp motion, the soldier drew a long sword from a saddle sheath and saluted Elidor.

The elf did not bother to return the gesture. He glanced to the right and left, backing away from the steed's advance. The alleys below were dark, sounds of marching feet echoing through the city. Elidor could see ranks of soldiers in the streets, marching inexorably through Aerendor's gentle lanes. Elven soldiers launched arrows from other rooftops, some closing ranks to fight against the undead warriors where they could. And always, they turned the undead toward the center of the town, slowly forcing them to follow Corrigan's route.

Then his eye caught a small figure below, and Elidor smiled.

"We have to jump," he called to Rina as they balanced on the edge of the rooftop. The spectral steed's claws pawed the patio floor, and the soldier raised its sword to strike.

"What?" she gasped. "The roof's too far! We'll never make—"

"Jump!" Elidor grabbed her by the waist and launched himself

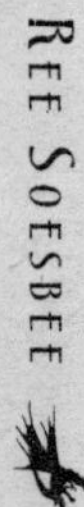

over the patio railing. He could feel the sharp swish of the warrior's weapon just behind him as they plummeted toward the alley floor.

"*Pfeatherfall!*" Their fall slowed, then stopped, leaving them hanging just a few feet above the alley floor.

"Sindri!" Elidor grinned as the kender stepped out from the shadows at the far edge of the alley. "Good job!"

"I saw you on the roof!" Sindri's face was smudged by ash, but his grin was larger than ever. "How did he get that beast up there?" The kender peered up, amazed.

"Sindri, take Rina to Kaja. She's hurt." He shifted his sister's weight over to his friend. Rina was light enough that Sindri could hold her up easily. "I've got to lead the legion closer to the center of town. They're spreading out."

"I watched them come into the city. They have two groups. Cat's in the plaza," Sindri said as he gestured, "trying to make the footmen reform with the cavalry."

"The cavalry," Elidor said, "were chasing me."

"Elidor, be careful." Rina pulled her bow and quiver from her shoulder, handing it to him. "Use this if you have to. Don't get close to them."

"Thanks." Elidor grinned. "Now get out of here."

Elidor dashed down the road, pulling up short at the edge of Aerendor's main plaza. There, around the fountain, Catriona, Corrigan, and a small group of determined-looking elves stood their ground against a group of undead swordsmen. Steel clashed against steel, and the undeads' weapons rang against elven shields. Corrigan stood on the edge of the fountain, head and shoulders above the others, calling out orders to keep the elf soldiers fighting in unison.

"They have no bowmen!" Corrigan shouted, pointing his sword at the undead. "Use this to your advantage! Keep your shields low, fight beneath their guard!"

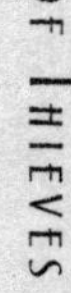

Meanwhile, Catriona waded through the undead, a blazing torch in either hand. Her face was lit by the billowing flame. The undead almost seemed to fear her, skirting her guard and flowing backward like a tide when she advanced. But for all that, few of the undead soldiers seemed in any way wounded or slowed. The people of Aerendor simply didn't have the means to permanently injure their enemy. Torches and small pools of blazing oil lay scattered across the plaza, forming a roadway through which the undead were forced to march. Elidor smiled. Corrigan had thought of everything, it seemed. Barricades for the cavalry, flaming ground for the footmen.

But where was Gieden?

Elidor nocked an arrow against the bowstring. He knelt at the end of an alley on the edge of the plaza, lighting the arrow's shaft in a small portion of nearby blaze. The bow wasn't his preferred weapon, but thanks to Set-ai's training, he wasn't a terrible shot anymore. He chose a target close to Cat and prepared to fire.

Behind Catriona within the elven defenders, Elidor saw Narath slipping away from the main group. The elf lowered the bow and darted into the darkness between two buildings on the near side of the plaza, dropping the flaming arrow in the dirt pathway. Neither Cat nor Corrigan seemed to notice. Elidor froze.

Where was Narath going, and why was he leaving his compatriots right in the middle of a desperate battle?

Elidor's eyes narrowed. Cat and Corrigan would be safe for a moment, and he didn't trust Narath. Stealthily, Elidor followed, slipping across the plaza without alerting the undead. As he moved through the city, Elidor kept Narath's shadow always in sight.

At last, Narath stopped by the side of one of the large towers, the meeting hall of Aerendor. A short distance away stood the school. Soon, Corrigan would draw the trap closed. But not yet. They had not yet found . . .

"*Gieden,*" Elidor breathed, peering out from his hiding place in the shadows. Narath approached two hooded figures on spectral steeds. They gathered in a small crossroads, hidden from the fighting in the plaza by a row of wooden stores. The huntsman greeted them warily, and Elidor could see Gieden smile.

"I'll give him to you," Narath said, glowering, "but you must spare the city."

"Of course. That is the deal we made last night." Gieden checked his nails for grit, flicking his fingers against his palm. "But I don't see that you've brought him to us. Perhaps we were too lenient, letting you go after our scouts found you on patrol—"

"No." Narath's response was quick. "I told you I'd hand him over, and you said you'd spare the city. Keep your part of the bargain, and I'll keep mine."

Gieden turned to the hooded figure beside him, spreading his hands wide. "I think he's not hearing me." Sharply, his head snapped back to Narath. "When you bring me Elidor, then the attack will stop. Not before."

"He wasn't with the main body of troops." Narath stumbled over his words. "He's alone in the city somewhere."

"Then find him." Gieden took up his steed's reins. "And let me give you a little incentive. I have yet to thank you for telling me about the knight's plans for the city. Allow me to show my gratitude." The black wizard raised his hands in front of Narath's baffled face. Words in a strange, magical tongue flowed from his lips, and Gieden's fingers shifted in strange patterns.

Within an instant, Elidor realized where Gieden was pointing, but it was too late.

A small spark of flame shot forth from Gieden's long fingers, streaking through the street.

As one, Narath and Elidor cried out, "NO!"

The spark entered the front door of the trapped school building

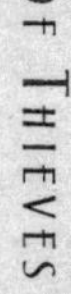

and exploded into a ball of massive, rolling flame. The building went up like a tinderbox. Dry straw packed around the inner walls caught fire in an instant, followed by kegs of oil placed in careful formation against the wooden columns. Flaming wooden beams exploded outward. Elidor stared as nearby buildings caught flame in the wake of Gieden's massive attack.

Corrigan's plan to destroy the undead legion—gone. And worse, Gieden's fireball had ten times the force and impact of Corrigan's planned ignition.

Aerendor was burning.

"You!" Narath's sword leaped up as he caught sight of Elidor standing in the shadow. Still stunned by Gieden's vindictive assault, Elidor froze for a second and faced his enemy on the other side of the crossroads.

"Ah, Elidor." Gieden smiled pleasantly. "So very glad that you could join us."

But it was the third man, the hooded figure at Gieden's elbow, who caught Elidor's attention. Green flame burned where his eyes should have been, flickering and rolling like faerie fire in the darkness of an empty face. A wave of hatred, anger, and palatable evil swept across Elidor, forcing his stomach to clench and driving a shooting pain through his brow. The crown on his forehead seemed to heat for a moment, then turned as cold as ice pressed against his flesh.

Narath raced forward, sword drawn back for a sweeping blow. "This is your fault!" he yelled, closing the distance between them while Elidor staggered back from the unexpected pain in his skull. "Aerendor would be safe if you hadn't returned, you half-blooded mongrel!"

Behind them, Gieden sat back on his steed and laughed, extending his arm to keep the hooded individual at his side still. "No," he murmured. "Let them play."

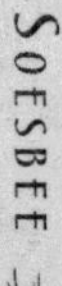

Elidor dropped the bow and pulled out a dagger in one swift movement. Narath's sword fell against Elidor's upraised dagger and was turned aside. Not to be deterred, Narath raised it again for another pounding overhand blow, forcing Elidor back against the wall of the alley. "You disgust me," Narath shouted. "You're impure. Weak!"

Elidor threw himself out of the way of Narath's third strike. "Narath, what are you saying?" he gasped, watching as several more buildings were ignited around them. "We have to get help. We have to put out the fire. You're wasting time!" Narath's strikes were wild and angry, and Elidor's arm grew numb from blocking ferocious blows.

"It's your fault, Elidor! All of it!" Narath screamed. "You brought them here! Why couldn't you have stayed away forever, you filthy half-breed?"

Elidor waited until Narath's sword fell, ducking so that the blade rang against the wall. Flame licked the rooftops above them, racing lightly up the walls of the wooden structures and blackening the silver sides of the tower itself. Elidor gripped the hilt of Narath's sword, squeezing with all his might against the other man's fist. He heard a sharp cracking sound. The sword fell to the side.

Narath turned, weaponless, his face filled with rage. He leaped to tackle Elidor, but Elidor was ready for him. A swift punch to the huntsman's stomach, a fist to his jaw, and a curled kick knocked out the other elf's knees.

The force of the blow left Narath curled on the dirt roadway of the plaza, gasping and trying to catch his breath. Elidor stood over him for a moment, dagger still in his hand, but then lowered the blade.

"I'm not going to kill you, Narath," he whispered. "And that's more than you would have given me."

"I think they've had their fun," Gieden purred, drawing Elidor's

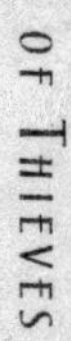

attention back to the two robed figures on their spectral steeds. Smiling, the black wizard raised his hands once more and began to chant as his hooded assistant rode forward.

The pain in Elidor's head intensified, white hot and terrifying in his mind. Images of a city that had not been seen by mortal eyes in hundreds of years flashed through his mind. The faces of people long ago turned to ash flickered and screamed. He gripped his temples, running blindly forward between two blazing buildings. He heard Gieden's chanting, but he didn't care. All Elidor knew was that he had to get away from the pain.

He ran through the city, half hearing Gieden's laugh and the scraping claws of his pursuers. The black wizard finished his spell, and a bolt of lightning coiled past Elidor, white and blinding. Elidor threw himself to the ground.

The lightning passed overhead and crashed into the central tower, blasting out stonework and impacting the structure like a giant hammer. The tower tilted crazily to the side, its roof aflame. Elidor covered his head as chips of stone rained down. With a groan, the tower walls collapsed, pitching the great tower into the main plaza of the city.

Elidor could see Catriona screaming to the elves. The defenders struggled to regroup around Catriona, and Corrigan yelled commands. Around them, the undead legions howled in glee, taking advantage of the confusion. One undead soldier thrust his sword through a defender, ending his life with a brilliant flash of blue-white light. Elidor stared in horror as the undead warrior froze for a moment, drawing the light into itself as the elf sank to his knees. The warrior seemed to be feeding from the dying elf, satiating itself upon the life energy of its foe. When it withdrew its sword a moment later, the elf crumbled to ash.

Yet even as Elidor stared, everything changed. The firelight became brilliant rays of sun, and the burning plaza changed into a wide white roadway through elegant arches of ivory and silver. He saw the soldiers of the undead legion, but in his mind their faces were not formed of bone and ash. Instead, they were youthful, long silvery hair gleaming in the light. Their weapons flashed, hunting horns sounding a clarion call.

For a long moment, Elidor was no longer in Aerendor, but somewhere else—a white city on a sunlit plain. Elidor rolled over, feeling the hard-packed white clay of the street beneath him, and saw two horsemen riding through the city streets.

Their white steeds charged between arches of ivory down a gleaming path. He saw a screaming commander ordering his troops—sober-looking elves with pale white hair—forward. Their uniforms were white as well, with the sigil of two crossed daggers over the symbol of a black moon enveloping a silver cresent moon. Elidor heard a shout echo as if from far away and . . .

Elidor's vision blurred. He shook his head to clear it and once again he was back in Aerendor. Gieden and his companion stormed closer, pounding a heavy beat against the soft loam of the city road. Elidor rolled as they passed over him, sharp claws cutting into the ground where he had lain. Gieden's laugh echoed with the ringing swords of the undead, their rotting arms holding aloft rusted weapons. Cat leaped into the fountain, defending one of the elves who had fallen.

Gieden turned his steed. It reared, shooting thin jets of flame from its nostrils. Gieden pointed down at Elidor, a strange light glittering in his cold eyes. "That one!" he commanded, his voice rising over the sounds of the fighting. "Bring me his corpse!"

The soldiers in the plaza turned. Their skeletal grins focused on Elidor, watching him struggle to stand despite his disorientation. To one side, another hunting horn sounded, and Elidor could hear the approach of more undead steeds—Gieden's cavalry.

Elidor caught Corrigan's eye as the knight leaped down from

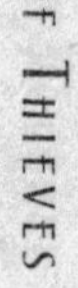

his position within the elven ranks. The knight pointed toward Elidor and Gieden, ordering the Aerendor defenders into battle even as the undead turned and focused their rage on Elidor. Elidor saw the elves struggling to raise bows and ready their swords in weary hands. The undead marched in unison, showing no sign of weakness despite their long conflict against the elves. Continuing the battle would only destroy the elves.

Elidor climbed to his feet and stepped backward, gripping his temples to try and fight the pain. He saw the undead cavalry charging down the wide street of the city, headed toward him—and their course would take them directly into the defenders from behind.

The elves scattered, some chasing their foes, others turning to brace themselves against the rush of spectral steeds. The battle for Aerendor would end as the one in his vision already had—in blood, fire, and death. Narath's words rang in his ears—"half-blooded mongrel!"—and Elidor knew that the other elves, the ones too polite to say it, had been thinking the same thing all his life. He froze, watching as the undead cavalry began to cut through the defenders' ranks. *This was his fault.*

But still, Elidor didn't move. He didn't owe them anything. The Silvanesti turned up their noses at him. He was nothing to them, nothing more than an aberration, a disease. A sickness of which they were ashamed. Narath was right.

Then his sister's face swam before his memory, clashing with the images of ancient ivory statues and magnificent towers of glass. "I am glad to see you again," she had said.

Aerendor. Even if the city hated him, it was still *home.*

Elidor hurled his last dagger and saw its tip bounce harmlessly from the deep velvet of Gieden's sleeve. The black wizard laughed eagerly, eyes widening as he enjoyed the fruits of his terrible power.

"You want me?" Tears stung Elidor's eyes, his hands clenched in rage. "Then come and get me!" Fear clenched his heart, but more than that, Elidor just wanted to get away—away from the vision, from the sight of Aerendor in flames, from everything that the Silvanesti and their town and their arrogance had ever done to him. He would give them what they'd always wanted ever since he was a child. He would simply *go away.*

Turning from the combat, away from the overlapping images of battle both in Aerendor and on the ivory streets of a long-dead city, Elidor did the only thing that he could.

He ran.

CHAPTER

10 When Home Seems Far Away

Wet leaves and fallen branches—remnants of yesterday's storm—twisted under Elidor's footsteps. Wind whipped the trees. There were no animals, no sounds other than the panting of his breath, the rough tread of his feet, and the heavy footfalls of the undead soldiers who pursued him in the dark. A light rain began to fall.

He was alone—alone and hunted.

Somewhere past the soldiers, Gieden and the cavalry followed. Or, at least, he hoped that they did. Aerendor would never survive a continued attack. The memory of an elf skewered on a skeletal footman's blade, his soul feeding the creature's undead hunger, dominated Elidor's thoughts. Not simply to die, but to be destroyed.

The soldiers were nearly upon him. They were faster than he was, and they weren't weary from fighting or tortured by memories. They had only one mind, and that was controlled utterly by Gieden's will. They were ordered to catch him.

Elidor saw a swordsman lumber out of the brush to his right. Elidor dodged, running beneath the warrior's blade, another to the left, and a third behind it. Elidor charged through a patch of thick brush to avoid them, wet branches slapping against his face. He had spent many hours in the woods as a child, but the passage of time and of the storm made it all seem strange and unfamiliar.

Suddenly, Elidor felt his feet sliding on the wet terrain. Mud shifted under his boot, twisting his ankle painfully and pitching him forward.

He burst out of the woods through the branches of a tall willow tree, catching a glimpse of a fast-running stream swollen by the rainstorms. He gripped one of the branches and swung out over the waters for a moment before throwing himself back on the bank. The cliff, though not much higher than the height of a man, was slick and muddy, the stream below deep enough and flowing fast enough to carry him away. In a moment, he could be lost in those waters, but his chances of surviving would be slim, perhaps even slimmer than his chances of surviving Gieden's troops. And he had to keep the undead busy and far from Aerendor—at least until the sun rose.

Something crashed through the brush behind him and Elidor turned. Two of the undead lumbered forward from the darkness of the woods, their bony grins shining in a stray beam of moonlight. Elidor's hand fell instinctively to his belt, but the scabbards that held his throwing knives were empty. They wouldn't be very useful anyway. Weapons didn't hurt Gieden's undead followers.

One swordsman swung, and Elidor leaped back. Gripping the willow branch again, he flew forward past the warrior.

Elidor leaped higher, grabbing the branch above him and pulling himself up. Carefully, he pulled himself to his feet on the light limb and ran forward over the soldier's head. The soldiers thrust their swords up at him, but they could not reach him. He teased them like that for a moment, dancing on the willow branch, waiting for one of the soldiers to step too close to the edge of the ravine. As soon as one did, Elidor grabbed the limb beneath him with both hands and swung. Feeling the rush of wind and sting of rain against his face, he circled the tree's trunk and planted his boots squarely against the warrior's back.

The undead plunged down the ravine and into the swollen stream. The waters swallowed him whole, sinking him quickly. Elidor saw the soldier struggle, fighting the water that sucked and raced past him. A last image of gleaming helm above muddied, choked waves, and then the stream tore the soldier away from the ravine and down into the forest beyond.

The second warrior swung but missed as Elidor swung back to the bank and dropped to the ground. He couldn't kill these lumbering monsters, but he could incapacitate them. The warrior's sword snapped through branches. Elidor spun and kicked his leg out to catch the soldier behind the knee. The warrior lost his balance and fell to the ground. Elidor snatched the sword from the creature's hand, twisting it away with a quick maneuver.

Two down, but more were coming. Hanging from the tree branch, Elidor could see four more soldiers among the trees, and the baying of the hounds was close behind, but there was no sign of Gieden. Elidor cursed. Surely the wizard hadn't remained behind in the village? He was hunting Elidor; he wanted the crown. Why wouldn't he follow?

Four undead broke into the clearing, rain dripping from their helms and dulling their glinting, silvery chain mail. Elidor gripped the unfamiliar hilt, testing the balance of the short sword as the undead approached. The warrior on the ground began to push upward. Elidor slammed his boot into its bony jaw and watched as the warrior's head spun to the side. The kick would have killed a man—the undead simply continued to try and stand.

Elidor reached out and grabbed the wrist of one of the advancing soldiers, jerking him forward over his companion. The warrior stumbled. Elidor spun and hurled it toward another, watching as the two collided. He leaped on the back of the one trying to stand, shoving it down into the muck, then leaped once more into the tree. The undead were strong, yes, and they were virtually indestructible, but they were slow. He nearly laughed at the sight of them stumbling in the mud and desperately trying to catch him. And he had been afraid?

Then, a wave of ice swept over Elidor. His heart froze, his knuckles clenched, and his breath turned to frost in the air. Everything seemed cold and pale around him. Indescribably, the world emptied of life.

At the edge of the clearing, just behind two other undead warriors, stood a robed and cowled figure.

"Gieden?" Elidor whispered. He felt his balance on the limb begin to fail.

The robed figure lifted its hands. The sleeves of its robes fell back, revealing twisted, leathery arms. It wasn't Gieden. It was the wizard's follower, the one who had ridden behind Gieden in the city. Gieden hadn't even bothered to chase Elidor himself—he had sent a servant.

Elidor's hands slipped from the limb, but he barely felt himself falling. He knew the swords were there, saw them lifted all around him as the warriors circled him, but nothing could pull his mind away from the numbing cold. The hooded figure stepped closer, bringing its arms forward in a gesture of attack. The soldiers closed in.

"No!" Elidor growled, struggling to fight despite the ice inside his bones. Still gripping the sword he had taken from a warrior, he pushed up against the willow trunk and found his footing. But the hooded figure stepped closer and reached toward Elidor's brow.

Ice crackled like electricity through its hands, and Elidor could see pale green globes deep within the blackness of the cowl. He staggered backward, teetering on the edge of the ravine. Every

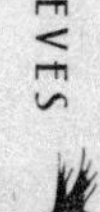

instinct told him to avoid the touch of this creature. Every fiber of his body wanted to run, to flee, to escape. But the stiffness in Elidor's bones and the cold within his mind numbed his every action.

The stream swirled beneath him. Another step and he would fall. Elidor tried to scream, but it came out as hardly a whisper. Before Elidor could yell, he found himself slipping down the bank. His limbs were heavy, and he dropped the warrior's sword. Staring up, he saw the hooded figure spin in slow motion, reaching out with one leathery hand. Clawed fingers missed Elidor by less than an inch, ripping his leather vest instead.

Then the waters stole Elidor's breath away, and there was only darkness.

CHAPTER

11 AFTERMATH

Aided by the light rain that had fallen just before dawn, the fires died quickly, the last ashes fading even as the sun overtook the land. The woods were still lush and green. Smoke rose like blood from a wound, marking the scarred, black area that had once been a city. The graceful towers of Aerendor no longer rose above the trees, but lay in crumbled ruins on the street. Most of the delicate wooden buildings were blackened and fallen. The city had been destroyed.

Elves in battered tabards, long overshirts stained in the lovely blue dye of Aerendor's council chamber, walked the streets. Some still carried buckets to put out the fires. Others knelt by a ruined building or devastated tree. A sketchbook, torn and stained with ash and water, lay beneath a singed bush. Catriona lifted a fallen door, placing it back against the opening of a still-standing house.

"It's going to take years to rebuild." Kelenthe rubbed her bandanna over one of the small statues in a burned garden, trying to smudge the ash away from a cherub's cheek. The city looked like a mockery of itself, a beautiful garden twisted and devastated by war. "Aerendor was a place for artists. We are painters, scholars, gentle people," she said mournfully. "It should never have known war." Her sister knelt beside her, uselessly trying to clean the soot from a child's doll.

Kaja shook her head. "It was that black wizard's fault. We couldn't fight his magic. Between his fire and the undead, we had no chance." Crestfallen, she lay the doll back down.

"Cat!" Rohawn's voice bellowed through the streets. "Cat!" He came into sight, panting and wild-eyed. "Corrigan found—I mean, Elidor—down by the stream. He's hurt."

Cat and Kelenthe stared, trying to make sense of the squire's words, but Kaja immediately stepped forward and grabbed Rohawn's arm. "Show me," she said firmly.

They raced through the streets toward the edge of town, down to a stream bed where a thick rivulet of water flowed beneath a footbridge. Corrigan and two of the Aerendor elves stood waist-deep in the water, pulling a body from the eddies at the pillars of the bridge.

Kaja stumbled down the steep incline, grabbing at the reeds that grew by the river. She waded into the water, taking Elidor's hand in hers, checking for a pulse. Kelenthe, Rohawn, and Cat stood by the footbridge.

"What are you doing?" Sindri trotted over to them, peering down the streambed. "Oh no, is that Elidor?"

Kaja knelt in the shallows of the water. She clutched her holy symbol in one hand, placing the other over Elidor's chest.

"Did he float all the way downstream? Where did he come from? Is he breathing?" Sindri tried to push past the others.

"Sssh," Kelenthe grabbed him, placing her hand firmly over his mouth. Below them, at the edge of the stream, a soft golden light began to shine from within Kaja's cupped hand.

Rina's scream echoed off the water. "Elidor!" One of the elven guards reached to hold her back, but she fought him and ran past.

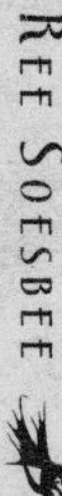

Catriona caught her, wrapping her strong arms around the elf's slight figure.

"Kaja!" Rina's voice was hoarse. "Please! Help him!" Exhaustion overcame her and she sagged in Cat's arms, tears streaking down her face.

"It's all right, Rina," Catriona said. "Elidor's going to be fine. Kaja can help him."

"He's got to be, Cat! He's got to be," Rina sobbed. "I can't lose my brother again."

Kaja looked up at Rina once, her eyes serious. She nodded, but didn't answer Rina, turning to stare back down at Elidor's silent body. Her hands touched his face, the golden light increasing, and her prayer never ceased.

"There's no use." Fallerian sniffed. "Leave him, Kaja, and tend to those whose lives are worth saving." His blue robes flared as he turned to walk away.

Kelenthe watched him go and realized for the first time that she hated him.

Rohawn caught her attention with an awed whisper, dragging Kelenthe's attention back to the river and her sister. "Is she going to bring him back to life?"

Kelenthe snorted. "If she could do that, we would have let her defend Aerendor all by herself. No, Elidor was still breathing when they pulled him out of the river. Kaja is going to heal him. Don't worry." Kelenthe shot the boy one of her dazzling smiles.

Kaja's sober face lifted, the lines of concentration fading from her brow. The glow over Elidor's chest faded, and slowly, Kaja removed her hand. Kelenthe saw Elidor's eyes flutter, confusion growing on his face as he realized he was being held by two elves in the middle of Aerendor's swollen stream.

Rina gasped and ran forward, breaking Catriona's hold. She took Elidor's limp hand in hers and turned to smile at Cat and Kaja.

"Rohawn," Corrigan called, and the boy was quick to step forward. "Come and carry him to the hospital."

The hospital was little more than a large manor house that had the good fortune to stand on the side of the city that had been away from the wind. Its walls were covered in soot, the wide porch fractured by the heat of the blaze that had enveloped Aerendor, but it still stood. The front doors were open, and a grizzled old elf in ill-fitting chain mail carried water back and forth between the injured. Wounded elves lay on the couches, the floor, and a few under the eaves of the porch.

Catriona walked with Rina. Rina's steps shook, but she refused to be carried. Cat steadied her with one hand on her shoulder, but let her make it on her own. When they reached the hospital, Rina sat down heavily on a chair by the door. Kelenthe stood in the doorway, watching as Rohawn placed Elidor on a lounging couch. Catriona took a wet rag from the old elf, placing it on Elidor's forehead.

Kaja put her hands on Rohawn and Sindri's shoulders. "The other injured people need my help as a cleric," she murmured. "Can you two assist me?"

"Oh, but Elidor's going to tell us what happened," Sindri began.

"I really think that's the best idea, Sindri," Cat was quick to agree. "Elidor's still very shaken. He needs rest. When he's ready, we'll come and find you." Rohawn looked over at Corrigan, who nodded. Kaja steered the two out the doorway, glancing back at Kelenthe with an uncompromising stare as she passed. Kelenthe sighed.

When they were gone, Kelenthe pulled up a chair near the couch and straddled the seat. She looked at Catriona and then over at Corrigan, his face pinched with concern. When it became obvious that neither of them were going to say anything, Kelenthe spoke up.

"What in the name of the Abyss happened?"

Elidor winced, running a hand over his badly bruised side. The tear in his leather jerkin spoke of a much more grievous wound, but Kaja's healing magic repaired all but the traces of the injury.

"I tried to draw them away from the city." As he spoke, Elidor coughed up water still in his lungs. "But they didn't follow."

"Some did," Catriona argued gently. "But Gieden stayed. I saw you running from the city, but Gieden stayed and unleashed his magic on the town. Oh, Elidor. It was . . . " Cat's face was pale. "It was brutal. The elves took a lot of damage. Aerendor is all but destroyed."

Elidor closed his eyes. "What have I done?" he whispered.

Cat gripped his shoulder. "You've done your best. If Gieden didn't chase you when you were right in front of him, then that proves your point. He would have come here and done this no matter where you went. Gieden's not nearly as interested in killing you as he is in killing everything that you love." Cat sighed. "For some reason, he can't touch you directly. So he has to find ways to make you surrender the crown of your own will."

Kelenthe raised her head from the back of the chair. "The crown protects you."

"I almost wish it didn't," Elidor groaned, falling back against the pillows. "I didn't ask for this. I don't want it—" His voice caught in his throat.

Catriona took the wet rag from his head and awkwardly dipped it back into a small bowl of water. "Be glad you're alive, Elidor. We still have a chance to get even with Gieden."

"Get even?" His eyebrows shot up. "His soldiers can't be killed. He's got some . . . some kind of wraith-thing that we can't even identify, hounds, cavalry. What exactly do you think we can do against him?"

Corrigan's voice was a low baritone rumble. "Wars have losses. But victory is not impossible." He stroked the thin goatee on his chin thoughtfully.

"Losses?" Elidor almost shouted, pushing the rag off his forehead even as Catriona tried to settle it on him. "Aerendor's in ruins! People are dead! We haven't even given Gieden a headache, and you call this an acceptable loss?!"

"Stop it, Elidor," Kelenthe shouted. "A lot of people died here, trying to fight off Gieden. If you give up now, they died for nothing. My grandfather . . . " She stopped, her face coloring awkwardly. "My grandfather . . . " Her voice, usually so gallant and strong, broke at last and she was silent.

"Councilor Hammon?" Elidor's face fell. The anger that had burned in his eyes faded into sorrow. "Oh, Kelenthe. I'm so sorry."

"Don't be." She wiped tears from her eyes, feigning a bravado she didn't feel. "He died fighting for his people, and he never gave up. Neither will you, Elidor, if I have to follow you from here to creation to make sure of it. My sister and I have nothing left in Aerendor now, and we've got a right to travel with you until we can find Gieden and put my grandfather's soul at rest."

"No, you're not. I'm not dragging you or your sister into this. You might get hurt too." He struggled to rise, wincing with pain.

Catriona pushed Elidor back down onto the couch. "Sit down before you undo all of Kaja's work."

Kelenthe stared at him sternly, looking for a moment very much like her dour sister. "One: you don't have a choice. Two: you need us. Where would you be right now if my sister hadn't healed you? Her magic is one of the few weapons we do have against these creatures." Kelenthe pointed a finger at him. "And how much did you know about these soldiers before I started looking them up in the scrolls? I figure I'm about as much of an expert as you're going to find on these particular obscure undead warrior things, so you can't afford to leave me behind."

"No." Elidor resisted. "Nobody's coming with me. I'm going alone."

Cat gasped. "Elidor, what are you saying?"

Behind her, Corrigan snorted. "He's feverish. Put the rag back on his head, Lady Catriona."

"I'm not sick." Elidor took the rag from Catriona and dropped it back into the bowl with a splash. "I'm just tired of watching people die. Aerendor's destruction is my fault. Whether they would have come here or not, Narath sabotaged the village because of me. I have to deal with that—and with him. He met with Gieden before the battle started."

Kelenthe felt her stomach lurch. "Elidor, are you sure?"

"I saw him with Gieden in the streets during the battle last night. He told them all about Corrigan's plans, where the trapped buildings were, the fire—all of it. I'm sure."

Corrigan said grimly, "Narath and Fallerian are addressing the council right now, deciding what is to be done."

"With Hammon's death," Kelenthe began, "Fallerian has a controlling vote in the council."

"We've got to stop him from taking over Aerendor." Elidor shoved himself up off the couch again, and this time, Cat didn't stop him.

Taking his arm and hoisting it over her shoulder to help him stand, Catriona turned to Kelenthe. "Show us where they're meeting," she growled. "At the very least, we'll make sure Elidor gets to tell them what he saw—what Narath did."

"And if they don't listen?" Corrigan murmured.

"We won't give them a choice." She pushed through the doorway, helping Elidor out into the sunlight.

Kelenthe and Corrigan paused, turning to look after the strong

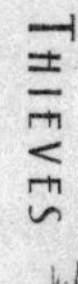

warrior and her limping friend. "Do you think we even have a chance?" Corrigan asked.

"No, not really." Kelenthe ran a hand through her dark hair, shaking loose some ash from the city's fires. "But I don't think that matters to either of them."

With a sigh, the two followed their companions from the room.

The city plaza was a far different place. Burned wisteria vines twisted across fallen garden arches. The central fountain still stood, but its sculptures were covered in thick, gray ash. Many of the branches of the carved tree were broken, scattered like bones around the fountain's base. The deer still stood, one leg poised, considering the choice between drinking and fleeing, but now it seemed that flight was certain. Its horns, once spreading and graceful, were gone, and only broken stumps remained.

All around them, the great garden was burned. Blood of elven warriors spotted the barren ground. All the beauty was gone, and only twisted vines and ash remained. The battle that Elidor witnessed had destroyed the artists' garden, leaving only chips of shattered pottery, a broken easel, and the fountain standing in a field of blackened growth.

Kelenthe drew a shuddering breath as she saw the elven crowd gathered at the base of the fountain to listen to their elders. Fallerian and Elyana stood on the fountain's tall rim, their reflections rippling dully on the ashy water behind them. Flanking them were Shalidrian, Fallerian's toady, and Motek. The squat, chubby elf wrung his hands. Hammon and Salaria were gone, fallen to the fires and the battle of the night before. There were four councilors—only four—where six should have stood.

At the front of the crowd, Narath held aloft his hand, a broken arrow clutched between his fingers. "Too many have died!" he yelled, and the crowd rumbled agreement. "We warned you that this would happen! This danger was not Aerendor's to bear, but *he*

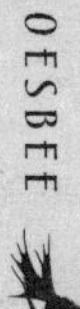

brought the evil to us!" The crowd nodded, a few excited villagers raising their fists with a shout.

"Oh, this is going to be bad," Kelenthe whispered.

"Fallerian warned us of the dangers of fighting these creatures, but Elyana would not listen," Narath continued. "And now look what they have done. The half-breed has always hated Aerendor. Now he has returned with that hatred and brought these undead to destroy us. I have seen him conferring with them in the woods! I saw him guiding them through our streets. Did they not avoid our traps, as though they had been forewarned?"

The crowd in the plaza yelled, several of the newly returned women clutching children tightly to them in fear. Wounded warriors stood in their still-bloodstained tabards, hands on their hilts as if ready for an attack.

"Don't you see?" Narath turned, obviously playing for the crowd. "Elidor brought them here deliberately. He came to us to lull us into trusting him and then gave them our plans. He delivered us into the hands of the undead—deliberately!"

"That is not true." Elidor spoke clearly, his voice rising over the howls and angry shouts of the elven crowd. Some of the gathered throng turned, angry eyes fixing on him as he and Cat pushed their way through to the council. "I tried to warn you about Gieden and his men. I tried to protect you, to help you fight them."

"By meeting with Gieden in the woods alone?" Narath sneered, tossing the broken arrow down at Elidor's feet.

"I never did that."

"By sabotaging Kelenthe's saddle, so that we would lose our best scouts to Gieden's forward guard?" Narath pointed an accusing finger at the half-blood elf.

Kelenthe breathed softly, "How did Narath know that? I didn't tell anyone what happened to us in the woods." She gasped. "It must have been him! Narath sabotaged my horse!"

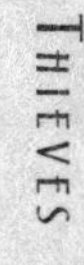

"But why?" Corrigan's frown deepened, and he moved closer to Catriona and Elidor.

"I didn't meet with Gieden." Elidor didn't waver. "But you did."

Narath laughed, and Fallerian raised his hands to bring the crowd to silence. "How dare you," the hawk-nosed councilor intoned, "accuse Narath, an elf of good standing in this village, of such treachery? Narath has lived his life in this village, protected it against many threats, and guarded it after Rerdhen's death. What have you done for this village, Elidor?

"I'll tell you. You have brought it nothing but pain. Your strange ways, your feral father, your insistence on rejecting everything that is Silvanesti. No, Narath's story does not sound so very difficult to understand." Fallerian's eyelids fluttered. "In fact, I think we have no alternative but to believe him."

"Fallerian," Elyana's indigo robes rustled slightly in a warm morning breeze. She seemed infinitely weary, her eyes carrying more than their share of pain. "That will be enough."

"No, Elyana. I do not think it is nearly enough." He turned on her like an animal, baring his teeth in a snarl. "You have protected the boy for too long from the Silvanesti and from the truth. I think it is time that the entire village knew.

"When you went to the Kagonesti as a missionary, Elyana, your parents were so very proud. How wonderful that their daughter went to teach and guide the poor, backward Kagonesti—*our cousins,*" Fallerian hissed scornfully. "But when you returned bearing a half-breed son, it was a different story. They wanted to hide you, send the mongrel child away, but you wouldn't have it. It was penance, you said, for trying to break the gods' commands and raise the Kagonesti above their state. It was a penance, yes, but on the entire village, not only on your soul. This is our *penance* for your foolishness, your pride. The elders were right in denying anyone else to go to the Kagonesti. They were right in turning away from those mongrel elves—and the half-breed son you cursed us with."

Motek wrung his hands, moaning, "Cursed, we're cursed. I knew we should have drowned the child at his birth, Elyana, but we pitied you. Oh, E'li, what has this brought upon us?"

"Be silent, Motek," Shalidrian hissed, hunching close to Fallerian's side. "Listen. There is much to be done, and we cannot hesitate." The elf peered up at Fallerian, eager to gain his master's good will.

"Fallerian," Elyana said, stepping between Elidor and his accusers. "Stop this."

"No. How many times have I seen you weeping over this boy? Pitying yourself for the circumstances of his birth, for the way he ruined your life? You, too, wanted to be rid of him. You prayed that he would die in the woods in some terrible accident as a child. When word came that he had been killed in battle, I saw your happiness—a joy that dulled as soon as he entered Aerendor once more."

"Enough, Fallerian." Her voice held the timbre of broken glass.

"No." He took her shoulders. "Think of all the pain he represents—no longer just for you, but now for all of Aerendor. I'm sorry, Elyana." There was little sincerity in the blue-robed elf's voice. "Elidor must be given judgment and executed for his crime."

"No!" Tears sparkled in Rina's eyes. "Elidor is my brother. We don't turn our backs on family. Mother, tell him so." A long pause punctuated Rina's desperate plea, and the crowd began to whisper. "Mother?"

Elyana said nothing, staring into Fallerian's compelling eyes with a strange, frozen expression on her features.

His hands tightened on her shoulders. "Elyana. Let the half-blood do something noble in death, as he has never done anything of worth in his life. There will be meaning in it."

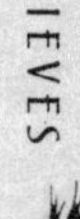

"I'll do it myself," Narath snarled. His hand on his sword hilt, he stepped close to Elidor and Catriona. "I'll take him to the wizard and see that the mutt gets what he deserves."

Swiftly, the red-haired warrior released Elidor, stepping between the two elves with her own sword drawn. "Over my dead body."

Bowstrings rustled by the fountain and the few guards of Aerendor that still stood watch pointed sharp arrows toward Elidor and his friends. For a moment, Kelenthe thought there would be blood drawn, that Catriona and Elidor would fight Narath in the city square and die by elven arrows. Fallerian did nothing to stop them, a faint smile on his face as he held Elyana's arms. "Let him go."

Elidor stood on his own, body arched slightly from the pain in his side. As one, Kelenthe and Corrigan surrounded him, standing by their friend. The sudden hatred of the crowd focused on them. Kelenthe could see it in their faces, hear it in their muttered words. The entire town seemed to agree with Fallerian. Elidor was the enemy.

"You're wrong!" Kelenthe sang out. "This anger you feel, it shouldn't be for Elidor. It should be for the enemy who destroyed your homes—the black wizard Gieden. Elidor's no ally to him. Look at what Elidor has already suffered. He came here, wounded and concerned for our safety—and we turned him away. Now we seek to blame him for the very thing he tried to warn us against?"

Kelenthe shook her head, black hair shaking around her shoulders. "We've known Elidor since he was a boy. I trust him. And I know you—all of you. I know this city. Aerendor is a place of peace, of art, and of mercy. Don't let Fallerian turn you away from those ideals."

A few of the elves seemed swayed by her eloquent speech, but the majority of them still spoke under their breath, hands on their bows and fire in their eyes.

"A brave speech, Kelenthe." Corrigan drew his rapier and readied himself. "But I fear this tide cannot be turned. I do not like harming innocents, but this goes poorly for us all."

"Narath." Fallerian drew out the word cruelly, a superior tone in his voice. "Take the guard and kill him. Kill them all if you must, but the mongrel traitor dies."

The crowd began to press in, bows twisting to a tense arc, but suddenly Elyana broke away from Fallerian's grasp.

"Stop!" she called out. The elves, used to obeying her commands, paused. Elyana pushed her way through the crowd. "You are right in one thing, Fallerian. My son must leave Aerendor. But I do not believe he is a traitor, nor do I believe that he is an ally to this Gieden."

"Elyana, the council has spoken," Fallerian said. "We voted while you were in town tending the wounded. You must accept what we have decided. This is our will." Fallerian folded his hands before him. "Stand aside."

"You voted . . . without me?" Elyana's face was as white as snow. "Have I no say in this matter?"

"You may cast your vote if you wish, Councilor. But it will make no difference." Fallerian glowered. "The rest of us have agreed. Elidor must be put to death so that Aerendor can be safe again. We will rectify the error of his life once and for all."

There was a long moment of silence, and then Elyana spoke again. "I want you to change your vote, Fallerian, from death to exile."

"Why would I do that?"

"If you do . . . " Elyana's voice broke for a moment. Kelenthe reached out to touch her hand, and the older elf took a deep, shuddering breath. "If you agree, then I . . . will vote to confirm you as the Royal Governor of Aerendor. You will need a unanimous decision to do that, Fallerian, and you shall have it."

Fallerian, intrigued, motioned for the archers to lower their weapons. "I have your oath, Elyana?"

"You do."

"And the half-breed leaves Aerendor—this time, never to return."

"I swear it." The wind moved Elyana's long hair, twisting the yellow braids. The warmth of spring seemed to fade around them as she spoke, leaving only the chill of an early winter.

Fallerian considered, and although it must have been only a moment, to Kelenthe it seemed like an eternity. When he spoke again, she realized that she had been holding her breath.

"Done." A long sigh rippled through the crowd. "Leave Aerendor, Elidor. Take your friends and never return.

"No!" Narath yelled, pushing forward as though to strike. "You told me Elidor would die! He deserves to die!" His eyes were wild and sharp, sword over his head with vicious intent. Catriona's weapon leaped up, blocking his overhand strike, and her boot slammed into Narath's chest. The elf staggered backward to the edge of the fountain. Cat fell into a fighting crouch, ready to take him on.

But as Narath stood and raised his sword again, Fallerian's hand struck out, slapping the younger elf across the face. The sudden pain shocked Narath, and he stared confused.

"Fool," Fallerian blurted. "You will not ruin my victory."

"But . . . he's a mongrel, an abomination." The elf made as though to raise his sword once more, but the gesture was half-hearted.

"He goes."

Fallerian struck Narath's face a second time, and Narath lowered the blade. Humiliated, he spun on one heel and stormed away from the gathering.

"You have one hour to leave the village." Fallerian gestured. "There will be horses prepared for you to speed your travel."

"But Gieden won't stop attacking Aerendor. I told you that." Elidor winced, holding his hand to his bruised side. "He knows that Elyana is in the city. And he's going to keep attacking Aerendor until he destroys everything that I love."

"Don't worry about Aerendor," Elyana said roughly. "There will be nothing here for Gieden to attack."

"You don't understand, Mother. You're in danger here."

"I will be in no more danger than you are, because I won't be here."

"What do you mean?"

Elidor's mother fixed him with an uncompromising stare. "I'm coming with you."

CHAPTER

12 Iron Hearts

The dream had begun gently, a continuation of the argument. Elyana's face swam before Elidor's eyes, as stubborn as she had been during the debate. He yelled, begged, cajoled—and nothing. And in the dream at least, Elidor was able to admit to himself that she was right. She wasn't leaving to protect him or to keep watch over him. She was doing what was best—for her people. Perhaps, Elidor yelled in his dream, they were the only thing she had ever loved.

They stood in a building that no longer existed—the tower of Aerendor—but Elyana seemed much younger than she actually was. Elidor pounded his fist on the table, refusing to allow her to come along, but she continued to pack her belongings into a bag that seemed much too small to hold an entire life.

"Why are you doing this?" he asked her.

Her only reply was a smile.

"Can't you understand that you'll be in more danger with us?" Elidor knew she wouldn't listen, but he tried anyway. "You have to stay where it's safe." But even as he spoke the words to his dream mother, he knew that she was right. Aerendor wasn't safe—not anymore.

He looked at the doorway of the tower, and it was a curling mass of vines. The woods. A figure rushed past through distant trees. His father?

But no. His father was dead.

Elidor walked away from his mother, leaving her packing, and pushed aside the vines. He stepped into a cool green glade. He tried to focus on the figure as it slid from tree to tree.

"Elidor. He's not finished with you. You're in danger; you can't stay here. Aerendor may hold nothing that you love, but he knows somewhere that does. Everything you love will suffer your fate, Elidor. Everything."

It was the ghost girl again, the one in the white robes. Were they robes? Rags, tattered, hanging below her knees in long, mud-covered strands. Her arms were dirty, smeared with dust and blood. Her hair, brownish like chocolate, seemed lighter than he remembered it, and this time, it was pulled back from her face by a thong of leather that barely contained her curls.

"What do you want?" he asked.

"You have to get out of here. They're faster than you. Narath has told them that you've left the village. He's gone somewhere else. He's gone where you should go."

"Where?"

The girl only stared at him, her eyes pained.

Behind him, he could still hear his mother packing. "My mother and my sister . . . "

"They're coming with you."

"I don't want them to."

"No choice. You have to keep the crown, Elidor. You have to. He's getting more powerful, stronger. You have to go. Do not fear. The shadows will go with you."

"Go where?"

But before she could answer, the wind whipped her away.

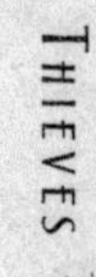

Elidor sat up with a gasp, sweat cooling on his forehead. The dawn had not yet broken, and the trees at the edge of the woods swayed mournfully. Sindri looked over from his perch on the tree branch, smiling down from his watch over the campsite. The others, Elyana and Rina included, still slept.

Elidor pushed himself up from his uncomfortable place at the foot of one of the trees, stretching and trying to shake off the lingering sense of unease. Sindri jumped down silently, moving across the campsite. When he reached Elidor's side, he whispered, "You should sleep. We traveled all night to get ahead of Gieden. You're going to be really tired at noon when we start traveling again."

"Yeah." Elidor tried to control his thoughts. "But where are we going?"

Sindri shrugged, ignoring a particularly large snore from Rohawn. "I don't know. I thought you knew. I mean, we've got your mother and sister here, right? That's your whole family, I mean." Sindri shifted from foot to foot. "Now we just keep traveling until we find a safe place, right? At least it was easy to leave. No long good-byes."

"Wait a minute . . . what did you say?" Elidor asked.

"Good-bye?" Sindri stammered. "You didn't have to tell anyone good-bye?"

Elidor closed his eyes, remembering. The words were familiar. There was a moment of memory that hung in his mind, of Vael's white hair flowing down her back, a summer laugh on her curved lips. The image had appeared as Gieden used his magic to infiltrate Elidor's mind. "E'li," he sighed. "I know where Gieden's going."

Sindri looked up eagerly. Elidor rubbed his eyes. "She told me that she didn't want to hear my good-byes." He ran a hand through his hair, feeling the thickness of soot still ingrained on his body.

"Who?"

"Vael." Elidor checked his knives once again out of habit. Nothing was out of place, but still he felt uncertain. He watched the sun peek up over the horizon and wished it would go back to its hiding place. The next day would be a long one.

"The baroness from the village near Navarre?" Sindri's eyes brightened. "Is she a white-robed wizard?"

"No." Elidor took his hand off the hilt of his hunting knife and turned away. "She's someone I love."

The ship journey back to Solamnia happened under restless skies, the sea rolling steadily beneath them. Every morning when he woke and every night as he slept, Elidor remembered the blackened streets of Aerendor. They haunted him.

Once ashore, they rode through the mountains toward the hidden village of Tarrent. Kelenthe and Kaja rode at the front of the group, Kelenthe telling a story about a kender pirate to pass time. On the back of her horse, Sindri laughed, feet kicking up on either side of the horse's flanks. Behind them rode Rina and Elyana, the elven noblewoman riding beside her daughter in silence. Cat and Corrigan were next, with Rohawn trotting along on foot beside his master's horse. At the rear of the group rode Elidor, his hands twisting the reins.

The mountains were high and jagged, with few paths and no road. Travelers did not come this way; there were no cities, no outposts or hunting villages in these high hills. The forest died out and became scrub and mountain pine, with boulders and steep cliffs to be navigated. They journeyed higher and higher into the mountains, fighting their way through untouched forest. Cat was the only one besides Sindri who never asked Elidor if he was on the right path.

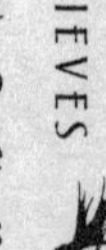

She had been this way before.

Catriona watched Elidor become quieter and quieter as they marched into the hills, leading their horses at intervals through canyons and thin paths above sheer drops. When they finally crested the last mountain, he paused at the top of the slope. She rode up beside him, wind rippling through her curly red hair. It was colder here than mid-spring in Southern Ergoth had been, the boulders icy to the touch. But below them in the canyon, spring had been in full bloom for at least a month.

The huts were primitive but well-tended, clumped together along even streets of grass and hard-packed earth. There were no roads out of the village, and the mountains all around provided natural protection against harsh weather as well as keeping the occasional traveler away. But around the outer ring of huts, a strange charred swath marked the village's edge. Thick, black and still smoking, it colored the sky with a hint of gray.

"There it is." Catriona stopped the others. Elidor kept silent, too filled with memories and fears. "We should be there by nightfall."

"And this is where we will find your . . . this . . . Vael?" Elyana seemed to be trying to keep the scorn from her voice.

"As I understand it," Cat said as she glanced at Rina, "Tarrent was created by the servants who fled the wrath of Asvoria, an ancient and powerful sorceress. The town has remained isolated in these mountains for hundreds of years. The people here don't like intrusions." She turned toward Elidor. "You're the only one they know, Elidor. You'll have to go first and talk to them."

"Vael," he sighed, kicking his steed forward. "She thinks I'm dead, doesn't she?"

Catriona nodded.

"Well, that'll take some explanation. And there's another thing." He turned toward his family. "You won't find any Silvanesti

here, or Kagonesti. In fact, I'd be surprised if you find any race you recognize. These people may have been of different blood in the beginning when they were all slaves, but now, they've lived together for too long to be any one race."

Rina stared down at the village, sunlight shining on her golden curls. "I understand." But her mother turned her face away, an obvious look of scorn written on her features.

Kelenthe smiled. "They've seen us." She stood up in her stirrups and pointed down a narrow path. "I see guards headed our way."

Elidor pulled on his horse's reins, taking the lead. "Let's go, then. I'd hate to keep Vael waiting."

Three guards dressed in leathers trod up the narrow path toward them, spears held at the ready. It seemed a small group to face such a large group of intruders—the companions numbered nine, in all. Yet Elidor saw the ripple of muscles in the men's arms as they held up their spears. Part ogre, he reasoned, but he couldn't tell how much—certainly enough for them to have inherited some distant ancestor's strength.

The biggest guard, a man whose face seemed tinted slightly green, stepped forward. "Travelers ain't welcome—" As soon as he saw Elidor's face, he stopped. "No, you're dead. The dead certainly ain't welcome here."

"I'm not dead." Elidor fixed the guard with a firm stare.

"Huh. Maybe so, maybe not. I'm not a wizard. How'm I to tell?" The guard squinted at Elidor.

Elidor had no memory of the guard, but knew that his own face was well known in the village. The last time he was here had been the day the baron died and left Tarrent in his daughter's hands. If he and Davyn had been unable to solve the mystery of his death, Elidor would have been executed.

"Take us to the baronness." Elidor spurred his horse forward a step, trusting in the good nature of the villagers, even if they did

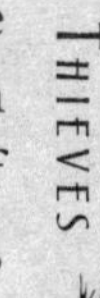

have spears readied for war. "We bring you news of a great danger. Vael . . . the baroness . . . will need to hear it immediately."

"Don't listen to him," one of the guards hissed to the other two. "He's dead, ain't he? Didn't they say so? He's bad luck for this village."

"I don't know much about dead," the first one replied, "but he looks like he's kickin' pretty strong to me."

"I was dead," Elidor explained. "But powerful magic has brought me back to life, and now I've returned to protect Tarrent—as I did before."

"Brought back from the dead. I told you they was bad luck," the second guard muttered as the leader lowered his spear.

Elidor winced as his mother began to speak, her voice as bold and commanding as it had been in the council chambers of Aerendor. "I am Elyana of Silvanost, a member of the council of Aerendor." Elyana gestured toward Corrigan. "And this is Sir Corrigan of the Knights of Solamnia. We ask respectfully that you take us to your Lady, so that we may treat with her in good faith. You will take us to her now."

The guard captain laughed, slapping his thigh, and Elidor turned red. "What do we care about the Silvanesti or Solamnia?" His stubby finger pointed out past the mountain range. "They live out there. We live in here. Your title is worthless in Tarrent, Miss High-and-Mighty Elf." Elyana looked shocked as the other guards added to the laughter.

"Please. Just tell Roland that we're here." Elidor cut off any response that Elyana might have made.

"Roland's gone on. The winter was hard for Tarrent. Been lean, and the old man's years finally caught up to him. Was a pity, too. Despite the madness his grandson caused, Roland was much loved here. He died in peace; at least fate gave him that much."

Elidor's heart sank. Roland, the kind seneschal of Tarrent, dead?

He had been Elidor's friend for many years, and a kind voice in troubled times. Even the protected canyon of Tarrent, it seemed, could not hide from loss. "What about Gerhalt?"

"Fit as ever, and if you're who you says, he'll be right on to see you, Elidor. He's the new seneschal now. It's him I'll send a man to. But you stay right here."

The guard captain eyed them suspiciously and the second soldier set his spear upon the ground. With a salute, the third soldier sprinted down toward the village.

Even at a distance, Elidor could see the man travel to a large rise where a building constructed of ancient wood and solid stone stood at the center of the village.

Within a few moments of his entry, the wide doors of the hearthstead opened and a small group came out. Among them, Elidor could see a woman with white hair giving orders to her followers. Vael. Does her face have the same softness, he wondered, as it did when last we met? Or have her duties hardened her?

One of the men at the hearthstead raised a white banner, signaling with sharp strokes to the right and left. The heavyset captain snorted. "For some reason, she believes your tale. The Lady'll see you."

Elidor let out a long breath. "Good."

They followed the guards through a hidden trail tucked against the canyon wall, their horses' weary hooves tromping out a slow cadence against rocky mountain soil. With each step, they approached the bottom of the canyon, a village of thatched huts, and the muddy riverbed. All of it was familiar to Elidor—especially the young woman standing on the bridge over the narrow river by the hearthstead.

They got off their horses a hundred yards from the bridge, letting the guards lead them away. Only a few citizens gathered in the streets to watch the large group move toward the center of

Tarrent. The faces of the people were familiar, but this time, they were pale with fear. Elidor saw injuries among them, and signs of fire and battle marked the outer ring of huts. Instead of greeting him with scorn, the villagers made the sign of lost gods before their faces, hiding their children and turning away from them as they made their way in.

When they reached the river, Elidor heard a friendly voice. "Elidor the Fallen."

He turned toward the greeting and saw a grizzled man limping slowly over the bridge. The man's wide shoulders were slightly stooped with age, but his stance was that of a soldier. An old wound slowed his steps, but they were measured and stately, and his mostly human features beamed welcome. "By Paladine, we heard you were dead."

"Not anymore," Elidor said.

Gerhalt, apparently believing it was a joke, clapped Elidor on the back with a loud bark of laughter. "Good to see you, lad. It does my heart no end of good to have you here." The old guard looked up at the building that stood on the rise. "But you go on now. She's waiting for you."

They crested the bridge, meeting the delegation from within the large hearthstead. At the head of four almost elvish-looking guards stood a white-haired woman. Her frame was slender, but she seemed taller than her five-foot height. Her features, like many of the citizens of the town, were a mélange of races—slender elven cheeks and high cheekbones surrounded a full-lipped, human mouth. Her eyes, blue and pale as ice, took in each member of the traveling group with a curious stare.

"Greetings, Baroness Vael." Elidor bowed slightly, and the rest of the group slowly followed suit. Rohawn nearly stumbled and fell trying to mimic Corrigan's stately movement; Elyana hardly moved at all, inclining her head only slightly.

Sir Corrigan whispered to Rohawn, "Who would have thought such beauty would grow in these cold backlands?"

"Elidor," Vael stood in the sunlight. "Elidor." She stared at him, tears cresting the edges of ice-blue eyes. "You're alive," she whispered. "And you've returned. But how?"

"It's a long story," he began tentatively. His mouth felt dry as a beach, and his heart twisted into knots. "I can't tell you all the details right now, Vael. I can tell you only that Tarrent is in danger. I need . . . we need . . . to talk to you immediately. Please."

"Again you come to us in troubled times, Elidor. But it is good to see so many with swords in your group. Tarrent will need them."

"What do you mean?" Elidor asked. "Is there danger?"

Sindri interrupted him before he could continue, pushing past Cat and Kaja to the front of the group. With a flourish, he swirled his purple cloak around his shoulders. "Hi! I am Sindri, Wizard Extraordinaire! Remember me? We fought Asvoria together!" Elidor tried to get a word in, but Sindri prattled on. "We've been fighting the undead in the elven forests. Have you met Elyana? And Kaja and Kelenthe?"

Catriona tried to grab the kender to shut him up. "Sindri, stop."

He muttered back, "You wouldn't let me talk to the elves, and see how that turned out?" Sindri lifted his chin and turned on a brilliant smile. He addressed the white-haired woman on the bridge, not sparing any time in his explanations. "You're in terrible danger, Baroness. We're here to help. But we might not be much use. The last time we helped, a whole town burned. But I think we have the hang of it this time."

Elidor winced. Elyana stiffened. Kaja half moaned, reaching to clutch her holy symbol and whisper a faint prayer. Sindri rushed on. "Kelenthe's a bard. She knows a lot about the undead. Kaja's a cleric. They run from her, mostly. And I have magic." He stood up even straighter. "So we can help you. See?"

Vael stared down at the little kender for a moment, and then her icy face crinkled into a faint smile. "Well, at least you have one truth teller among your group, Elidor."

"I'm sorry, Vael," Elidor said.

Vael raised her hand to silence him. "Do not apologize. Truth, and quickly told, is exactly what is needed. Come inside the hearthstead. These are matters to be discussed alone."

Sindri grinned, bowing again and walking beside her as she led the group into the large building across the bridge. Elidor caught a glimpse of his mother as she stared into the face of one of Vael's guards. The man's heritage was stamped clearly across his features—a blend of ogre, human, and elf, which held Elyana's eyes. Elidor saw Kaja step up to her, taking his mother's arm and speaking to her in low tones. The two elves fell behind the others, standing on the bridge as the rest of the group followed the baroness into her audience room.

The chamber was much as Elidor remembered—wide and dark, the broad fireplace providing warm light at all hours of the day. Wide windows near the ceiling allowed sunlight through open shutters. Vael's guards walked over fur-covered floors, keeping their hands on their spears. Elidor followed, wincing as he watched Sindri bound by Vael's heels. The room could easily hold a hundred people. Tables and benches stood by the walls, ready to be taken out for use during festival days.

Today, the chamber showed signs of wear—sleeping rugs still balled up on the ground, several weapons placed conspicuously near the fireplace and the large oak doors. Scurrying peasants carried pots of water and food from the village into the room, hurrying with them deeper into the hearthstead to the kitchens.

Vael walked toward a fur-covered chair at the end of a large table. She sat down heavily, steepling her fingers.

"Forgive me, your Excellency." Corrigan bowed. "But before we

bring you our business, I cannot help but be concerned for your people. You were saying you need swords. Has the village been attacked?"

Vael nodded. "Last night, a group of strange creatures on horseback attacked the outer huts of the village. We gathered everyone into the hearthstead, save for the members of the watch."

"They didn't destroy anything?" Sindri asked excitedly.

Vael looked at him strangely. "Not significantly. There were only a few of them—perhaps ten—riding steeds of ash and smoke."

"Gieden's cavalry," Elidor broke in, frowning. "They're just an advance guard. There are others coming."

"You know these attackers?" Vael stared at Elidor, ice-blue eyes riveted on him. "I wonder, Elidor," Vael shook her head wearily, "if fate will ever allow me to simply be happy to see you." She reached for a glass of water that stood on the table. "It seems that, living or dead, bad luck follows you everywhere you go. Tarrent is a small village. We can handle only so much trouble."

"Don't be mad at him." Sindri sat down at the foot of Vael's throne, grinning up at her. "We're here only because Gieden found out that Elidor loves you."

Vael choked on her sip of water, setting the glass down with a thump. Silence fell over the chamber. Corrigan coughed uncomfortably. Both Vael and Elidor colored, pale faces turning unmistakably red.

"Well," Elyana said crisply, stepping out from where she stood near the back of the group. "I expect I should be more properly introduced, then, to the young woman who loves . . . my son." Her tone was cold, her demeanor stern, and she swept across the fur rugs on the floor with an air of command. Pitiless, Elyana stared at Vael.

"Elidor . . . is your son?" Vael rose shakily, facing Elyana from her throne.

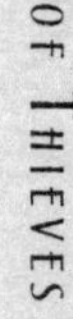

She and Elyana stared at one another, frozen, until Kelenthe and Kaja swiftly stepped between them. "Your Excellency," Kelenthe drew Vael's attention with a flourished bow and a resonant. "How did you manage to defend your village from the attack?"

Still silent, Kaja merely took Elyana's hand with a taciturn frown. She shook her head *no* and drew the Silvanesti woman to the side.

Plainly grateful for the intrusion, Vael turned to Kelenthe. "Gerhalt knows much about the undead, having traveled the catacombs of Asvoria in these mountains. The legacy of the sorceress left many such creatures. We set fire to an outer ring of the village, piling every available scrap of firewood that we had to form a ring. Tarrent is small, but it took every effort to keep the village safe. I thought the specters were no more than remnants of Asvoria's catacombs, but you are telling me that these creatures have something to do with you?" Vael's eyes kept drifting to Elyana.

Before Sindri could start talking, Kelenthe cut in. "Yes. They are hunting Elidor. The crown he wears is cursed with a terrible past. They can't take it from him. He must give it up of his own free will. So the black wizard who wants it is destroying everything . . . " Kelenthe paused, trying to find an eloquent way to phrase it.

"Everything he loves," Elyana finished coldly. "No matter how base."

"Mother." Rina matched Elyana's sharp tone.

"Silvanesti." Vael clenched her hand on the arm of the wide throne. "Your people's bigotry is legendary, Lady. Some of the people in this village were driven out of their homes and away from their families by your kind. They were given no choice. They came here to seek refuge from hatred leveled against them for no better reason than their heritage." Although the baroness's voice was

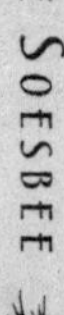

sharp, her eyes held no hatred. "The few who were not born in this canyon came to Tarrent to find shelter. And now, war and bigotry comes to their very doorstep." She rubbed her forehead, taking the golden circlet from her white hair. "And I can't protect them."

Catriona whispered, "I'm sorry."

"By E'li!" Elidor exploded, making Rohawn jump nervously. He kicked one of the fur rugs angrily. "Everywhere I go, I bring pain."

Corrigan crossed his arms. "Don't bring judgment on yourself, Elidor."

"What? You think we can save Tarrent?" Elidor turned on the weasel-faced knight. "Aerendor burned."

"Tarrent will not burn." Vael was a pillar of ivory, pale and white against her seat of dark bearskins.

"Vael, I didn't come here to save Tarrent. I came to save you. You have to come with us."

"Leave my people? Leave my home?" Vael laughed without humor. "No."

"Then you condemn them," Elyana said.

"No." Vael's white hair rippled against her pale skin, eyes flashing. "I fight beside them. We stood up against them last night and we can do so again."

"Don't be a fool," Elyana said. "What was true in Aerendor is still true now. The only way to save your people is to flee, to keep moving. Gieden and his men will follow us. If you come, they won't attack Tarrent. You must leave—immediately." The councilor, certain that her words would be obeyed, cast a haughty gaze around the group.

"How do you know this for certain? What if he comes even if I'm not here? No, I cannot leave my people to suffer some unknown fate. They need me. Elidor," Vael turned to face him. "Do you really want me to abandon Tarrent? You do not believe that together, we can stand against this evil wizard?"

All eyes turned toward Elidor. Catriona's were all but pleading, and Elidor could see that she was willing to stand beside whatever decision he made. Sindri, Rohawn, Corrigan, the others—all of them, ready to stay or flee based solely on his word. Was this what his old friend Davyn had felt when he led them against Asvoria? It was a weight settling about Elidor's shoulders, pushing the breath out of his lungs. Whatever his choice, no matter which way they went, Gieden might kill them all. Desperate to find an answer, Elidor looked up at the pale baroness on her throne. Vael's gaze spoke only of her faith, an honest understanding that harbored no compromise.

"I can't fail you again." Pain broke his voice, and he flushed.

"You won't," she replied with certainty.

Elidor stared into Vael's eyes, and he loved her.

Until he heard his own voice, Elidor didn't realize he was speaking. "We fight."

Elyana's features hardened. "Fool," she whispered under her breath.

Rina took her mother's arm, clenching tightly, and guided Elyana in a smooth motion toward the door. "Perhaps we should go outside, Mother."

Elyana shook off her daughter's hand haughtily. "Yes, Rina. Let us leave this place." She turned, indigo robes flowing with the sudden motion. "There's nothing of value here."

He watched the two elves leaving the hearthstead, recognizing them by the distinctive golden braids and indigo robes of Elyana's garb. Her daughter walked beside her, curly blond hair shining in the afternoon sunlight.

The rest did not exit.

That was all right. He didn't need to see the others to know that they were inside. The half-blood traitor would be with them. And as a bonus, he could eradicate all of the mongrels in this god-forsaken town. Not only was he about to gain his revenge, he was about to perform a valuable service to society.

On the hillside outside Tarrent, Narath sharpened his blade and waited for the sun to go down.

CHAPTER

13 DISCOVERIES

Only a few short hours later, Corrigan strode through the village of Tarrent. The city's fifteen guards were eager to help, and the citizens had chopped down several trees to form a haphazard circle around the perimeter. Corrigan and Rohawn walked the streets, gathering the information they would need to defend the town.

Aerendor had been a challenge. It had no walls, the streets were crooked, and visibility was limited outside the city perimeter because of the dense woods. There were three high towers, several low buildings with arched roofs of wood and clay shingles, but no central building, no defensible position, and nowhere to keep the body of the population. The town was not built to be defensible —it was an open chest waiting for Gieden to plunder.

Tarrent was different. The town was built like the spokes on a wheel, with four main roads leading directly into the center of the village. The river cut through the hub and circled a rise upon which the hearthstead had been built. Preparing for cold winters, the builders in Tarrent had unwittingly made a small fortress of their meeting hall. The building was made of stone and thick oak, with only one way in over the river—a single bridge, and then a stronghold. Beautiful.

Outside the hub, the huts were made of clay and stone. The roofs were flammable, thatched. Many of the villagers contributed their own roofs to the barricade, breaking them down in order to hand the dry timber and thatching to the blockade. Roofs could be rebuilt.

"Hail, Orrin," Corrigan saluted one of the ogre-faced guards that escorted them into the village.

The man grunted, looking up from binding a square of thatched roof to a fallen tree. "Making it round. Can't reach the northern side, not enough trees to drag there. We cut most of them down this morning." He flexed, and greenish-black skin tightened over huge muscles. Delicate elven ears pointed up through his hair. "Got the barricade up by the river, though. Readying the bridge to burn on Gerhalt's order."

"Well, we're mostly trying to defend the hearthstead this time, not the main body of the village. Gieden isn't interested in wholesale damage. He's interested in specific targets. If we keep them within the hearthstead, he will come to us."

Rohawn squinted. "Sir," he said to Corrigan. "Where is Gerhalt?" Curious, the squire scanned the workers.

"Meeting with one of them elven women." Orrin spat on the ground, black tobacco spattering the dusty ground.

"You disapprove, I see." Corrigan raised an eyebrow.

"T'aint my place to agree or not. I follow orders. That's all." Leveling his shoulders, Orrin went back to work.

Corrigan and Rohawn walked on down the road, away from the hearthstead. Corrigan frowned, stroking his short goatee thoughtfully.

"They don't like us here, do they, sir?" Rohawn asked, uncharacteristically subdued. The squire trotted along beside his slender

master, the strap of his greatsword lying against the sweat that covered his bare chest.

"They have no reason to, Rohawn. We're outsiders here."

"But we're trying to help them," Rohawn said. "Why doesn't anyone understand that?"

"People don't take change easily. As long as they can deny it, they will. Everyone wants their life to stay the same. We represent change, squire, brutal change. And what follows us . . . kills."

Corrigan saw Gerhalt then, walking with Elyana and her daughter through the bazaar. They stopped at stalls, talking and listening to the villagers there. Gerhalt still had the stocky body of a warrior, but a wound in his leg left him with a permanent limp. A thick cane decorated with carved faces of tree spirits, helped him keep up with the steps of the lithe elven women. He pointed to and fro, obviously talking about the village, though Elyana seemed to hardly listen.

She paused at a weaver woman's loom, her fingers tracing the delicate colors with something akin to surprise. Rina spoke to the old woman behind the loom. The old woman, her face showing signs of both elven and dwarvish blood, grinned widely. Elyana said nothing, but moved on.

"Lady Elyana," Corrigan bowed as they drew near. "How are you finding the city?"

Elyana sniffed. "City, Sir Corrigan? Hardly. It is little more than a bump on a very poor log." Behind her, Rina rolled her eyes.

Gerhalt smiled kindly. "It is not as pleasant as Lady Elyana's homeland, perhaps, but Tarrent has its own simple beauty." He seemed unperturbed by Elyana's comment, and Corrigan tried to smile. "I have been showing her the village as best I can." He thumped his cane on the ground.

Corrigan politely offered the Silvanesti woman his arm. "Tarrent does not have the advantages that Aerendor may have had, but it is simple and peaceful." He glanced over at the loom, the

old woman's shuttle clicking easily back and forth between the threads. "And there is art here nonetheless."

"Yes," Elyana admitted grudgingly.

"Elidor certainly seems to see something here worth saving," Rohawn blurted out, trailing behind with Rina. "These people remember him. A lot of the guards know him by name."

"Elidor told me he stayed in a village in the mountains after he left Aerendor," Rina twisted a curl of golden hair around her finger, spinning it idly. "He must have meant Tarrent."

Gerhalt spoke soberly. "He was happy here . . . for a time. He wished to marry the baroness, but he was given a terrible choice by her father—marry Vael and she would be removed from succession, or break the engagement." He shrugged. "He left that night and we thought never to see him again. When he did return, it was on the day of the old baron's death—a death of which Elidor was unjustly accused. When he found the real culprit, he also saved Tarrent from falling into the sorceress Asvoria's hands once more. She would have destroyed us all. Tarrent owes much to Elidor the Fallen." The seneschal stared at the ground for a moment, raising his eyes at last to meet Elyana's. "I owe him my life, that's the truth." He clomped his cane on the ground. "I took this wound fighting beside him, and I'd do it again, any day."

"Elidor did not need to find a home in Tarrent," Elyana said. "Aerendor would have accepted him, but he refused to act like a Silvanesti. He turned away from his heritage."

Rina scowled. "Don't you see, Mother? He couldn't pretend to be Silvanesti, not any more than you could pretend to be an ogre."

"Lady Elyana," Corrigan smoothly interjected. "Elidor could not be what you wanted him to be. But does that mean that he is not a good person?" The knight looked up toward the tall hearthstead, his eyes seeking the pale shadow that stood near the wide oak doors.

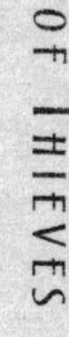

Shaking his head, Gerhalt paused. He bent down, picking up a small rock from the roadway and turning it between his fingers. "Vael is a baroness. Her people trust her." He looked up from the rock, staring intently at the elven matriarch. "She loves your son. I don't think a woman like her would care for a man without worth."

"Vael's still sweet on him too," said Rohawn. "I overheard one of her ladies-in-waiting talking to her. Everyone knows the story of how Elidor saved them from the sorceress. They think he's going to do the same thing against the undead—save them all."

"He didn't do it all by himself," Rina muttered. "His friend Davyn helped."

Rohawn didn't pause. "Still, he saved their lives and risked his own to do it. This village means something to him, like Aerendor did, but . . . different." The young squire spoke honestly, tripping over his words as they stumbled out of his mouth. "Lady Elyana, I—I'm sorry if this is rude, but Aerendor was Elidor's home because he was born there, and he tried his best to save it. Tarrent is Elidor's home because he *chose* it. And he's going to fight for it too. No less than he did for Aerendor." His face was earnest. "You're mad at him because he couldn't save Aerendor, but that wasn't his fault—the Silvanesti didn't listen. It's not his fault, but you blame him anyway. And I . . . I just want to know why." Suddenly the squire realized that the others had fallen dead silent and were staring at him. Rohawn stuttered a bit. "I . . . I'm sorry."

Elyana paused, taking the squire's measure with a long gaze. "No," she said at last. "You're correct, Squire Rohawn. I am angry. Elidor didn't fight for Aerendor. He wanted to run, and run we did. But he fights for Tarrent." The façade of calm sternness fell away and Elyana looked aside as though ashamed to meet the squire's eyes.

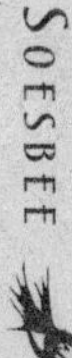

"Don't you see, Mother?" Rina murmured at her elbow, "He came to Aerendor out of duty. He came to Tarrent out of love."

Elyana lowered her head, tears touching her dark blue eyes. "How can he love this place? These people? When he could not love his own?"

Corrigan took the Silvanesti councilor's hands in his. "My lady. I pray thee, if you wish to ask that question, then you will find the answer not with us" —Corrigan gestured toward the old woman at her loom, the soldiers dragging fallen trees to shore the barricade by the hearthstead, and the white plume of Vael's hair as she helped the villagers prepare the building— "but with them."

"Gerhalt." Elyana smiled very faintly, her face growing studious. "I need your assistance."

"Yes, my lady?" He thumped his cane on the ground lightly. "What would you have me do?"

"You can start by introducing me to . . . " Elyana looked around, seeking a place to begin. At last she pointed at one of the soldiers working on the barricade. "Him."

"I can't get this!" Kelenthe pushed the scroll away with a groan. "Maybe if we had the libraries of Palanthas, or the translators of the Clerist's Tower. But here? On the run?" She lay her head down on the rough wooden table. "It's impossible."

"Nothing is impossible, Kelenthe!" Sindri sat in the window of the hearthstead just above her, his feet swinging out into the wind outside. "Hard doesn't mean impossible. Look at me! Everybody said I couldn't do magic, but I can!"

Kaja rose from where she had been helping the villagers stack wood by the large fireplace. "Sister," she said quietly, "how can we help you?" The cleric reached out to massage her sister's shoulder.

"The scrolls that talk about Gieden's legion—I've gotten everything I can from them. Oh, they go on and on talking about some lost city named Taeloc, how beautiful it was. This one," she scrabbled among the papers, "even has a poem about it. Bah." Kelenthe tossed the scroll down again. "A few of them mention the fall of the city and how the Defiler made the warriors that Gieden is using. But none of them—none!—tell us how to destroy them."

"Maybe nobody could write it down. Nobody knew. I mean, nobody's ever destroyed them before, right?" The kender's words made Kelenthe grimace.

"I'm certain there is a way. Magic made those creatures, and magic has flaws. It is the gods' way of reminding us that we should not be proud." Kaja smoothed the old scrolls, her eyes flicking over the scribblings.

Sindri pulled a coin out of his pocket, spinning it idly over his knuckles in the sunlight. He perched on the window ledge, the shutters behind him knocking softly in the wind. "So, just like some things don't burn, there has to be something that the spell that raised the warriors didn't cover?"

"Sindri." Kaja stared up at him. "What do we know about the burial site? Perhaps there was something in the barrow, something that seemed small, which you or the others neglected to mention."

"I don't know. It was really dark and we saw only one room. That one was round, with lots of graves. They were like alcoves in the wall, and the bodies were all in headfirst. They had weapons, armor, all sorts of stuff—just like they do now. When Gieden rang the gong, they all just stood up and started fighting. And they haven't stopped since." The sunlight twinkled over Sindri's coin.

Kelenthe's eye fell on it. "Sindri, you said you picked up that coin in the barrow, right?"

"Oh, yeah. Piles of them. The soldiers were buried with them.

They also had gold buckles and stuff too—ornaments, dagger hilts, things like that."

"Let me see it." Kelenthe reached up to catch the spinning coin as the kender tossed it through the air. It landed in her palm with a heavy thunk.

"Gold hasn't been used to make coins in centuries." Kaja stared at the disk as her sister opened her hand. "It must be very old."

"Old, and important enough to be buried with," Kelenthe said.

"But not important enough to keep with them when they rose as the undead?" Kaja completed her sister's sentence. "I saw no ornaments like that on the warriors in Aerendor. They wore no gold at all."

Sindri cocked his head to the side, his shadow stretching out over the table. "What would the undead buy? And with a gold coin, they couldn't get much. People don't deal in gold anymore. It's pretty, but worthless."

Kelenthe scattered the scrolls again, pulling out one with a drawing of a wide gate. "Look at this." She held the coin beside it, and the pictures matched. "One thing about the undead, Sindri, is that they don't leave things behind. Everything they're buried with has significance to them. If they didn't bring those gold daggers and buckles, there's a reason for it."

"Look at this," Kaja pointed to the sketch of the gate again. "Here, the symbol of a black disk swallowing a silver crescent moon—Nuitari crushing Solinari. Elidor said he saw that same symbol in the barrow too."

"He used the power of the moons to create the undead." Kelenthe pointed at one scroll, then another. "The scrolls all agree on that point. The power of Lunitari and Nuitari and the darkness of night, just like the ash that trails behind them."

"Darkness, silver . . . silver moon, black moon. What does it mean?" Kaja frowned, trying to follow her sister's mental leap.

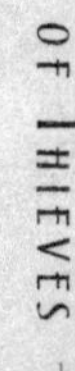

"And didn't this scroll—the other one, over here—didn't it say something about the legions of the Defiler being forged by moonlight?" Kelenthe leaped up again, knocking scrolls from the table in her growing excitement. She pulled one of the scraps of parchment closer, scanning the text for answers, and then stared once again at the drawing of the gold and ivory gate. Moon surrounding moon, night, and darkness.

"They carry silver weapons. They run only by moonlight. They fear the sun." Kaja's hand went instinctively to the golden symbol around her neck, the sign of Shinare. "The golden sun."

Sindri sat up in the window, the last of the day's light making a halo around his shoulders. "Are you saying that gold . . . might hurt them?" He looked excited, scrabbling down the wooden wall toward them.

"I don't know, Sindri," Kelenthe grinned. "But we're going to find out."

CHAPTER 14

Beneath a Scarlet Moon

Echoing off the high cliffside, a lonely horn sounded in the mountains. A second joined it, and the baying of hounds provided rhythm to the impromptu music. As Lunitari slipped above the highest peak, its scarlet light uncovered shadows that were not like the others. They moved away from the rocks, moving at breakneck, fearless speed down through the passes.

The horn sounded again, and the riders wheeled, taking their positions at the top of a hillside. Below them, fires burned in the village.

Gieden's black steed chomped at the bit, its claws striking sparks against the stone. "Our cavalry had little luck against them last night. These mountain folk are hardier than the elves. They will not fall as easily."

Behind him, the hooded figure drew in a shallow, rattling breath. "Elves shatter like porcelain. Men crumble like clay. There is no difference."

"No, no difference other than the sound they make when breaking." Gieden smiled. "I look forward to hearing it." He laughed. "Soon, we will rejoin our legion, and then we will see destruction as we have never caused it before."

"This is a waste of time. Killing his family will not make him return the crown. It only makes him run." The figure crossed his arms beneath voluminous robes, clawed fingers curling against one another with soft clacks of bone.

"The plan will work. You are stuck in an archaic dream, my friend. Those old ways don't work anymore." Gieden simpered in a courtier's pout. "Don't you trust me?"

The hooded figure suddenly turned its head, listening for something in the wind. "We are not alone." The voice was dull, like breath forced through rotten tubes.

"I know. I've already seen him." The wizard's steed danced again, but he did not bother to draw up its paces. "Perhaps this time, he will make himself useful." The undead steed reared and turned, charging down the mountain. "Now just watch, and learn." Gieden's laugh echoed with the third sounding of the horns as the legion charged.

Huge wooden logs burned around the hearthstead, creating a wall of fire and light. Archers stationed on the rooftop and before the wide oak doors launched volley after volley into the undead as Gieden's legion stormed through the empty streets of Tarrent. The last of the villagers raced from abandoned huts, carrying precious bundles in their arms. They were all but jerked through the barricades by Gerhalt's guards.

A man with a brown cloak pulled high over his hair was the last of them. After he had passed, Gerhalt yelled the order from his perch on the roof. "Seal the hearthstead!"

The wide doors slammed shut with the force of many hands. Gerhalt could see Vael's pale hair flash past behind one of the closed window shutters. Those, too, would be sealed—all but one. And that last, just to the side of the door, would seal as soon as the archers left their posts and climbed inside. They clambered across the rooftop, launching their arrows fruitlessly beyond the fire and into the undead.

Rina and Elidor shot arrow after arrow, their faces grim. Gerhalt tromped across the roof to Elidor's side. "When we run out of arrows, the archers will go within. *All of us.*"

Elidor nodded. Rina muttered in agreement, hunching her shoulders.

"The arrows do nothing more than slow them. The real battle will be at the main doors. They won't hold against Gieden's magic." Elidor shot another arrow, knocking back one of the hounds that attempted to leap over the barricade of fire.

"I know. But everything's ready inside. The populace is being moved to the underground chambers, and Sindri swears he's got spells to counter anything Gieden might cast. Not that I fully believe in the small wizard's powers," Gerhalt thumped his cane on the roof, "but he's persistent."

"That he is." Elidor's last arrow hissed from the bowstring, thunking into a warrior's shoulder plate. It did little to harm the undead, but caused the creature to drop the flaming branch it was trying to drag away from the barricade. Around Elidor, other archers were standing, making their way in through the high window and dropping down to the floor beneath. "Let's go."

Inside the hearthstead, villagers rushed into a tunnel that led to pantries and underground storage rooms. Vael gave quiet orders, her voice calm despite the horns sounding just outside the doors. Unlike her earlier garb, now she wore a suit of bright chain mail and a helm with a reddish plume upon her head. A short spear hung on her back.

"Vael, what are you doing?" Elidor stood still when he saw her, eyes widening.

"The same thing you are," she said, fixing him with a level stare. "I'm defending Tarrent."

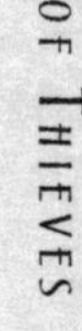

"But you can't—" Before Elidor could continue, Kelenthe, Kaja, and Sindri rushed up from below, holding two small satchels.

"This is all you have?" Kelenthe yelled. Another horn wailed somewhere into the night, and there was a crash as flame broke through rotting wood outside.

"Yes, that's all." Vael took the satchel and dumped its contents on the ground. Golden chalices, necklaces, plates, and other baubles fell onto the bearskin rugs. "The last of Asvoria's treasure, stolen by her servants as they escaped Navarre and founded our city. None of it is magical. It isn't even worth trading. Gold is useless." She shrugged. "I don't know why you even had them find it. It's been rotting away in some back storeroom for centuries."

"Useless to you." Kelenthe knelt, reaching into the pile to lift a heavy golden scroll case. "But not to us."

"We hope," Kaja whispered, her hand touching the symbol of Shinare.

"Mother, you must go below." Elidor caught sight of Elyana standing at the stairs that led down into the underground chambers. "Rina, go with her."

"I don't want to," Rina began, but Elidor cut her off.

"This isn't a request. Someone has to protect Mother. If Gieden's men get through here, they will come for three things—Vael, you, and Mother. Do you hear me?" Elidor put his hands on his sister's shoulders and shook her gently. "I need someone downstairs who can fight."

"All right." Rina tried to smile. "I'll do it." Taking her mother's hand, Rina pulled Elyana down the stairs toward the rooms where the other villagers were hiding.

Elidor watched them go. "Are they going to be all right down there?"

Gerhalt glanced over. "They'll be fine. Gieden might get in here, but I doubt he'll make it downstairs. They're barricading the passages fairly well, and there are secret corridors below this building that will give them extra space to hide—just in case."

"I didn't mean Gieden," Elidor said. "I was wondering if the villagers are going to strangle my mother before the night is over. I know I'd want to." He unsheathed a dagger, playing with it in swift fingers.

Gerhalt paused a moment. When he spoke again, his voice was low, so only Elidor could hear him. "We spent the day in Tarrent, you know. Your mother, Corrigan, and I. Your sister and Rohawn too, for that matter." The old guard listened to the howl of the undead outside the hearthstead, the steady crackle of the barricade's flames outside the door. "You'd be surprised, Elidor."

"Surprised? By my mother?" Elidor snorted. "I'm only surprised she's managed to hold her tongue long enough to keep herself from being stabbed by the villagers."

"You do her no credit."

"She doesn't deserve any," Elidor shot back.

Grimacing, Gerhalt shouted orders to some of Tarrent's burly guards, directing them to reinforce the main doorway. The sounds outside were growing louder, the clacking of claws now punctuated by a sound that could only be a battering ram against the burning barricade. Soon, Gieden's warriors would be at the door. Once his men were in motion, Gerhalt turned back to Elidor. "Your mother told me she was a missionary to the Kagonesti before you were born. Have you ever asked her why?"

Shaking his head, Elidor replied, "I never thought it mattered."

"You should ask her. I think you'd be surprised by her answer." Gerhalt walked away, yelling to his men to stack large logs against the shutters of the lower windows.

Elidor stared after him, unsure what to say.

He strolled over to where Catriona and Corrigan stood, peering out a crack in the shutters.

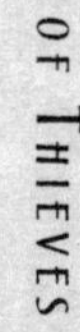

"We have a few hours, no more," Catriona grumbled. "The fire won't last longer than that. Already, Gieden's warriors are doing what they can to cause a breach in the fallen trees that we set on fire."

Corrigan pointed beyond Elidor to where Kaja, Kelenthe, and Sindri sat in the corner of the hearthstead, passing golden bric-a-brac back and forth as if trying to solve a jigsaw puzzle. "Any idea what those three are doing?"

"I think they have a plan," Elidor reasoned. "But I have no idea what it is."

"Let's have Rohawn join them." Corrigan smiled, teasing his young squire. "That'll sort it out."

Rohawn sat near his master's feet, sharpening his blade. He smiled thinly. There was sweat on the boy's forehead, and his eyes constantly strayed to the doors that led below.

Rohawn was afraid. And rightly so, Elidor thought. Gieden's legions destroyed the elven archers at Aerendor and nearly bested Elidor and his friends in the barrow. What chance, really, did a little town of misfits in a mountain canyon have against them?

Rohawn gulped, the stone moving faster over his blade.

"Have no fear, boy," Corrigan said. "There are no flaws in my plan. All will be well come morning."

Catriona turned away from the window. "Don't feed the boy that idiocy. When Gieden gets here, everything will change, just like at Aerendor. We don't have the ability to fight Gieden's magic. Corrigan can't outmaneuver raw power, and Sindri isn't the wizard that Gieden is. If you're lucky, your death will be painless—not 'noble,' not 'honorable.' Just painless and quick."

Rohawn blanched, jaw gaping. "How can you say that?"

"I'm telling you the truth, and that's more than the Knights of Solamnia will do for you," Cat snarled bitterly. "Their pretty words and stories of heroes don't cover the fact that for every Huma, there are ten thousand soldiers dying uselessly on the battlefield below. Heroes climb over everyone else, Rohawn. Wake up."

"Cat, stop it." Elidor cut her off with a sharp exclamation. "This isn't the time." She fell silent.

"We'll know when Gieden arrives," Elidor continued, "and we'll fight him when he does. There's never been another choice. All the running we've done, from the barrow to Aerendor to here, but we can't lose him. We can't outrun him."

Catriona nodded grudgingly, her red hair shining in the glow of the fire. "We don't have a weapon against Gieden. We may fight, but we cannot win."

Kaja looked up from the fireplace where she had set a pot to boil in the massive stone hearth. "I pray that you are wrong, Lady Catriona," she said as she made a gesture of blessing over the metal cauldron. "I pray that you are wrong."

"Cat, I thought that avenging Elidor was impossible." Rina stood to the side of the others, arms crossed over her chest. "I thought Asvoria would kill us all, that we'd die there. But I saw you fight, and I knew that we had a chance. Not because you were the best warrior in the world, but because you never gave up. You didn't let me fall when I went over that cliff back then, and I'm not going to let you fall now."

Catriona looked overwhelmed. "You're right. Maybe . . . maybe there is a chance. Not much of one, but . . . " Taking her dragon claws from her sides, Catriona swung the swords experimentally. "We'll see."

A sudden chill, biting and vicious, thundered against the front wall of the hearthstead. Snow hailed down against the flames of the barricade, snuffing out the fire. The old logs and fallen trees were swept back by a tornado of ice and battered into the wall of the hearthstead.

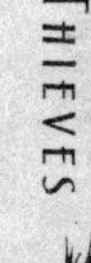

"Gieden," Elidor whispered as frost whitened the shutters and crept under the heavy oak doors.

Vael stood in the center of the room, her chain mail glinting in the firelight. "Be not afraid!" she called to her people. Yet even as she did, the beating march of armored feet pounded near the doors. The oak barrier shook once with a loud thud, as though something heavy slammed into it from outside.

"He'll send in the warriors and footmen," Corrigan called. "His steeds are of little use in here, and he won't assume he'll need them. Use the terrain as I taught you! There, behind that table. Archers, release one volley only as they enter the door. More, and you risk hitting our own men." Ordering Rohawn to the center near Vael, Corrigan readied himself for the inevitable.

"Elidor!" Sindri yelled from near the fire. "I need one of your daggers!"

"What?" Elidor looked back over his shoulder. "No!"

"All right, fine. No time to argue." Sindri raced over to Vael. "Give me your spear."

"Now I know you've gone crazy," Catriona stared. "Sindri, we need your magic. Stop playing around."

"I'm not playing. Give it to me! Hurry!" Sindri reached for the spear in Vael's hand and the baroness let him take it from her. Instantly, two of the ogre-like guards stepped closer to her. Sindri ran back to the fire at full tilt, with Kelenthe gesturing for him to make haste.

The doors shuddered once more, cracking from top to bottom as the wood shrieked in protest. The blows continued, pounding against the hearthstead, shaking the very building with insistent demand. Then, the blows ceased.

"Here they come." Elidor crouched.

The silence was ominous, almost worse than the steady pounding.

Then, with a terrible howl of wind, the doors exploded inward.

Rows upon rows of warriors in black plate armor stood just beyond the door, ash churning in their wake.

The first volley of arrows was launched from the rear of the room. They left bright arcs of light in their wake, flames detonating as the arrows struck their mark.

Behind them charged the soldiers of Tarrent. With swords, pickaxes, and scythes raised, every able-bodied warrior in the village stood against Gieden's undead troops.

Elidor raced forward, a dagger in each hand. Beside him, Catriona charged with a fierce cry, Gerhalt and Rohawn close behind them.

A brilliant glow radiated through the room from the rear, and Kaja's chanting rose over the sounds of battle. Soft rays of sunlight struck two of the undead and caused them to fall screaming to the ground. Corrigan took advantage of their fall, tearing off their helms and ripping their weapons from grasping undead fingers. He hurled the swords back to the fighters of Tarrent, arming them as best he could against their enemies.

"Sindri," Elidor screamed. "Do something!"

But the warriors swept into the room. Ash thickened in the air, black and swirling, obscuring Elidor's view.

Rohawn's greatsword rose and fell, covered by ash and hurling shards of bone across the room with each massive cleave. Though he could not harm the undead, the sheer force of the young squire's muscular arms swept warriors to either side.

Elidor tore his gaze away from the boy, certain that Rohawn was in no immediate danger, and tried to find Sindri in the room.

"Corrigan!" Elidor caught the knight's eye as the Solamnian assisted a man with a scythe. "Find Sindri! Get him out here! We need whatever magic he's got!" He spun and suddenly saw Vael.

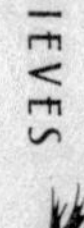

She stood with three of the guards of Tarrent, a few capable soldiers fighting among the farmers and woodsmen. Undead surrounded them, but neither Vael nor her men showed any fear. Sindri slid between her guards and thrust Vael's short spear into her hands. She glanced down at him, smiled, and leaped into the fray.

"No, Vael!" Elidor gasped, trying to push his way through the warriors.

Elidor threw his daggers, striking the undead, trying to draw their attention and keep them off-guard. It wasn't a fight to win; it was a fight to waste Gieden's time, to keep his soldiers busy until dawn could come. Elidor growled, kicking the feet out from beneath another undead minion, tossing him to the ground with a vicious shove.

One of Vael's guards fell to his knee, a bright blossom of blood spreading across the gray-skinned man's chest. Elidor pushed closer, but one of the undead warriors hurled him to the ground, raising a sword over his throat to kill him. Elidor tried to roll, but in the close quarters of the fight, there was nowhere to go. The skeleton's grin leered at him through the ash.

But as it brought its sword down with a violent thrust, the creature jerked. The sword hung in the air, inches above Elidor's throat. The bony grin never wavered, but the hand shivered, twitched, and then released the hilt of the sword. The weapon slowly fell from the warrior's fingers, clattering to the ground.

The undead shuddered. Ribs slipped off beneath the plate armor, and the warrior's fingers fell to the earth beside its sword. The warrior rattled once more, and then toppled over and lay still.

Behind the creature, standing over Elidor, was Vael. Her spear was thrust forward, the tip still piercing the undead soldier's back plate.

Elidor stared at the head of her spear and saw a thin layer of gold shining in the firelight.

CHAPTER

15 A Glittering Dawn

Dawn broke over the hearthstead, bathing the wooden structure in shimmering light. The last of the warriors had vanished into the earth, deep within the forest nearby, leaving a dark trail of ash over the mossy ground.

The villagers of Tarrent cheered, celebrating their victory—such as it was. Several were dead, many more wounded, but Gieden's men had not been able to penetrate any farther into the hearthstead than the main chamber.

"Corrigan's tactics proved their match!" Catriona grinned, stepping out into the sunshine. Her arm was bloody from a fresh wound, but her step was light. By her feet, Sindri trotted with a tremendous smile plastered over his features.

"He had a little help!" Sindri laughed. "Even though we could only coat a few weapons with the melted gold, we actually killed some!" He stopped in his tracks, staring up at Cat. "Can you technically kill the undead?"

Beside him, Elidor sighed, saying nothing.

"Gieden's not finished," Cat replied. "Not by a long shot. He hardly used any of his magic last night—"

"No doubt wearied by using it to get his army here so fast," Sindri broke in.

"—and when the army rises again tomorrow, Gieden will be ready. How many gold weapons do we have?"

Sindri struggled to keep up with her long strides. "Three. And I scraped up the gold that fell out when I threw the melting pot at one of the undead. Corrigan thinks we can make a few arrowheads out of what's left."

"Gold makes for poor weapons." Gerhalt looked back at them, leaning on the bridge over the river. "The ones dipped in it last night are already chipping. They aren't permanent. We'd have to forge weapons of gold, like those arrowheads Corrigan and Rohawn are working on, or we'd have to pour gold layers over the weapons we have. Even at that, it doesn't make for a very sturdy—or balanced—blade."

"Elidor!" A scream from inside the hearthstead startled them all, and Elidor spun warily.

"Elidor, come quickly!" Kelenthe stood in the doorway of the building, a wild panic in her voice. "Elidor!"

Without hesitation, Elidor raced back up the hillock toward the building. Cat and the others followed behind.

Inside the building, a crowd gathered around the open door to the lower chambers, and Elidor could hear Vael's voice speaking slowly and evenly. "Put away the weapon."

As Elidor approached, the villagers stepped quickly out of his way, allowing him to approach the stairway that led down into a torch-lit corridor.

He saw Vael standing at the bottom of the stairs, a guard behind her in a fiercely protective pose. The baroness stepped forward. "Put away the sword and we can talk. There's no need for anyone to be hurt."

"There's every need," growled a voice just beyond her. "There's a need for every one of you mongrel, mixed-blood dogs in this village to die in fire."

"Narath," breathed Elidor as he reached the bottom of the stairway and the scene came into view.

Narath stood in the corridor, the sword in his hand pressed against the back of a village woman. His brown hood was pushed back, the look in his eyes enraged.

The whimpering woman was his captive, a young mother whose children were being held back at the top of the stairs by Catriona and Sindri. The woman's hair was clutched in Narath's hand, her back arched, the sword ready to plunge through her heart with the slightest push of his blade. "You want to save her?" he growled. "Then trade your life for hers."

"Still serving Gieden, Narath?" Elidor drawled, trying not to show his nervousness. He stepped forward in a leisurely manner.

Narath jerked the sword up against the woman's back. She let out a shrill scream.

Elidor froze. Now that he was closer, he could see why Vael's face had paled. Narath seemed barely a shadow of himself—his skin was gray, his features gaunt, and the nails of his hand blue-tinged and strange. "Narath, what's happened to you?"

"Not one more step," the elf snarled, his face contorting, "or I will kill her."

"No," Vael's voice wavered, and she began to step forward, but Elidor caught her by the arm.

Aware that half of Tarrent was standing on the stairs above them watching the spectacle, Elidor whispered into the Vael's ear. "Let me handle this."

She paused and nodded.

"What do you want, Narath?" Elidor asked.

Narath laughed. "Want?" In a fraction of an instant, the laugh died and Narath's face became serious. "I want you—and all of

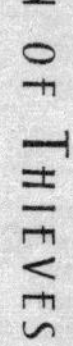

these half-breeds—dead under my feet. I made a deal, Elidor. Your life for my own. And I plan to pay in full—with extras." He jerked the woman toward him for emphasis. Behind Vael, two of her guards leveled bows at Narath, afraid to fire lest they hit the village woman. Vael gestured for them to stop.

Elidor tried again. "It's not her you want. It's me. Now, why don't you let her go?"

"When you're dead, she goes free. End of deal." Narath's grin was sickly. "Now the question is who's going to do it. Elidor? Do you have the courage to fall on your own blade to save this wretched, worthless creature? Or maybe I should take on that mongrel behind you instead." He gestured roughly toward Vael.

Elidor nearly lunged at him.

"Narath." For a moment, Elidor thought that Vael had spoken. But the voice was lower, more calm. Educated.

"Elyana?" Keeping his sword close to his hostage's spine, Narath looked over his shoulder at the figure standing behind him. "Here to watch the half-bloods die?"

"This isn't you." Elyana spoke evenly, her chin lifted in a gesture Elidor remembered from the council room in Aerendor. Narath seemed to remember it as well, and he faltered slightly.

"You don't belong here, Elyana," Narath grinned. "You're like me—pure. You're worth more than everyone in this village combined. Help me, and I'll make sure my master rewards you as well."

"With what?" As she stepped forward, Elidor could see faint dark circles beneath her eyes. The night had been a difficult one for her, he could tell, but there was no trace of weariness or doubt in her movements. "Gieden has nothing to offer me."

"He can free you of the son you despise. Fallerian was right, you've suffered too long."

"Never." Something seemed to break within Elyana then, and she took three quick strides forward. With a movement swifter than Elidor would have imagined, she gripped the hilt of Narath's blade and twisted the sword away from him.

Her hand struck out, slapping Narath across the face.

"These are people, Narath, no matter what their blood. I believed that when I left Aerendor to live among the Kagonesti. When they saved my life, they did not turn me away because of my heritage. They accepted me, they taught me, and they risked themselves to keep me safe when I chose to return home. And yes, I loved one of their people. When humans came and enslaved their tribe, I was released because of my Silvanesti blood.

"I could have tried to free them, but I was a coward. I chose to run back home, to pretend that it never happened, all because they were not Silvanesti. I was afraid, but no longer." Elyana faced Narath eye-to-eye and never wavered.

"I returned to Aerendor not because we were a better people. I returned because I was not strong enough to be more than I had been raised." Tears touched her eyes. "I tried to hide myself where I did not have to think about those memories of happiness among the Kagonesti. But coming here, seeing these . . . people . . . ." She breathed a deep, shuddering breath and continued, "has made me remember. I will never again hear you, or anyone else, blame someone for their blood. I bore my son out of love. I raised him, and I was ashamed. It was of my own weakness, not his."

Elidor stared at her, stunned.

Tears trickled down Elyana's porcelain cheeks. "I was ashamed, and I was wrong to be. My son is a good elf, better than I deserve."

"Mother," Elidor whispered. "I never knew."

"Get out of here, Narath," Elyana murmured, placing her hand gently on the elf's shoulder. "Go home, where you belong."

Narath seemed to wake as though from a dream, staring up at her. "Elyana?" She smiled at him and he shook his head slowly. "I can't go. I can't . . . " He pulled away from her and bent to pick up

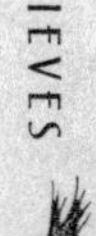

the sword on the ground. "My master . . . he knows where I am. He can see me . . . "

Narath's sword wavered, the sharp point floating between Elyana and the crowd on the stairs.

Elidor bristled instinctively, flinching toward his knives. Only Vael's hand on his wrist stopped him from launching to the attack. "He'll kill her before you take a single step," she whispered, frightened.

"What have you done, Narath?" Elyana spoke softly.

"He gave me something to carry into the building. A magical trap," he whimpered, the tip of his sword falling an inch lower. "This building will be destroyed."

"Have you set it?" her voice was quiet. When Narath didn't answer, she snapped, "Tell me!"

He shook his head, one hand reaching into his vest pocket. He withdrew a small orb, metallic, covered with delicate etchings. "He gave me this."

"By E'li," Elidor's mother murmured. She reached out her hand. "Give it to me."

Tension crackled through the air, and Elidor heard several of the villagers behind him draw in shuddering, frightened breaths. Elyana did not waver, keeping her palm steady before the distraught elf. "Give it to me."

"I can't." Tears ran down Narath's cheeks, and he gulped for air. "He . . . commands . . . me . . . "

He jerked then, as though compelled by some outside force. His skin, already gray, sickened further with a strange pallor. He clutched the orb close to his chest. "I promised him Elidor's life . . . or my own. I don't want to hurt you, Elyana. Please, please . . . leave." His irises turned for an instant to an unnatural white. Robotically, he lifted his sword again, blank eyes searching the crowd.

“I’m not leaving.” Elyana stood frozen, her hand just inches from the orb.

“Then it will be my honor to die with you.” Tears running down his face, Narath saluted Elyana with his sword, his hand clenching around the orb.

“NO!” Elidor held out one hand instinctively, a sharp pain splintering through his mind. Without understanding his own actions, Elidor jabbed one finger toward Narath.

A dark, shadowy pulse emanated from the crown, shifting down Elidor’s arm like rolling snakes of darkness. It flew forward and enveloped Narath in a tangle of thick, shadowy tar.

Narath jerked sideways, slamming into the wall so hard that the orb was flung from the elf’s hand.

Elyana leaped for it. She landed on her shoulder and caught the silver ball on her fingertips just before it hit the ground.

Narath recoiled. Seeing Elyana fall near him, he grabbed her.

He clutched Elyana close to him and slowly stood. Within the twisting black coils of Elidor’s spell, Narath’s eyes flickered. “I cannot resist him!” His body spasmed, twitching like a puppet on strings, and the white began to return to his eyes.

Catriona jumped from the stairs and raised her sword as if to attack. She paused just before landing the blow, aware that Narath held Elyana’s life in his hands.

“Let her go!” Cat growled. She punctuated her words with a threatening jerk of her sword.

“Narath!” Elyana fought to break away, trying to grasp the Silvanesti’s shoulder.

The elf spun, pale cataracts taking over his eyes once more. The shadowy tentacles that contained him snapped, shattering into fading shards of darkness.

As they did, Elidor fell to the ground in agony. His hands clutched the crown on his forehead. Whatever he had done, he

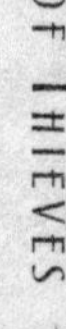

didn't know how to control it.

"Elidor!" Narath screamed, releasing Elyana and raising the sword above his head. "The Lord of Taeloc commands me!" It was half battle cry and half a plea for forgiveness.

Elidor struggled to his feet, uncontrolled energy still flowing through his body. Another coiling serpent of darkness, thick and slimy like tar, writhed from his outstretched arm. It launched out of his fingers, wrapping around Narath's chest.

Narath jerked like a marionette, pitching forward and then back with a moaning cry. Fighting the magic in his mind and Elidor's power, Narath turned toward the closest target—Elyana.

He thrust the sword into her side. As he staggered back, Elyana fell to the ground, hands clasping her side.

Rina screamed. Vael ordered her guards to fire—but they were too late.

Unable to reach Elidor before the archers fired, Narath twisted in the air and tried to flee. His body shook, lost in the convulsions of the Defiler's magic. Elidor's black tentacles swarmed over him, covering every inch of his skin. They wrapped around his arms, tearing away his sword and stretching Narath spread eagle above the floor as the elf screamed.

"Elidor! Make it stop!" Elyana screamed.

But he couldn't. The magic was out of control. Shadows rippled and plunged over Narath, engulfing him completely. They dragged him through the air, away from Elyana and toward a patch of darkness on the wall of the passage.

Pressing him against the wall, the shadows began to spread, fusing with the darkness there. Elidor could hear muffled screams from Narath, terrified calls—but then they became whispers, then echoes, then faded into nothing more than real shadow against the wall.

Narath was gone.

"Where did he go?" Sindri piped up curiously from the stair.

"I don't know," Elidor shuddered. "The Crown has taken him . . . and I don't think we'll be seeing him again."

"Wow! Cool!" Sindri's fist punched the air in cheery victory. "Now that's magic!"

Elidor was glad that Sindri didn't notice the sick feeling in his stomach as the elf touched the crown on his forehead, nor the way Catriona stared at him as though he'd suddenly grown another head. Suddenly, he remembered Elyana.

"By E'li." Elidor ran to Elyana, taking his mother's head in his arms as she wept. The darkness that emanated from the crown faded, shifting into striped bands of shadow that were no more than bands of black against the stone wall. Elidor ignored them, holding Elyana tightly.

"Are you all right?" he asked.

She nodded, wincing. "I am bleeding, but it could have been much worse. He didn't want to hurt me." Elyana choked back a sob. "Gieden made him. Oh, poor Narath."

Elidor touched his mother's hair protectively. "Don't pity him. He chose this path long ago, and nothing could have made him change it. Some people never change." He paused. "I never knew the story about the Kagonesti."

"You never asked." She forced a smile, pain evident in her features. "Some day, my son, I'll tell you the whole story, but not today."

"No, not today."

"How did you do that, Elidor?" Sindri said with wonder. "You made the shadows come to life! That was real magic!"

"It wasn't me," Elidor said shakily, his face red. "The crown just . . . acted. If I'd been able to control it, Narath wouldn't have gotten near her." He pressed his cheek against Elyana's hair. "I'm sorry."

"No, Elidor." She gave him a pained smile. "You saved my life."

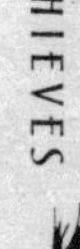

"Whatever you did, however you did it, we are all grateful." Corrigan sighed in relief. "What is that thing he carried?"

"Oh, right! The magical bomb. Can I look at it?" Sindri hopped down the last few stairs and trotted to the baroness's side. He took the silver ball from her hand, rolling it across his fingers. "I've seen these before! You put them somewhere, and then hit them with magic—any kind of spell, really—and boom! They blow up!"

"Gieden isn't playing around anymore," Gerhalt said. "We can't take the risk of holing up inside the hearthstead again . . . " He trailed off, the rest of his sentence written in the grim lines of his face. "This bomb is just a safety measure. He knows we're vulnerable."

"I understand. And we have few means with which to fight him." Vael frowned. "Kelenthe? Kaja?" She turned her pale blue eyes to the top of the stairs, seeking out the elven twins.

"Here." Kelenthe pushed through the crowd. "My sister's working with the small amount of gold we have, hoping to coat a few more weapons."

"It won't be enough." Vael looked to Elidor. "Gieden knows we have a way to hurt his soldiers. He's not going to play with us anymore. Gieden likes to be feared. What he did to Narath is only a taste—controlling people's minds, turning them into his puppets. He knows we can fight him, even hurt his men. I know how minds like his work. He won't let us feel as though we have the upper hand. We're going to lose that advantage very quickly, Elidor."

"You're right. In Aerendor, he fought with huge, fiery spells. He could burn this hearthstead down around our ears if he wanted to. This isn't just about the crown. It's about his pride too." Elidor sighed, brushing a lock of hair from his serious eyes. "So what now?"

"Gold is the key," Kelenthe said. "But we don't have nearly enough, even if we had the smelting and metalworking tools . . . "

As she spoke, her sister pushed down the stairs with clean rags and a skin of water. Kaja moved to kneel by Elyana, pressing cloth against the stateswoman's wound.

From the top of the stairs, Corrigan mused, "We don't need those. All we need is a great amount of the raw quantity, and we can find a way to fight with it."

"Raw quantity," Vael mused. "There may be a way. I hadn't thought of it before, but there is a mine, some distance from Tarrent. In the age of Asvoria, her slaves would work the earth to bring up gold from deep veins and make her treasures. Long ago, after Tarrent was founded by those who escaped her, the mine was closed."

"Can you find this mine?" Corrigan asked. "How long would it take us to get there?"

"Not long. Perhaps a few hours. But I don't see how it could help us. There is gold there, of course, but it's in the earth. The gold veins are wide and deep, but still embedded. It would take days to mine it and bring it back here."

The thin knight shook his head, a smile spreading beneath his wispy mustache. "Mine? Oh, no. We won't need to mine, and we won't be bringing it back here."

"You've got that look again." Elidor raised an eyebrow. "The one that says you've got a plan."

"Don't worry, lad," smiled Corrigan. "I think you're going to like this one."

"Whatever the plan is, Elyana's not going anywhere." Kaja was wrapping cloth around Elyana's waist, binding the wound that she had received from Narath. "I have no magic left from the fight last night, and I will need all the healing I have if we are to fight Gieden when the sun goes down again." Before Elidor could protest, she held up a hand to stop him. "Your mother is fine, Elidor. Her wound is not grave, but it will not heal if she leaps onto a horse

and rides though hill and vale with warriors at her back. No. I will not hear of it."

Elyana raised her head. "Go without me."

"What?" the sound came from three voices at once—Rina, Elidor, and Vael. Elidor shook his head. "We can't leave you here."

"Yes, you can," Elyana insisted stubbornly, rising to stand with Kaja's help. "Gieden knows how many people entered this village. He's going to be looking for that many to leave. You'll be one short." Turning to Vael, she said, "We are of a similar build; our hair is very close in length . . . "

"Mother, what are you suggesting?" Elidor asked.

"Gieden would never imagine that Vael would leave her village. It will be easy enough for her and me to exchange places. I can remain here, wear her armor, be seen at a distance here within the hearthstead. She can darken her hair, wear my robe . . . "

"How do we know he'll follow us at all?" Kaja frowned. "Why not just stay and destroy Tarrent? Without us here to defend it, it would be an easy target."

Elidor grimaced. "He doesn't want Tarrent, or you, or any of this, really. Gieden just wants one thing—me. He wants this crown, and he's willing to do anything to get it. I'm the bait. If he thinks I'm getting away from him, he'll follow me all right. He can't afford to lose track of me, or he's lost the crown forever. But that still doesn't mean we can leave you, Mother. It's too dangerous."

Elyana took Elidor's hand and squeezed it. "Though I may not know much of war, I know a great deal about soothing panicked people. And if Gieden is concentrating on you and your group, Elidor, then he won't leave many soldiers behind to attack us."

"Tarrent won't listen to you, Mother."

"I think you'd be surprised." Vael reached out and took Elyana's hand. "Many of my people heard your words just now, Elyana. Your bravery saved the life of a woman of this town. That will not be forgotten."

"It could work." Corrigan smoothed his mustache thoughtfully. "If we leave the village as a large group, Gieden will follow. He may be obsessed with his pride, but at the heart of it, he wants the crown, and his pride means that he wants to make Elidor pay." Corrigan looked over at Vael. "But this all depends on you going with them, Vael. Are you willing to do that?"

The baroness looked at Elyana, and then at Elidor. "I am."

Elidor sighed. "Why do I have the feeling that the decision's being made for me?"

"If you have a better idea—" Elyana began.

"No." He rubbed his face regretfully. "No, I don't. But that doesn't mean that I'm happy about this. I know what we have to do to stop Gieden." Elidor looked significantly at Kaja standing at his mother's side. "And I know that you're capable of taking care of yourselves." A faint pounding in his head was blurring Elidor's thoughts, whispering like a distant humming behind his ears.

"Then what's the problem?" Kaja stared up at Elidor with solemn intensity.

"I . . . " Elidor held his fingers to his temples, trying to will the headache away. It didn't seem to help. "I just need some time alone. I'm tired."

The crowd parted on the stairway as Elidor walked through them, still holding one hand to his temples. Behind him, there was an awkward silence before Vael began giving orders to her men. He heard Elyana offering quiet advice, her cultured dialect a counterpoint to the chattering relief in the villagers' voices.

"Elidor?" Cat followed. "Are you all right?"

They walked outside. The bright morning sunlight hurt Elidor's eyes, making him blink repeatedly. He sank to his knees by the river at the base of the bridge to the hearthstead, clutching his

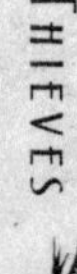

pounding temples. "Whatever I did in there—it wasn't me. It was the crown."

"I know," she murmured, squatting beside him. "You countered Gieden's dark magic."

He shook his head. "When I felt the power of the crown move through me, I somehow touched Narath's mind." Elidor's voice fell. "I don't think it was Gieden controlling Narath."

"What?" Cat sat down in the dirt beside him. "Then . . . who?"

"I don't know. Maybe one of his servants."

The river flowed at their feet, trickling over mountain stone and simple earth. It ran beneath the high arched bridge, which was covered in ash from the barricade fires and the passage of Gieden's soldiers. Small white flowers blossomed in the shadow of the hearthstead. The wind ruffled their resilient petals, darkening them with touches of black ash.

"Elidor, what you did in there . . . it was kind of scary. You don't use magic. That crown, what else can it do? Or more to the point—" Cat tried to cover the fear in her voice, but he could still hear it.

He shook his head. "You're asking questions I can't answer."

"If you can't answer them, who can?"

A small pair of pale feet walked along the riverbank, tattered white rags trailing behind them. The feet stopped at the water's edge, the ripples of Tarrent's river flowing around each toe. Elidor looked up and stared into the spirit's face as she spoke.

"I can."

CHAPTER

16 Answers and Deceptions

Elidor rose, reaching out his hand as though to touch the spirit that stood before him. Unlike the other times, when she had seemed completely solid and real, now the girl was faintly transparent. The edge of her white robe faded away in the sunlight. Her brown hair was more a shadow than a tangle, yellowy green eyes matching the color of the grasses on the hillside behind her. His hand went through her shoulder, clenching into a fist beyond the girl's form.

"Tell me what the crown can do." Elidor dropped his hand.

Cat froze. "You're talking to that ghost again, aren't you? The one Sindri told us about?"

He nodded, taking a step to follow as the spirit began to back away. "Tell me what happened in there," he said forcefully. "I need to know."

"I can help you, Elidor," she whispered. "But you have to trust me—"

"Trust you?" he cut her off. "I've trusted you enough. Where were you when Gieden attacked Aerendor? Where were you last night?" Elidor thrust his hands in the air, his voice rising. "If this crown gives me power against them, then why can't I *use* it?"

The spirit hunched down and clapped her hands over her ears. "Stop, please, stop! I'm trying to help you."

Cat reached for the hilt of her sword. "Elidor?"

He waved his hand back at his friend and advanced toward the spirit. "You're connected to the crown. You're a part of it. Why? What holds you to it? And why can't you just tell me how to use it, how to defend myself and my friends against Gieden?"

"I . . . I can't. There's more to it than you know." The ghost fell backward, bare feet churning against the mud, but leaving no marks on the damp earth. "I can't answer your questions. I am forbidden."

Elidor yelled, "Forbidden by what? What don't I know? Whatever it is, I don't know it because you're not telling me! You keep saying that you're here to help me, but your riddles and your games aren't helping—they're just distractions. How do I know you're not working for him too?"

If he had any real doubt, it was erased by the horrified look on the spirit's face after he said the words. Her skin paled, her mouth widened, and tears sparkled in the corners of her eyes.

He lowered his arms. "I'm sorry," he muttered. "But I'm tired of dreams and puzzles. I want the truth."

Catriona stared at him with open curiosity. "What's she saying?"

"Nothing." He crossed his arms.

"Ask her about that weird shadow, the one that killed Narath."

"Yes." He turned to the spirit. "Tell me about that. If you're so eager to help, then teach me how to control that." A wind blew softly through the flowers on the hillside, and in the silence, the river seemed as loud as raging rapids.

"I can't." It was little more than a whisper. "I cannot tell you things directly. I can only lead you to them and hope that you understand. I am restrained by the burden of the crown itself, even as my soul is bound to it. You bear the Crown of Thieves. Thieves who move . . . ”

“In shadow,” he guessed.

She nodded, hiding her face.

“The crown has some power over shadows, but you can’t tell me any more than that. So, what can you do?” He snorted.

“I can help you save yourself.” She looked up. “No magic is invulnerable. You already know how to defeat the soldiers. The sun destroys them; the sun born in the earth can kill them.”

“Gold.”

The spirit nodded. “But it isn’t enough.” When Elidor didn’t interrupt her, the spirit continued. “You made the crown do something in there. But you also made a ripple. Like this.” She pushed her hand into the water. Though it did not shift to her presence, Elidor nodded. “You pushed. So he pushed back.”

He knelt beside her, trying not to stare at the edges of her form where she faded into nothingness. Talking to a ghost was a bit disconcerting. “That’s where my headache came from when it happened.”

“Yes. He saw you.”

“It was worth the cost. My mother is alive.” Elidor considered this for a moment, and then frowned. “How can I do it again?”

“You just have to *be*. Not here, but there. Not here.” When Elidor did not respond, she stomped her foot in frustration. “It doesn’t work here. You aren’t here, and neither is he. You don’t understand. You’re in danger. He *saw*.”

“ ‘He’ who? Gieden?” When the ghost only stared at him forlornly, Elidor shook his head. “How are you supposed to be of any use to me if you can’t talk to me? What’s keeping you from just telling me the truth?”

Slowly, cautiously, the ghostly girl reached up and brushed her fingers across the silver crown. It was like a shock ran through

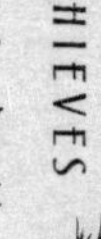

Elidor at her touch, and he closed his eyes.

Images flowed through his mind of ivory streets and tall towers, thick walls broken by a single ivory and gold gate; the girl, standing before the symbol of a black moon crushing a silver one, holding her arms open as if blocking the way into the city. He opened his eyes.

"Kelenthe told us there was a sacrifice—a precious gem—placed into the crown. But I don't think the scroll meant a stone. I think the sacrifice . . . was you. Wasn't it?"

The girl turned away. "I have to go." She scrambled to her feet, refusing to meet Elidor's eyes.

"It was you, wasn't it? That's why you're here. That's why you're helping me. You're trapped in the crown, aren't you? Whatever magic is keeping me alive, it's keeping you from death."

"Elidor, what's going on?" Cat leaned forward, fingering her sword hilt. "I don't understand what you're saying. Who's trapped in the crown?"

"I have to go." The ghost repeated again. "He's going to find out that I'm talking to you."

"Gieden can't command you. He's not that powerful. If he could just take the crown, he'd have done it already." Elidor brushed aside the spirit's argument, refusing to let her fade away.

"You don't understand." Tears streaked her dirty cheeks. She whispered again, "You aren't *here*."

Ignoring her, Elidor pushed for answers. "You know about our plan for tonight, to run through the woods to the gold mine and use it to fight Gieden's soldiers. Will it work? What can the crown do to help me? Can it teleport us there? Can I put a protective spell around my mother? Or Vael?"

The girl shook her head. "Please, Elidor, I—"

"Is the crown capable of using magic against Gieden? Or taking control of his undead minions?" Elidor grew angrier with each question, refusing to back down even as the ghost cowered away. "It has to do something or he wouldn't want it!

"I can't tell you!" she cried.

"Then leave me alone!" he yelled, pounding one hand into the riverbank. The pain of stone digging into his flesh made him jerk away, and pulled his bleeding palm against his chest. It only stole his attention for an instant, but when he twisted his attention back to the girl, it was already too late.

She was gone.

The horse shied beneath the Baroness of Tarrent, tossing its head in the fading sunlight.

"Vael," Elyana said from the doorway of the barn, "Take this." She approached the baroness, placing her purple cloak across Vael's saddle. "It is my cloak of rank. He'll be expecting to see it."

Vael's hair had been dyed a soft gold, the color strange against her too-pale skin. She wore a blue gown, chosen to match Elyana's robes, and the braids against her neck were a perfect imitation of the Silvanesti's coils. "This is precious to you. I can't—"

"No, dear," Elyana took Vael's hand, looking up from beside the horse. "You are a baroness, after all. It suits you."

"Thank you," Vael whispered. She pressed her hands against Elyana's. "Take care of them."

"I swear that I will." Elyana permitted herself one last smile. "I'll make sure you have a home to return to. You make sure," she said, glancing at her son's brooding posture on his roan steed, "that you both come back to it."

Vael said nothing, only nodded.

"Are we ready?" Corrigan asked. He moved his steed closer to Vael and patted her shoulder. "Don't worry, my lady. I'll be right beside you."

"So will I," Rohawn grinned, his shoulder nearly higher than her horse's saddle. The squire glanced back at Rina, who kept her own steed at Vael's side. "They'll be expecting us to protect you, and we will. Don't worry about that."

"I know, Rohawn," Vael tested out her smile. "Everything will be fine. The mine isn't far, only about an hour north, through the box canyon and over the ravines. We'll make it."

Elidor's horse lifted its head, catching a whiff of some foreign scent, and its ears flickered back and forth uncertainly. Elyana and the guards of Tarrent said a last good-bye, then slipped out the door of the barn and hurried toward the hearthstead. The barricades of last night had been rebuilt—as much as they could be. This time, they weren't designed to keep Gieden's men out for very long, only long enough for him to see the fleeing group and give chase. From the hearthstead, men came with torches lit by the great indoor fire, lighting the barricade with pitch and tar and trying to force it to rage as it had the night before. Vael watched a hooded Elyana slip up the hillside and into the main building, and wondered if she would ever see that fireplace again.

Vael stared at Elidor. His legs tensed around his horse's barrel. He'd hardly said three words to her since that morning. She sighed.

"Vael?" Sindri caught her attention. "Don't worry about the villagers. Elyana will take care of them." He grinned, waving his hands in the air. "Even if he leaves some troops behind, Tarrent is going to be safe."

Vael nodded. "Elyana knows what to do now." Her hand touched the hilt of her spear, feeling the hard wood, smooth and ready, beneath her fingertips. Her father taught her how to use it, but she was certain he'd never have predicted these circumstances. "I'm glad we left them half of the gold weapons."

"Yeah, but that's still only three weapons for them, and three for us." Sindri sighed. "I wish we could have made more than that, but it was all the gold we—"

"Hsst." Elidor silenced them. "It's time."

The light of the sun faded and died, and there was only shadow. Rohawn pushed forward, slamming back the door of the barn with one solid shove. Elidor's horse reared, the scent in its nostrils now apparent to them all.

The undead.

Gieden's troops clawed their way up from where they had sunk the night before. Cruel bone fingers shot up from the earth, followed by shining armor, soil crumbling from breastplate and helm. Steeds of ash and fire broke free of stone into the night.

"Now!" Elidor shouted, spurring his panicked horse. The animal needed little encouragement. It pounded out into the street.

Catriona was the second to react. A master rider, she released the reins, letting her horse follow Elidor while she drew her blades. Sindri yelled a battle cry from the rear of her saddle.

"Our turn." Rina, beside Vael, wasted no time. She slapped her horse's neck with the reins and the animal charged. Elyana's steed, accustomed to running beside Rina's, leaped instinctively to follow. Vael clenched her hands in its mane, not trying to guide the horse at all but trusting the animal's instincts.

Rohawn jumped with her, his booted feet slapping against the ground in tandem with her horse's hooves. For all his huge height, the boy was nimble, bounding along with giant strides as his huge greatsword clanked in its sheath on his back. He kept himself just at the rear of Rina's horse, always keeping his eyes on the elven girl.

Corrigan was on Vael's other side, his Solamnian war horse as burly as his squire. The horse was one of the few that had not succumbed to panic. It followed Corrigan's every order with instinctive trust. It was fast—faster than she would have thought—but then again, Corrigan was perhaps half the size of a

normal knight, his thin frame significantly lighter than most of those in his brotherhood.

At the rear of the group rode Kaja and Kelenthe, defending their flank from attack. Kelenthe's steed made little sound even on the hard-packed earth. Kaja kept one hand clenched around her holy symbol, her mouth whispering soft prayers to Shinare.

The sound of a battle horn echoed over Tarrent, and the wind from the south blew a great cloud of ash over the city. Vael gulped, her steed rocking beneath her.

Clawed hands reached up, grasping at the horse's ankles, trying to shred flesh. Her horse staggered, and for a horrible instant, Vael thought it was going to fall. But the steed righted itself, tumbling forward on unsteady feet until it once again picked up its stride. Vael hung on tighter.

Rohawn cursed, leaping over a half-fleshed warrior whose torso was now completely uncovered. The undead warrior swiped at him, ripping its weapon up from beneath the sod in order to swing. The squire leaped forward, diving over the flashing sword and rolling to his feet with a heavy grace. Still, the move cost him. Rohawn fell behind. Vael half-turned in her saddle and saw him resume their fierce pace, losing no more ground. He might not be able to catch up with them, but he wasn't going to be left behind.

"Rohawn!" Rina screamed.

"Keep going, girl!" Corrigan chastised her, reaching forward to slap her horse's flank with his hand. "He's right behind us."

Vael looked up at the hearthstead. From the outside, the bonfires that had seemed so large and comforting the night before now seemed like tiny specks of light. She gritted her teeth, refusing to let the tears flow down her cheeks. This was going to work.

They rounded a corner, riding down the single road that led north toward the forest. Ahead of them, Vael saw more of the undead, their steeds breathing gouts of greenish flame toward an ash-filled sky. Among the gathering riders on their spectral steeds, Vael could see two hooded figures. One wore the velvet black robes of a dark wizard, his hands spread in command. Gieden. She steeled herself and clung low against her horse's neck.

The next few moments were a blur. Wind whipped through Vael's hair as she tried to keep Elyana's hood pulled tightly about her face and shoulders. The others, weapons drawn, charged toward Gieden's cavalry with reckless abandon. Just before they collided, Vael heard Kaja's voice rise as the cleric completed her spell.

Golden light poured from Kaja's outstretched hand, swelling through the group like a wave. Everything in Vael's vision was touched with amber and illuminated by the light of Shinare. It was as if the entire group was suddenly bathed in sunlight.

The undead screamed. The ash and bone steeds reared and fell back, several panicking and trampling over foot soldiers in their frantic need to escape the ball of sunlight. Gieden's steed leaped away, causing the mage to clutch at the reins.

"Stop them!" Gieden commanded his voice high pitched and furious. "Do not let them escape!"

"What are you doing?" Vael screamed, seeing Elidor slow his steed and fall back. He did not seem to hear her, or at least, did not care. With a fluid motion, he made a mocking bow toward Gieden and his men.

"Good-bye, Gieden!" Elidor laughed. "Burn it if you want! But you'll never see me—or the crown—again! She's told me how to destroy the crown, and I'm going to do it!"

"What's he saying?" Rina gasped. "Who told him?"

Catriona turned, the wind whipping her voice back toward the others. "He's bluffing. For Paladine's sake, *ride*."

Gieden's face flushed, the golden glow of Kaja's spell casting sickly shadows across his face. Beside him, his lieutenant raised leathery hands. The words he chanted twisted knots in Vael's stomach.

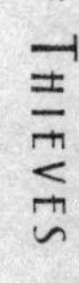

Vael felt a push of great pressure against her skin, singeing the cloak she kept tight around her shoulders. It suddenly built up as though to detonate, crackling around them and crushing the wind from her lungs. She saw Rina clutch her throat, a startled look on her face. Corrigan choked, trying to cough, but nothing came out. Then, with what sounded like his last clear breath, Sindri yelled something in response—bless him, thought Vael, he's trying to counterspell—and there was a clap of thunderous sound.

The horses renewed their pace. With desperate agility, Cat's horse cleared the last rank of scattering undead first, then Vael, Corrigan, and Rina, followed by Kaja and a widely grinning Kelenthe, and at last Elidor and Rohawn, side by side at the very edge of Kaja's sphere of golden sunlight.

"I got him!" Sindri guffawed. "I got him!"

"I don't know what you did, but by Huma, I'm grateful!" Corrigan shouted.

"There's the edge of the village." Vael pointed over her steed's shoulder, indicating the opening into the woods. "That path will take us to the mine."

Kelenthe looked back as the glow cast by Kaja's spell faded. She reached out to steady her sister. "It looks like they're following it."

And indeed, Gieden's cavalry were regrouping, their riders leaping to saddle and mount. Warriors flooded to Gieden's side, marching forward in half-controlled ranks. Gieden's voice could be heard above the sound of booted foot and bony claws, commanding them to follow. Vael thought she saw a grin on Elidor's face, illuminated by the last flickering glow of Kaja's magical sun.

"Now all we have to do," Corrigan growled softly to himself, "is outrun them."

Vael's horse leaped over a pit in the road. At their speed, any stumble would cause calamity. She clung to its flowing mane desperately, hoping that her skill as a horsewoman would keep

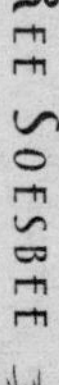

her on its back no matter what came next.

Elidor's horse pushed past her, headed for the front of the group. He grinned as he passed her. "Follow me. I know the way."

Vael kept one hand on her horse's mane, the other on the staff of her spear. She followed the others with a last look back at her beloved village. They needed her to be strong. They needed the gold that the mine would provide. For them, she would do anything. The baroness summoned her courage and rode on.

The woods were dark, the long limbs of the trees shutting out what little light was left in the sky. Soon, Solinari would rise and bathe the ground with silver light, but for this hour after dusk, the sky was bare and overcast. Branches slapped against Vael's face. She caught glimpses of the others ahead of her, following the same path as her own horse. Time passed in a haze, counted only by the pound of each cantering gait.

An undead steed burst out of the trees to their right, forcing Elidor to lead them to the left. Swords clashed as the cavalryman swung toward Catriona, nearly pushing her from her horse. She kicked, burying her boot in the ash of the other creature's cheek, and the spectral steed staggered to the right. It had to rear suddenly to avoid crashing into a wide oak tree, and the undead rider was thrown.

"There are more of them!" Cat screamed.

"Keep riding!" Elidor did not turn to look.

Another horseman—two, three—broke out of the woods behind them. Rina twisted in her saddle, bow gripped in her hand. Two quick arrows flew, sinking into the saddle strap of the first warrior. Damaged, the leather snapped and the saddle was flung backward off the creature's flanks, rider and all. The other two dodged, one leaping over the fallen soldier at full speed.

"Got any spells handy, sister?" Kelenthe said, her eyes sparkling with excitement.

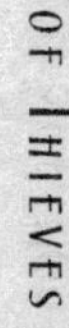

Kaja shook her head soberly. "None that I won't need once we reach the mine."

"Pity! Guess we'll have to do it the hard way."

Kelenthe pulled her horse's reins around, the quick-footed steed rearing and pirouetting mid-stride. She whispered in its ear, and the gray steed struck out with both front hooves. The impact collided with a warrior, bolting him from his creature's back and hurling him beneath the third steed's feet. The spectral steed screamed in panic, unable to stop in time to prevent colliding headlong into the armored solider. All three—steed, rider, and fallen solider—went down in a messy tumble of limbs. Kelenthe's horse spun again, gathering its rear legs beneath it, and sprinted. She caught up with Rohawn at the rear and winked.

The thick smell of ash hung in the air, and horns echoed over the sound of the scraping claws of the spectral steeds.

Gieden's men followed closely, and the thick, twisted forest kept Vael's horse from reaching a full gallop.

"They're gaining!" she cried to Rina. Vael pulled out her spear, holding it like a javelin in one hand as they rushed onward.

"Only a little more," Elidor called back. "I see the edge of the canyon ahead." The stone wall, covered in ivy and moss, rose from the forest floor.

"The mine is just a little farther." Squinting, Vael tried to gauge where the opening was. While trying to avoid the undead, they had veered west.

"That way!" Her finger stabbed toward a gap in the trees, but even as she pointed, four undead soldiers crashed through the brush, weapons lowered. Vael spun her steed, holding on tightly. Behind them, more of Gieden's soldiers crashed through the trees.

Vael plunged her spear into the shoulder of one of the undead as it reached for her. The clawed, bony hands sank into her thigh, tearing the hem of her tunic. Her gold-tipped spear shoved through the withered ligaments of the creature's arm, punching into armored plate and rotted flesh. The warrior chopped at her weakly, slicing strands of Vael's dyed hair. Her steed reared and carried her away with great leaping strides.

She pounded her feet into the horse's flanks. With a shrill whinny, it jolted backward to where the others were packed against the canyon wall.

"How far is the mine?" Cat swung back and forth in her saddle, trying to control her panicky horse.

Vael tried to keep steady. "Perhaps twenty yards. That way."

"We can make it at a run. Get off the horses!" Elidor threw one leg over his saddle, leaping to the ground. The horse reared and raced back into the woods. "They're panicking. It's too dangerous. We need to be able to fight."

Gratefully, Vael fell from her horse onto unsteady feet. Her horse almost kicked Rina. Rina ducked beneath it, smacking her own steed in the rear and watching them both charge forward into the brush.

The others quickly joined them, standing with weapons drawn in a loose semicircle, their backs to the canyon wall. Tree limbs hung over them, dark and sinister in the night.

"What do we do now, Corrigan?" Rohawn whispered, as the undead soldiers surrounded them.

"You die."

A dark hooded figure stepped out from behind the trees, two of the fire-breathing hounds shadowing his footsteps. Gieden's smile held victory in its subtle curve. He raised one hand, and a greenish orb flickered between his fingers like a supercharged firefly.

CHAPTER

17 Drowned in Shadow

Gieden stepped delicately between his men. In the eerie green light, the bones of his undead minions glowed.

"It's over, Elidor. There's nowhere else to run." The wizard tossed his long braid back with a flounce. He stared at each of them, obviously relishing the anger and fear on their faces.

"Get on with it, Gieden," Elidor growled, readying a dagger in each hand.

The dark wizard laughed. "Oh, I will. You're so impatient!" He turned and stared at Rina, obviously recognizing her as Elidor's sister. "I think I'll start with her."

Two of the undead warriors took a step forward.

Rohawn charged. "You won't touch Rina!" he roared as his greatsword struck the first of the undead. The gold coating on his blade sparkled in the dim light. He dragged the sword through armor and bone, down past the soldier's sword. The undead fell, cleaved in two.

The second undead cracked Rohawn's jaw with a swift punch. His head snapped backward. The greatsword fell out of Rohawn's hand, stuck deep in the forest floor, and the squire fell to his knees.

"Well, well! A volunteer!" Gieden chuckled. "I didn't expect that."

He gestured, and three other warriors surrounded Rohawn, their swords out and ready. The sharp tips of the blades were only inches from the boy's skin. "What do you say, Elidor? Give me the crown, and you won't have to watch him—or any of them—die."

"You'll kill them anyway," Elidor growled, crouching.

"I know. But this way you don't have to watch. Isn't that merciful of me?" Gieden turned away, looking down at Rohawn with sick glee.

In the shadow of one of the larger trees, Vael glimpsed a second hooded figure. From beneath its black hood shone an eerie reddish-green.

"Elidor, no!" Vael grasped his arm just before he sprang on Gieden. Elidor jerked back, rage in his eyes. She glanced over at the figure by the tree. Elidor followed her stare, and then rocked back on his heels, one hand rising instinctively to touch the crown. Pain brushed across his face and he leaned suddenly against her.

"Elidor?" she whispered, frightened.

He squinted, trying to stand solidly. His pulse raced against Vael's hand. Vael helped him as quietly as possible, hoping that Gieden would not notice Elidor's agony.

"You will not touch the boy."

Gieden's head snapped up. "I know that voice." He frowned, scanning the faces of Elidor's companions until he found . . .

"Sir Corrigan Stormwatch of Lees." Gieden laughed. "Well, well. Tell me, is this big ox your new squire? I'm surprised they let you have another one after what happened to your son."

Corrigan drew his thin sword, standing before the others with a murderous look on his thin-featured face. "You want a volunteer, Gieden? You have one. I challenge you to a duel—for your life."

"A duel?" Gieden raised one hand to his cheek. "Oh, Corrigan! How funny! What do you plan to do, use your magic on me? Set me on fire? Oh, no. That's right. All you have is a sword." Gieden's face twisted into a savage smile, and the green flickering light around his fingers exploded into a ball of flame. It rippled over Gieden's hand, igniting his fingers with evil light. "You want a duel, Corrigan? All you're going to achieve is your own death—*just like your son.*"

Without saying anything else, the slender knight raised his sword and charged. Gieden extended his hand, and a shield of green flame appeared between them, circling from the wizard's fingers into a half orb that reached above his head and down to his knees.

"I will enjoy this, knight." Gieden signaled to the warriors. "Throw the pup back in the bin. I'll have his master first."

The undead, forced to obey, removed their swords from Rohawn's throat and backed away. Rina pushed past Cat and Elidor, grabbing Rohawn's hand and tugging the boy backward to the relative safety of the canyon wall.

"Don't let them fight," Rohawn pleaded, staring up at Elidor. "Gieden will kill him. Don't you understand? *He killed Corrigan's son.*"

The green flame spread to encompass both Gieden and Corrigan, sealing them in a bubble of fire. Through the flames, Vael could see the slender knight charge again, sword held in both hands as he struck toward the wizard's chest. Gieden laughed, spreading his arms as the steel ricocheted away from his body as though his skin were made of stone.

"Take your time, knight. We have hours to go before the sun rises. And your squire will be next, I assure you, just as the other one was." Gieden continued to taunt Corrigan even as the knight twisted his sword and stabbed again.

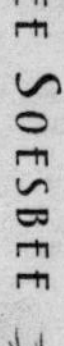

The wizard lowered his hand, wrapping Corrigan's blade in a whip of fire that sprang from his fingers, nearly jerking it from the knight's hand before Corrigan could pull the steel away. "Your son was protecting innocents too, you know. I needed the blood of a certain young girl for a spell—I can't remember which spell now, it's really not important. But while you were away receiving accolades from the Knights for your tactics in some battle or another, I killed him."

"Shut up!" Rohawn screamed.

"He has a right to know, don't you think?" Gieden laughed. "How his son begged for the girl's life, how he tried to fight me in the end, and how I broke him like a twig in the wake of my power."

The wizard's fire roared from Gieden's fingers again, burning the spot where Corrigan had just been standing.

Vael gripped Elidor's elbow. It was clear that the knight, so clever and intelligent, was not nearly the fighter that Catriona or Elidor was. Didn't anyone else see what he was doing? Corrigan dodged another of Gieden's flaming bolts, letting it ricochet past, just inches from his face.

"By Shinare, stop this," Kaja called out, holding her symbol close and readying a prayer.

"Wait!" Vael pushed Kaja backward, drawing her attention. "Do you have any spells that can shield us all? Last until the sun rises?" Kaja shook her head, and Vael hurried on. "Then think! Corrigan's giving us the one thing we need most—*time*."

"The only sunlight spell I can cast right now is a wall, not a globe. It won't be enough to protect us out here in the open." Kaja's knuckles were white around the holy symbol.

Vael couldn't keep her eyes from returning to the fight. Already, Corrigan's strikes seemed to be slowing, the taunts making his arm fly wild with anger. He was a strategist, not a soldier. Corrigan's

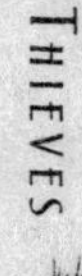

life—and their own—could now be measured in seconds and sword blows. "Think . . . *think* . . . " Vael gripped her spear in one hand, fingernails sinking into the wooden staff.

"What's . . . wrong . . . Gieden?" Corrigan wove back and forth through the flames, refusing to cease his attacks even as his skin turned red from the heat of the fire. "Can't you even kill an old man?"

"Are you weary of living, Corrigan? Very well, then. I shall accommodate you, as you have been such good sport." Gieden leveled his hands toward the knight, chanting in the tongue of magic.

As he did, Corrigan suddenly straightened. Vael gasped.

With speed and strength she hadn't known Corrigan to possess, the weasely knight ripped around in a full circle and hurled himself toward the wizard. Vael realized that Corrigan had been faking his weariness, overcompensating in order to make Gieden underestimate him. He was not the fighter that his squire Rohawn was, but the knight had managed to get a tactical advantage over his opponent.

Gieden's spell exploded on the ground where Corrigan had been standing, burning the forest floor black with its heat. At the same time, Corrigan darted close to Gieden, stepping behind the shield of flame. He sliced at Gieden's throat, but the wizard's magic prevented most of the damage, leaving only a thin trail of blood to mark where the sword cut his skin.

"Your protection is fading, wizard." Corrigan kept one arm around Gieden's neck, forcefully pulling the wizard back and forth so that Gieden could not prepare another spell. "Soon my sword will find your heart."

Gieden shrieked in fury. The bubble of flame around them both expanded and then began to contract as the wizard lost his concentration. Above them, the first rays of Solinari's light broke through the covering trees, touching the ground with a latticework of silver. The undead that surrounded them flinched, instinctively drawing back from the light. Shrieking, they covered their bony faces from the touch of the moon. Vael saw Elidor and Corrigan exchange a glance. And then, she knew.

"Get ready to run," Vael told the others, reaching down to drag Rohawn to his feet.

"Run?" Rohawn cried. "We can't leave Sir Corrigan!"

Nodding to Vael as though understanding her plan, Elidor reached for the squire's other arm. "I don't think we're going to have a choice." Before Elidor could complete his sentence, Corrigan's sword arced forward once more, plunging deep into Gieden's back. The tip thrust through the front of the black wizard's robes, red blood trickling down the pale steel. Gieden screamed in agony. "Kill me now, Gieden," Corrigan yelled. "I dare you."

Gieden choked, blood tinging his lips. "Soldiers!" he commanded, sliding to his knees. "Destroy . . . Corrigan!" His hand clenched as he sank, falling into the dirt. "Avenge me . . . "

Obeying their master's last command, the warriors turned from their prey. They stepped away from the canyon wall, pointing their weapons toward Corrigan as they closed in. Suddenly, Vael and the others were unguarded, the way along the canyon wall toward the mine clear of enemies.

"Run!" Elidor shoved Rohawn forward toward the northern edge of the wall. "Make for the mine!" Cat and Sindri were already on the move, the kender's booted feet bounding over stone and tree limb.

Rina paused at the edge of the clearing, staring back. "Rohawn?"

Forcefully, Elidor shoved the boy again. "Get out of here! Rina needs you! If we don't leave now while the undead are confused, she'll never make it."

Rohawn took three steps forward, freezing by a tree just at the edge of the bubble of flame. "Corrigan?" he shouted, uncertain.

The knight answered without haste or fear. "Go, son. Find your dream. Be a knight. You'll make a fine one." Corrigan half smiled as the bubble of fire from Gieden's spell faded and died. Gieden fell forward onto the earth.

The warriors gathered in a tight circle, armor clanking softly beneath the silvery moon. Between their ash-laced helms, Vael could see Corrigan readying himself, drawing his sword from Gieden's body and sinking back into a battle stance.

She caught his eye as the others ran. Although Vael had expected to see fear or desperation, instead the knight's face looked peaceful. He raised his bloody sword in a salute and winked one last time. In an instant, the undead swarmed him and Vael could see him no more.

CHAPTER

18 The Dark of the Grave

One by one, they darted into the mine, their feet echoing on cold stone. Inside it smelled of dust and animals. Elidor stared back into the darkness, listening to the sounds of the forest. Somewhere out there, regrouping, were the undead warriors. What would they do without Gieden? Return to Tarrent? Follow Elidor and seek vengeance?

"Safe at last!" A faint glow danced to life, lighting his face as Sindri blew on the tinder. The spark became a soft flicker of flame, casting long shadows against the cave wall.

Inside the abandoned mine, broken mine carts covered in moss and mold lay on their sides. The wood was rotted away, leaving only caskets of iron that once held weighty burdens rolled from deep beneath the earth. The walls of the cave glittered intensely, wide golden veins standing out sharply against the dark earth and stone.

Small chunks of gold ore, dug up from the earth long ago, lay abandoned on the ground inside. Once, men dug these caves and tore the yellow material from the walls. Now there were only cobwebs, unused and rusted mining equipment, and old smithy tools. Nothing else remained, no other trace of the men who had once given their lives to mine the sorceress Asvoria's gold. Elidor picked up a piece of gold, marveling at the yellow color of the metal ore as if in a daze.

"Aren't you happy, Elidor? Gieden's dead! It's over!" The kender raised his torch and hopped in a circle. "We won!"

Vael snatched the torch out of the kender's hand. He fell silent, staring up at her, and Elidor was struck by the sight. Vael's face was quiet, her hair falling loose from the Silvanesti braids and drifting around her shoulders. In one hand she held up Sindri's torch; in the other hand was her spear, the tip shining faintly with gold. "It's not over."

Elidor nodded, aware that his heart was pounding in his chest. He turned away from Vael, unable to look at her.

"What do you mean?" Sindri asked.

Elidor glanced away from Vael, aware that his heart was pounding in his chest.

"Gieden's lieutenant—the one in the robe." Vael handed the torch to Catriona. "When Gieden was fighting Corrigan, he was watching Elidor as if he'd like to have attacked Elidor himself. You should have seen his eyes."

Vael stepped closer to Elidor. "If he has any power left after Gieden's death, he'll be here. He'll come for you."

Kaja knelt at the mouth of the cave, readying herself to cast a spell. "I can block the mine shaft, but the spell will last only as long as I pray, and no more than an hour."

"Kelenthe," Vael began. "Were there any references in the scrolls that might help us know about Gieden's assistant? Any powerful captains among the Taeloc guard, or any . . . " Her voice suddenly fell. "Kelenthe?"

Kelenthe's face was white as she slowly sat down on a rock. "E'li. I don't know why I didn't think of it before."

"What?" Elidor and Catriona asked together.

Kelenthe scrabbled in her backpack, tearing out one of the scrolls she carried there. "He can't touch you—not directly. That's the key."

"What key?" Vael knelt beside Kelenthe as the bard dumped her backpack on the floor of the mine.

"Don't you see?" Kelenthe turned the scroll toward them, pointing at the picture of the gold and ivory gate. Within it was a figure that Elidor had not noticed before. It stood in the distant background, an abstract against the city wall. Draped and hooded, it raised its hands to the gate as though to place the final stone. The robes were rich and sumptuous, drawn with careful consideration to what must have been delicate threading. The eyes of the figure beneath the hood were drawn with bright tongues of flame.

Elidor's dream flashed into his memory. Bloodstained floors and roadways lined with the dead. Once more he saw the figure that had haunted him that first night in camp. Black robes drawn in close against a gaunt frame, the hood pulled low to hide shadowed, angular features and the burning eyes of flame.

Not noticing Elidor's hesitation, the kender jumped forward. "That's Gieden's assistant!" Sindri cried.

"Is he an architect? Someone who built the city?" Vael asked hopefully.

Kelenthe lowered the scroll. "You could say that. He built it—and he tore it down."

Catriona stared out into the darkness, shielding her eyes as Kaja's spell filled the entrance of the cave with golden light. "The Defiler. But you said he couldn't touch the crown."

"That's why he was using Gieden. The crown has to be given to him in order to retain its power. He has no ability to simply take it. Gieden knew that, and he was playing a delicate game. Gieden wanted Elidor to give the crown to him—to Gieden—and then he'd make a deal with the Defiler, probably for power." Kelenthe

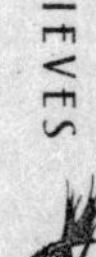

sighed, tapping her chin with the rolled-up paper. "Gieden was just a pawn too."

"Yeah, that sounds like Gieden," said Rohawn, his voice hoarse. He did not look up from the ground. He was slumped against the mine's wall with Rina kneeling over him. "Corrigan always said he'd do anything for power, including making deals with demons. Corrigan . . . " The boy's voice broke, and he put his head down on his arms.

"The Defiler's not a demon. He used to be an elf, but now . . . well, I don't know what he is." Kelenthe stared out past the protective spell. "But it's got to be him. If Gieden alone were controlling those warriors, they'd have fallen to ash when he died, but they didn't. That means they're drawing on someone else's power. I don't know what deal Gieden had with the Defiler, but now that he's dead the Defiler has full control over the legion."

"She tried to tell me," Elidor said as his fingers ran over the smooth silver coronet. "She told me . . . " He struggled to remember. "She said, 'You aren't here, and neither is he.' But I don't know what it means." Elidor paced at the front of the cave, trying to rearrange his scattered thoughts. "I've been seeing Taeloc in visions, overlapping the world around me."

"How long has this been happening?" Catriona asked.

"Ever since you found me in the Jade Tower. The visions have been getting stronger and stronger with every day. I think it's the ghost. She's been trying to show me something that I've been too stubborn to see."

"Then you should try listening." Vael put her spear back in the sling that held it. She walked to his side, taking Elidor's hand in her own for a moment. "The rest of us will gather whatever gold we can find in the mine. We need weapons."

"I can't leave the opening of the mine." Rohawn stood up suddenly, stubbornly planting his feet. "What if Corrigan comes and he can't find us? I can't leave him alone in the woods. He's my . . . he's . . . my knight . . . " The boy's voice quavered and he wiped tears from his eyes with the back of one grimy hand.

"Rohawn." For a moment, Elidor thought that Catriona would chide the boy about his misplaced honor, but the warrior's voice was surprisingly quiet. "Corrigan would be proud of you." Cat placed one arm on Rohawn's shoulder, squeezing the boy's arm. "But now, we need you. The gold's going to be very heavy, if we can even find any. You and I are the only ones strong enough to move it—and we're going to need a lot of it. Corrigan . . . he's not coming back."

"He has to come back." Rohawn gulped. "He's teaching me to be a knight. There's no better teacher than Corrigan. He's . . . " The squire looked up at Cat. "I made him a promise. What am I going to do without him?"

She took a long breath as if readying herself for battle. "I'll teach you, Rohawn."

Rohawn was not the only one who gaped at Catriona's words. "What?"

"I know how to fight. I know the code of the knights, and I know that Corrigan would have wanted you to continue your training, to be the best knight that you can be. Until we can find someone to squire you, I'll teach you what I remember from my time in Solamnia. I was training to be a knight too, you know." Cat tried to steel her face to hide her emotions, but Elidor could see tears brightening her eyes. "I'm not a knight. Maybe I'm not worthy of being a knight. But I know what you need to know, and I can help you until . . . until you find another way."

"You will?" he whispered.

"Of course I will," Catriona said seriously. "For you, and for Corrigan."

"Come on, Rohawn." Rina reached forward and shyly took the youth's hand. "I saw a mine cart down the tunnel a little way,

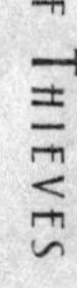

before Sindri lit that torch. I bet we can use it to transport any gold we find up to the front of the mine."

The boy nodded, looking at Catriona one more time. She gestured for him to go on, and he followed Rina into the mine.

"Cat, are you sure?" Elidor pulled her aside. "That's a big responsibility."

"I owe him that much. Corrigan, I mean, but Rohawn too. When it came down to it, Corrigan gave his life for us. Most Knights of Solamnia only talk about honor—they don't live it. Corrigan did." She sighed. "Corrigan proved to me that it was possible to live the dream that the Knights preach. If there's any chance Rohawn could be as great a knight as Corrigan, well, then maybe that will prove that I was wrong about them."

"But a squire, Cat? Can you really do that?"

"Oh, it wouldn't be recognized by the Knights, but until he finds someone else, I know what to do. I was a squire myself, you know. I remember the lessons they teach." She tried a grin, but the sadness showed through. "I gave Corrigan a tough time, but he always treated me kindly, no matter how horrible I was to him. I guess I owe it to him to take care of Rohawn."

Cat and Vael followed Rina and Rohawn down into the mine, leaving Sindri and Kelenthe with Elidor in the light of Kaja's wall of sunlight. "Elidor?" Sindri said hesitantly. "What are we going to do with the gold they find?"

"I don't know yet, Sindri." Elidor closed his eyes. "Getting it back to Tarrent isn't going to happen, not if we only have an hour of safety and no horses to load the gold on. But at least the village is safe."

"That's great for them," Kelenthe said wryly. "But bad for us."

"Corrigan had a plan. I wish he'd told me what it was." Elidor paused to think, staring at the wide yellow veins that striped the mine wall. "Maybe we can find a way out the back of the mine, down into Navarre. We could lead the Defiler there, and lose him . . . or something. We've been down there before—it's a dangerous place. The legion might run into some of the traps there."

"No," Sindri said.

"No?" Elidor cranked his head around in surprise, staring at the kender. "What does that mean?"

"It means we can't run anymore," Sindri said with unusual seriousness. "That's what we've been doing, right? Running from Gieden, from Aerendor, from Tarrent. Even now, you're running from Vael. I saw how she looked at you, but you wouldn't look at her."

"Sindri, cut it out," Kelenthe began. "Now's not the time—"

"Now's the *only* time. When else?" Sindri pushed himself onto one of the broken iron carts. "Think the Defiler'd be willing to come in for tea and chat when he gets here? I mean, I'd invite him, of course, but I don't think he'd want to. I'd love to hear what Taeloc was really like. And what has he been doing since it fell? Being an undead guy must be really boring after a while, unless you do something interesting like adventuring. I'd go adventuring if I were undead. It'd be kind of anticlimactic and all, but think of the great places I could go!"

Elidor held his head in his hands. "Sindri, you're not helping."

"Yes, I am."

"How?"

"You're the leader, Elidor. So start leading and stop running away."

Shocked, Elidor and Kelenthe stared at the little kender. "You sound like Cat."

"Cat knows what she's talking about. You're a thief, Elidor. Thieves take things and they run, just like you've been running since the day you left Aerendor in the first place. Now you've got everything you love at stake—including your own life—and still you keep running. If you spent half the time thinking about ways to defeat the legion as you do thinking about ways to run from them, we'd be safe by now!"

Exasperated, Sindri kicked his feet against the iron cart. The thum-thum echoed lightly in the mine corridor like little thunderclaps. In the silence that followed, Sindri dropped down from the cart and grabbed Kelenthe's hand. "Maybe you're not a leader, Elidor. But right now, you *have* to be one. You don't have any choice. We need you."

A pause, and then Sindri's bright smile returned as if nothing was wrong. "Come on, Kelenthe. Cat's going to need us to carry up gold."

Reluctantly, Kelenthe followed the kender down into the mine, looking over her shoulder at Elidor. "Think about it, Elidor," Sindri called back as they turned a corner and went deeper into the earth. "Just think about it."

"Think about it," Elidor sighed. "As if it hasn't been haunting me all my life."

The cave felt strangely empty, lit only by the faint amber light of Kaja's sunlight spell. Outside in the darkness, the Defiler's spectral troops were gathering, but there was nothing they could do except wait.

Elidor closed his eyes and focused on the dream that hovered just at the edge of his memory. White streets, wide and lined with graceful trees, circled through a city as beautiful as it was ornate. Elegant archways of ivory and silver rose in slender spires over the road. Elidor rested against the arch, feeling the smooth white marble against his back. He knew it, this city. Taeloc.

"I know what you've been waiting for me to ask," Elidor whispered. "I understand now."

The girl stood in the roadway, her arms crossed defensively. Through narrowed eyes, he watched her. Brown hair, still a tangled mass, caught a ray of long-ago sunlight. The streets were empty, not even echoes of city bustle disturbing the silence. He could hear her breathing, see the slight shift in her tattered robes as a breeze passed them by. It was as though the mine did not exist at all, and yet somewhere, it did.

"We're really here." He looked up into a startlingly blue sky. "Taeloc. Your city."

"His city," she whispered, still afraid.

"His city," Elidor agreed. "But you lived here too. And that's why you keep telling me to run, isn't it? Why you keep warning me about him. You know him."

The girl looked down. "Yes."

"Why couldn't you tell me?"

"He can't touch the crown, Elidor."

Understanding at last, Elidor sat back against the marble arch. "And you can't touch him, is that right? It's a two-way street because you *are* the crown."

"It was once a beautiful city." Her voice was soft. "But now it is as dead as stone. You bear the mark of its king, the Crown of Thieves. Let me show you." She lifted one arm, her smooth, white flesh shining in the sunlight. Time around them sped forward, and the city bloomed. Elidor saw again the night that haunted him in Aerendor, soldiers in white marching through the streets. But this time, above them, he saw a pulsing green light growing in the night sky. With each innocent death, the light increased. Elidor saw soldiers in white leather armor, fighting with daggers so swiftly that his eyes could barely follow the movements. Thieves, skilled beyond anything Elidor had ever seen. The city of Taeloc—it was a city of thieves, and the soldiers were destroying the populace around them without any sign of regret or mercy.

The crown on his forehead grew warm, as though feeding on the strange illusion of Taeloc. The girl continued, "He destroyed Taeloc to gain more power for himself. 'To become a god,' he said.

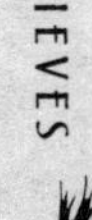

And he believed the crown would make him so."

One by one, the ghosts of Taeloc faded, leaving behind nothing but the marks of scarlet blood on the pale city streets.

"And you were the last sacrifice," Elidor continued. "His most 'precious gem' as the scroll said. But it wasn't a gem at all. It was a soul—your soul." Elidor shook his head. "Is that why you're still here and the others are gone?"

She didn't answer. "The crown is part of Taeloc. And now, you are part of the crown. You are here. And he is here."

"That's why you kept telling me to go 'there.' But you meant Taeloc, didn't you? You wanted me to see *this* world and to be part of it somehow. I don't understand what's going on. How can I be both here and in the real world?" Elidor struggled to make sense of her words. "Is that why you say I can't beat him?"

"It's why they" —she gestured at Elidor, Catriona, Rohawn, and Rina, and suddenly he could hear the echo of voices in the mine— "cannot beat him. They can only attack the part of him that is there. Not here."

"But I can."

"Only if you are there and here too."

Elidor shook his head in confusion. "I don't know how to be in two places at once. I'm not a wizard."

She sighed. "You only have to be exactly what you are. But you have to be you in two places."

"Argh." Elidor thumped his head against his hand in frustration. "And that will destroy him?"

"No. But it will give you a chance."

"And that's more than we had before." Elidor sighed. "He was using Gieden, wasn't he?"

She nodded. "The king—the Defiler—told that one that he was looking for an heir, a prince who could prove his power by seizing the crown and returning it to him."

"How do you know this?"

"Sometimes," she whispered, staring at the bloodstained marble of the ancient streets. "I can hear him."

"But you can't fight him. " Elidor suddenly shook his head. "No, that's not entirely right. Like the way he used Gieden to fight me. You can't fight him, but you can help me—to a point." Elidor began to smile slightly, the truth dawning on him at last. "And that's why all the puzzles and riddles. Because if you can hear him sometimes, then that means that he can also hear you."

For the first time since he'd seen her, the girl smiled. It slipped across her face lightly, curving her lips, and in its wake, something changed. Her robes shifted, the mud stains lightening to faint touches of gray against the white. The tears in the cloth healed themselves, and her brown hair moved in the wind. She nodded, and said nothing.

"I think I know what to do now." Elidor pushed up, standing in the roadway. "Thank you."

"Good luck, Elidor." She lifted a hand to salute him.

He turned away from her and the streets faded. White marble became dark stone, silver tracings turned to rivers of gold trapped within cold rock. Kaja still knelt by the opening, her body encased in a golden light that kept the darkness at bay. Elidor breathed in a long, shuddering breath of cold night air, and then yelled.

"Sindri! Cat! Rohawn! Everyone!" He yelled into the mine. They came swiftly, perhaps hearing something unusual in Elidor's voice.

Sindri was the first to arrive from the depths of the mine, his hair covered in dust. "What's wrong?"

"Nothing." Elidor ruffled his ash blond hair with both hands, assessing the time they had before Kaja's spell failed. "I have an idea. I think I know how to defeat the undead legion, and the Defiler too."

"That's great!" Sindri danced lightly on the stone floor of the mine. "What can we do?"

"We've found some gold, but it's not much—not to fight a whole legion." Rohawn dropped two big sacks with a shrug on the cavern floor.

"That's just it. I want you to stop trying to find ore. It's not gold that we need." Elidor grinned. "We need clay."

CHAPTER

19 The Path Between Two Worlds

A light glowed steadily in the forest, shedding amber across moonlit leaves. On a wall against the side of the canyon, the golden light merged with the stone as one. Nothing could be seen beyond it; no sound came from the cave that lay on the other side.

The light flickered once.

The shadows seemed to creep forward, hesitant in the glow. There was movement in the tree limbs, making the leaves shudder.

The golden light flickered again and dimmed.

Then, with a wink, it died completely.

One by one, the undead approached. They waited in the clearing just outside the cave, cutting off any point of exit, and turned their heads to await his command.

Through the press of soldiers, a man in a hooded robe swept forward. Terrible, clawed hands coiled beneath black leather. Under the cowl, his eyes emanated hatred for all living things, but especially for those who hid within the cave before him.

Gieden was dead. There would be no more games.

"Destroy them." His voice was a rasp of air forced from long-dead lungs. "Bring me the crown."

The undead marched forward from the woods, their boots treading over leaf and twig, crushing the life from the forest floor. They amassed at the front of the cave, gathering in loose ranks. The first boot fell on the stone floor with a decided click.

"You're a bit late." Elidor's voice came from the darkness. "We were getting tired of waiting."

A torch burst into life, illuminating Elidor, Vael, and Rohawn standing with their blades bared and ready. Behind them, Rina and Kelenthe leveled their bows beside Catriona. Kaja stood at the far rear of the group, her hands clasped around the symbol of her god.

Sindri grinned, holding aloft a spear just behind the rest of the group. He winked at the Defiler as if he knew a secret.

The Defiler raised his hands. Ash swept from every soldier's bones. It gathered together like a black swarm and swirled through the Defiler's claws.

"Kill them all."

The soldiers obeyed instantly, charging into the mine. Swords flashed and a war horn sounded just outside the cave. The hounds bayed, flames flickering at the corners of their mouths.

Elidor struck first, the gold edge of his dagger sinking into a swordsman's arm. Only he, Vael, and Rohawn had weapons edged with the metal. Sindri and Catriona held hastily made clubs topped with stones of ore, and Kelenthe and Rina readied a few precious arrows whose dulled heads were formed of rock-beaten chips of ore.

The soldier screamed as Elidor's dagger bit deeply into bone and ash. The undead's sword trembled as it swung toward Elidor, allowing him to duck beneath the blow.

Vael cried out in anger, her spear plunging through a soldier's breastplate and shoving the undead backward. She stepped forward and pitched the soldier from her spear much as a farmer would use a pitchfork to shovel hay.

He fell against his companions, knocking them backward. As he tumbled, his bones shriveled to ash and his armor crumbled. The others simply marched over their fallen companion, no sign of fear or doubt showing in the bone sockets of their eyes.

Beside her, Rohawn fought like a tiger, his greatsword narrowly missing the cave ceiling with each tremendous swing. Elidor darted in and out around the field of steel created by Rohawn's weapon, his dagger seeking armor joints. Where his dagger bit into the undead, they faltered, easy prey for Vael's terrible spear thrusts.

Behind them, Rina and Kelenthe chose their targets cautiously, using metal arrows on the hounds and saving the gold-tipped ones for undead that came too close for Rohawn's sword to drive away.

Kelenthe grinned as she shot her short bow into the throng, laughing lightly despite the danger all around them. Rina, on the other hand, was grim-lipped, her face gray and angry. She whispered to each arrow she shot, as though praying with every one.

Sindri, however, did nothing. He stood on a rock near the rear of the mine shaft, just where the shaft turned to the left and struck deep into the earth. He held the torch high, its light dull against the empty clay walls of the cave. No light refracted back save the twinkle of steel weapons and the dull gleam of armor. He grinned, watching the desperate battle slowly fall back into the cave.

The Defiler slammed his hands together with a resounding clap. The ash that swirled around him crashed like ocean waves between his hands. It exploded forward and slammed into Elidor and the others. They were all hurled back to the rear of the cave, bodies cracking against the unmarked clay wall of the cave.

Kelenthe and Elidor struggled to their feet first, helping the others stand as the soldiers rushed forward. Hot ash hissed past

Elidor's face, singeing his skin and setting the ends of his hair on fire. He jerked Catriona to her feet.

"Get out of here," he told her, shaking Catriona out of her momentary stupor. "It's time."

Catriona nodded. She gripped Rohawn's wrist and pulled the burly youth to his feet. They raced toward one of the mine shafts. From a distance, the corridor appeared to turn sharply, leading deeper into the mountain.

"Sindri?" Elidor grinned down at the kender.

"Ready for the first part, Elidor!" The little wizard spun toward their enemy, facing the opening of the cave and the legion of soldiers with a brave smile.

"Hey, Defiler! I heard you liked playing with fire." Sindri fluttered his hand over the torch he was carrying, letting his fingers dip lightly down into the flame. Behind him, the rest of the group charged down the mine toward the steep turn that lay ahead.

Sindri chanted, staring into the flame. The fire flickered, leaped upward, and then began to chase Sindri's hand as he passed it in circles around the torch. "Try this on for size!"

He flicked his hand toward the front line of warriors, and the flame detonated forward. As though a spigot had been opened, a short cone of flame sprouted out of the torch, temporarily blocking the soldiers from sight.

More importantly, it prevented the undead from watching *them.*

"You really are a wizard, Sindri," Elidor whispered gratefully. The kender grinned, obviously enjoying hosing the enemy down with brilliant fire.

Elidor was rewarded with a wink and a wide grin. "I told you so."

Cat and Rohawn paused where the mine shaft took a sharp

turn, pushing themselves against the wall of the cavern. Although it wasn't apparent from a distance, the wall actually folded in, revealing a passageway behind.

"Get in, squire," Cat shoved him, helping Rina enter the hidden corridor immediately after the youth. One by one, as swiftly as they could, the entire group ducked behind the clay covering over the alcove, hiding behind it while the undead were blinded by Sindri's light.

In only a few seconds, Elidor was alone in the passage save for Sindri, who stood ready at Elidor's side. "Are you sure you're up for this, Sindri?"

"Absolutely." The kender puffed his chest out with pride.

"All right," Elidor grinned. "Let's go."

Sindri closed his fist and the brilliant light of his fire was cut short in an instant. The torch glowed only faintly.

The undead at the edge of the flames surged forward. As Elidor's eyes adjusted to the dim light, he was grateful for his elven heritage—and their exceptional gift of sight. Movement caught his attention, the faint light from the opening of the cave reflecting from steel swords and armor. Elidor yelled loudly, making a rude gesture toward the troops at the mouth of the cave.

"What's wrong, Defiler? Your men afraid of the grave?" He laughed, then turned and raced down into the mine shaft. Sindri followed close behind him, his feet pitter-pattering over the stone.

Behind them, a war horn sounded and the undead flooded down into the earth with weapons bared. Elidor could hear the booted tromp of their feet, the clay ceiling of the mine reflecting nothing of the bare and glittering green light of their eyes. Even the hounds' baying seemed muted, echoing only faintly against the dark and muddy walls.

Sindri started murmuring again, pointing forward. A host of

noises sounded out ahead of them: footfalls, steel ringing against stone, faint shouts and muffled yelling.

Elidor and Sindri raced through the darkness, trusting in the path they'd traced before Kaja's wall fell. The undead behind them remained tight on their tail. Not one turned aside, and for that, Elidor was grateful. Sindri's spell kept an array of sound echoing ahead of them, sounding like everything from yells to the tromp of running feet.

"They're falling for it!" Sindri hissed between deep breaths. "They think the rest of our group is down here!"

"I know," Elidor gasped. "Keep running."

The undead hounds closed the distance rapidly. Elidor felt their hot breath on his heels, heard their clawed feet scrabbling against the floor of the mine. One of them leaped forward and slammed into Elidor's calf. Its teeth scraped against his flesh, tearing both skin and leather pants. Elidor screamed, struggling to keep his footing. It was impossible.

He fell and tumbled over both Sindri and the hound, the three of them in one large ball of kicking feet. Elidor felt a sharp crack, and white hot pain lanced through his skull. His vision blurred.

Sindri dodged to his feet, snatching Elidor's dagger. He plunged the blade between the hound's shoulders, forcing the creature to let go. The hound jerked back, screaming in agony. The animal roared and fire erupted out its mouth. The flames brushed the walls of the mine shaft, washing away mud and clay to reveal a thick swath of gold.

"We've got to keep running!" Elidor pushed himself despite the pain, gathering his injured leg beneath him and jerking the dagger out of the dying hound. With a kick and a curse, he spun the dog back toward its fellows. Two more leaped on them, forcing Elidor and Sindri to jump to the side.

"This way!" Sindri pointed down a branch in the mine shaft.

Elidor tried to peer down the corridor, his mind still stunned from the fall. Two shafts, one left and one right, wavered before his eyes. "Are you sure it's not the other one?"

Sindri looked back and forth, and Elidor heard the other hounds scrabbling to their feet. "I'd bet my magic on it!"

Sindri grabbed Elidor's hand and pulled him down the corridor. The hounds were only a jump behind them.

They gained a few steps on their enemies, racing down the passage at full tilt as though daring fate to block their flight. The soldiers, heavily armored, pounded behind them eagerly, realizing that their prey could not continue to run much longer.

"Only a little farther!" Elidor panted. "The other exit to the mine is just down this passage."

Elidor and Sindri rounded a corner and met with a wall of solid stone.

"Wrong corridor." Elidor stared at Sindri.

"No choice then," Sindri sighed.

They looked at each other in the fraction of a second before Sindri raised the silver, egg-shaped bomb that they had taken from Narath.

He held it aloft at eye level, staring down at it with a curious, expectant grin. On the walls around them, the clay coating was sliding off to reveal thick stripes of gold. Sindri's torch made the wide bands of gold dance, sparkling like liquid sunlight against the stone of the mine.

"We had a lot of fun, didn't we?" Sindri said with a smile.

Elidor replied wearily. "Yeah, we did, Sindri."

Sindri wrapped his hand around the egg. He whispered a word, and the small bomb began to glisten and glow in the kender's hand. The silver shimmered. Sparks flew. The little egg swelled and glowed with magic, turning a brilliant and luminescent blue.

The undead legions gathered, filling the corridor with the creak of armor and the stench of churning ash. They raised their weapons and advanced, relishing each step and readying killing blows.

"It looks just like a robin's egg," Sindri said, wide eyed.

And then the bomb exploded.

CHAPTER

20 A Journey Without End

Vael pushed herself up from the ground, brushing clay and moss out of her long hair. The shock of the explosion still rumbled through the mountain, making dust and dirt fall from the ceiling onto the group of friends. Beside Vael, Catriona straightened to her feet, reaching to push back the cloth that held up their false clay wall.

"They did it!" Rina gasped with relief. "Elidor and Sindri did it!"

"Praise Shinare," Kaja said. She looked weak and pale, her spirit drained from the long session of holding alight the wall at the mouth of the cave. She leaned heavily on her sister, stepping gingerly wherever Kelenthe led.

Vael stepped out into the corridor. A light behind them illuminated the mine shaft. Rohawn lifted the small torch gingerly, and Vael's eyes, a mark of the faint elven blood that ran in her veins, quickly adjusted to the view.

To the north toward the cave opening, the mine was dark, with only the faint outline of Solinari's light shining some distance away. The clay they had used to cover the wide gold veins in the walls was crumbling, knocked loose by the explosion. It didn't matter anymore, Vael thought to herself. The deception was enough to lure the Defiler's troops into the mine and give them no indication of the danger. Gold, to destroy them, just as Elidor said. She steeled herself and looked the other way.

To the south, there was only rubble. The mine shaft had collapsed. Everywhere Vael looked, she saw gold piled in the rubble, filling every crack in the newly fallen stone.

"Elidor was right." Catriona reached out and touched the stone blocks gingerly. "The undead are trapped under all this gold."

"They will never be able to make their way to the surface. The gold is too thick. Blessed Shinare grants her strength to our endeavor. It is an end at last to their evil." Kaja smiled.

"Do you think they'll make it out?" Rohawn kept one hand on the hilt of his greatsword, the weapon's blade still gleaming faintly with its overlay of poured gold. He stared at the rubble as if expecting a skeletal hand to push aside the stone and an undead soldier to climb toward them. Then again—Vael gulped—she half expected that herself.

Vael eyed the collapsed rubble thoughtfully. "The crevice we found in the mine, the one that led to the surface, was pretty deep. This rubble's far closer to us than I would have thought. The explosion must have been huge."

"But . . . they're all right?" Rina's eyes looked worried. "They made it out?"

Vael cleared her throat, trying to find the words.

Catriona quickly cut in. "The crack will provide them plenty of shelter. We'll see them outside, I'm sure." Cat roughed Rohawn's shoulder. "Now let's go and meet them."

After the close quarters of the cave, the faint hint of breeze that blew across the cave's mouth seemed like the touch of heaven. Vael's steps lightened as she walked into the clearing.

Then suddenly, something struck her from behind and she

tumbled to the ground. She heard Rohawn cry out. Vael kept her hand tight around her spear, rolling on the ground and lifting her weapon as she regained her footing.

A shadow moved in the darkness at the edge of the clearing. Vael caught a flash of fiery eyes, and then another slam knocked her to the ground. Ash swirled around her like a swarm. She coughed, choking. Rina tumbled beside her. The ash flew to the edge of the clearing, slowly swirling together to reveal a darkly hooded form.

Kelenthe gasped, holding her sister gently with one arm while reaching for a dagger at her waist. "It's him! The Defiler!"

Kelenthe stepped between Kaja and the hooded specter. Catriona and Rohawn stopped just behind her at the edge of the cave.

The specter raised his hands, black ash curling up from the ground and filling the bottom of its rotted leather robes.

"Did you think that you could escape me so easily?" The ash in the air whipped Vael's face and stung her eyes.

"Quick, back into the—" Vael's warning was cut short as ash choked her lungs. She heard Rina scream and saw the girl clutch her throat.

"Rina!" Rohawn raced toward the fallen elven girl, lifting her in one strong arm. Rina buried her head in his shoulder, using the cloth of his sleeve to shield her face from the cloud of ash.

Pushing Rina back toward the cave, Rohawn screamed a battle cry. He lunged forward with his gold-edged greatsword in two hands, tears streaking the clay and dirt on his face.

"For Corrigan!" he yelled.

Rohawn took three steps toward the cowled figure, sword arcing. The hooded man did nothing to prevent it; he did not raise an arm to shield himself nor step out of the way. The youth's sword plunged down with the fury of all of his anger and struck the figure broadside.

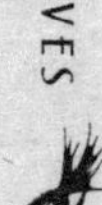

When the sword struck the figure's robes, there was a brief clap of thunder. Rohawn's greatsword snapped in half, the steel flying past its intended target.

Rohawn staggered, still holding the hilt and part of the blade. The rest of the sword fell to the earth, skidding uselessly past the Defiler and into the trees.

"It is not so simple to destroy me. You can tell that tale to those who have gone before you, once you meet them in death." Scorn dripped from every word.

The Defiler raised one hand lazily, a trail of dark ash swirling around it. Rohawn was lifted into the air by some invisible force, then hurled backward so hard against the stone that Vael believed she heard the very rock crack with the impact.

Kaja pushed away from her sister, sliding to her knees beside Rohawn's body. She pressed her fingers to his chest, feeling for a heartbeat. She slid her hands over the boy's torso and began to pray.

The hooded figure began to laugh. Vael felt her stomach turn over at the sound of it. Despite the pain, Vael tightened her grasp on her spear. She pulled herself to one knee, her spear shaking in her hand, and leveled the tip of the weapon at the Defiler.

"You too, little one?" the Defiler asked. "Very well, then. Fight all you want. I prefer the suffering."

Pain wracked Vael, her stomach suddenly contracting with dark and bitter bile. Magic poured through her system, turning her blood to acid, destroying her from the inside. She heard a scream—Rina—and saw the elven girl fall to the ground near the cave.

The battered Rohawn, still clutching the hilt of his broken sword, toppled over like a tree struck by lightning. The others cried out, caught up in the spell. One by one, their legs buckled and they fell to the ground.

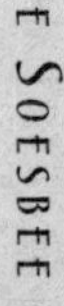

Vael struggled to keep herself upright, swaying back and forth on one knee. She pressed the butt of her spear to the ground, pushing up against it, and stared at the Defiler.

He clenched his outstretched fist, and the pain redoubled, tearing a sharp cry from Vael's throat.

"Show me where the thief is hiding. Give me the crown."

"You'll never find Elidor!" Vael spat. "He's going far away from here, beyond the mountains! Without your soldiers and your wizard pawns, you will never find him!"

The Defiler lifted his head, smelling the air like sniffing hound.

"Perhaps not," he growled. "But if you scream just a bit more, I sense that he will find me."

Deep beneath the mountain, a small bubble of air lay buried in the rock. It was small and circular, completely surrounded by wreckage and stone. The falling mountain covered the little open area, stone pressed tightly against the magical force that protected Elidor and Sindri. No light came from the walls of the bubble, only a very faint electrical static that Elidor could feel against his fingertips and his back when he leaned against it.

In the darkness, Elidor could hear Sindri's labored breathing hissing in and out of the kender's mouth.

"I didn't know a little spell could hold up so much weight," Elidor mused, not knowing what else to say.

"Small things . . . can do a lot more . . . than you think they can." Elidor could hear the smile in Sindri's voice.

Elidor twisted in the darkness, feeling the sharp poke of stone against his back. "Do you think we got them all?" He listened, but even with his keen elven hearing, he sensed nothing moving beneath the stone.

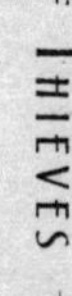

"It was a good plan," Sindri murmured. "A really good plan." He coughed, voice raspy from the dust. "You did a really good job, Elidor."

"A good job?" Elidor laughed bitterly. "I can't believe you can say that while we're trapped in a bubble of force under a collapsed mountain."

"We destroyed them," Sindri said, his irrepressible humor showing despite their dire situation. "All of them, I think. Whatever we didn't get, I'm sure Cat and the others will handle on the other side." The kender's voice fell, a touch of sleepiness creeping in. "I do wish I could see them again. Rohawn and I were . . . were going to . . . see Solamnia together . . . "

"Hey, don't fall asleep, Sindri. Sindri?" Elidor reached out to touch the kender's soft hair, and he felt the head tilt. Sindri seemed for a moment to nod off and lean back against the tingling wall of the spell.

"He can't help it. The air's getting thinner. Soon, there will be nothing for him to breathe."

Elidor jumped. The voice was familiar—female, soft and compassionate. In an instant, he knew who had spoken.

"Spirit or ghost," he whispered. "You have to help me. I can't let him die."

Thinking that Elidor was speaking to him, Sindri muttered softly, "I think I would have liked Solamnia. It's such . . . a big place, you know . . . " Then the head nodded backward again, and Elidor listened to Sindri's breathing grow even more shallow.

"Why is he suffocating, but I'm not?"

"Because you don't need air to sustain you. The Crown of Thieves keeps your life intact. Its power is all you need." Though he could not see her, Elidor remembered her face, heart-shaped and sweet. He wondered if her white dress was as tattered as he remembered, her chocolate-brown hair wild and tangled.

"So I'm to sit here while he dies?" Elidor felt hot tears stinging his eyes. "And what about me? How long will the crown keep me alive?"

Her answer was long in coming. "Forever, Elidor. Or until you remove it, or are killed in battle, or die in some other way. But you will never simply *die*."

"By E'li." He laid his head back on the jagged rock. Elidor felt the coldness of the stone, the dirt beneath his fingers. Sindri's labored, shallow breaths echoed from their small, cramped space. Between each one, Elidor felt his heart freeze, hoping that there would be another. "There must be a way out. You said the crown is powerful. Tell me how to use it."

Her hand touched his in the darkness, shivering, cold, and small. Fingers wrapped around his hand gently, twining with Elidor's own. "I can't tell you. You have to discover for yourself."

"But why?"

"Because I am constrained by the rules set upon me when the crown was made. I cannot disobey them. I cannot work against him. I can only try to help you in small ways and hope that you will understand."

"What can you tell me, then?"

"Only what you already know." The spirit's voice did not echo in the cave like Elidor's did. She was only in his mind, he reminded himself.

"You are not here, Elidor. You are there and here both." Her hand tightened around his. "Remember what I told you, Elidor. You just have to *be*. Not just here, but also there. In Taeloc."

"Not here, but there." He considered this. "You keep saying that. That's what you told me when the crown used its power to save my mother. You said I wasn't here. I was . . . there."

"Both."

"And that's how I can defeat the Defiler. Because . . . because

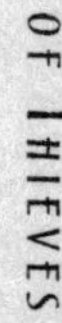

he lives both in the Taeloc of the past, and in the here and now."

Elidor's eyes searched the darkness, and for a moment he saw her face, pale and concerned, hovering next to him. He blinked and saw again the darkness of stone. "I saw Taeloc on the streets of Aerendor. I was there."

"Yes." Her voice lifted, filling with hope. "Yes!"

"Are you saying that I can go there? Into the past, somehow?" Elidor touched the coronet on his forehead.

"Yes and no. You can walk both worlds at once, as he does. And only there can you defeat him."

"I can go there? I . . . can I take Sindri?"

"If you want."

"I'm not going to leave him here." Elidor placed one arm around the limp body of his friend, drawing the kender close to him. "But how?" He struggled to understand.

"Say this word: *Untharis.*"

"*Untharis.*"

"Good." The spirit's voice was soft, gentle in the warm darkness. "Now, remember the city. Remember the sky and the light and all that goes with it. Think about Taeloc . . . and then . . . just . . . be."

Elidor thought back to those white streets, the high ivory arches that lined the twisting roadways of the unfamiliar city he had seen in the visions. He remembered the feeling of the golden sun on his face. Huge walls, white and clean, surrounded a city of curves and spires, wrapping about the buildings like a serpent through the desert. And the gate . . . the black gate with the symbol of a silver crescent beneath a black disk.

"Be," she said again, and this time, her voice did not seem as ghostly. Elidor opened his eyes and saw.

He lay on the white street, the earth beneath him warm from afternoon sunlight. Around him, villagers went their way, seemingly unable to perceive that he rested in the middle of the road. An ivory arch rose above him just as he had pictured it, the white standing out clearly against the dark sky.

Sindri rested on Elidor's lap, his chest rising and falling faintly.

"Why isn't he getting better?" Elidor demanded.

"He is still in the stone, still *there*. Just because you can bring him to this world doesn't mean that you can free him of the other."

The spirit's white robes were nearly whole, Elidor noticed, tattered only at the edges of the smooth white sleeves and the hem. He could see now that her clothes had once been very formal—a toga-like robe. Her hair, brown and long, now lay in light curls on her back, tangled only at the edges and where it hung against her cheeks.

Elidor stood, lifting Sindri in his arms. The kender was even lighter than usual. Elidor felt as though he was carrying only a figment of his own imagination. "I need to get him out of here. Out of the cave." For a moment, he felt the pressure of stone against his back once more, the close tightness of the small chamber created by Sindri's ring. He shuddered and tried to focus on the warmth of an ancient sun.

"Then follow me," whispered the spirit, "and I will lead you. Every step you take here, you move in the real world around you as well. When you have walked far enough, you will be outside the mountain. Do you understand?"

"I . . . I think so." Elidor walked down the road with her, wincing at the brilliance of daylight. After the darkness of the mine, it seemed almost unbearable. Something moved in his mind, and he could feel the solid stone around him, sense the pressure of thousands of pounds of rock even as a warm wind blew against his skin. Staring at the city street, Elidor could also see the faint outline of stone and earth surrounding him. "I'm still in the mountain?" he murmured.

"You are here," the ghost put both hands out, reaching to pull him along. "But you are also there, just as you are dead and alive. Taeloc exists within you, and you within it. The crown just lets you enter the shadow world, where Taeloc's spirit exists. This mountain isn't there, so it can't stop you. But it is there for him. He is able to move only because you carry him."

"This is strange magic, and I'm not a wizard." Elidor struggled to make sense of it. "The power of the crown lets me walk through shadows—the shadow . . . of Taeloc?"

If he failed now, lost concentration now, both he and Sindri would reappear within the depth of the mountain, their bodies crushed within the stone.

Elves walked past him on the road, carrying fruit and cloth. Their laughter echoed like a memory of his childhood, and he could smell fresh flowers on the breeze that touched his face. The world flickered and changed, then snapped back to this reality, his eyes locking on the willowy gaze of the spirit. He followed her through the street, toward a tree that hung low over a bubbling fountain where children played.

Elidor staggered. "I can't . . . " He fell to one knee, protecting Sindri with his body as a sudden pain pulsed through him. "What's happening?"

"*He's* close—outside the mountain." Her eyes were wide and frightened.

As Elidor watched, her robes grew suddenly more tattered, tearing away at the hem, their white folds turning gray and filthy once more. She fell to the ground.

Around him, the image of the city wavered. The purity of her robes diminished as the city's ivory walls darkened.

"Get out," she whispered urgently to Elidor. "Leave the city.

He's . . . he's here. He'll find us." Elidor felt another pressure, greater than the imagined weight of the stone and the mountain. It was as if a great wind blew against him, sweeping down with a bitter, oppressive cold.

The figures in the road shifted and vanished, their footprints left in the dust where they had been. Across the clearing, near the fountain, Elidor caught a glimpse of a man in thick leather robes.

Elidor closed his eyes, another sharp pain from the crown shooting white hot within his temples. When he opened his eyes again, he stood inside the mouth of the mine, Sindri limp in his grasp. The kender suddenly seemed heavier, his body sagging in Elidor's arms. With a groan, Elidor sank to one knee, placing Sindri on the stone.

When Sindri breathed a shuddering, deep breath of clean air, Elidor smiled.

Then, from outside the cave, he heard a scream. It cut through both his heart and his mind, a sharp stab of pain from the crown.

Startled, Elidor jumped forward into the silver light of the moon, reaching to draw his daggers from their sheaths.

The Defiler stood where the figure in his dream image of Taeloc had been, leathery robes black and covered in cloying ash. The clearing was disjointed in Elidor's mind, overlaid both with the silver light of the moon and the blinding radiance of the Taeloc sun. The mine opening was an ivory arch; the wind in the forest trees whispered, echoing the distant noises of peasants and children on a busy city street.

"Just be," he murmured to himself. "Just . . . be."

Vael knelt on the ground before the shrouded figure, leaning heavily on her short spear even as ash choked her breath. Elidor could see her fighting not to scream again, the sound dying on her lips. She fought, resisting the lich's magic with her last ounce of will. Around her, his friends lay on the ground—some unconscious,

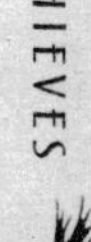

others writhing and whimpering in pain, their bodies encircled by rings of char and ash.

The Defiler lifted fiery eyes from his prey, seeing Elidor in the cave. *"At last . . . "*

Elidor dropped one of his daggers on the ground scornfully, keeping only the one that Kaja had treated with gold. He tried to look beyond the dark night, see through the forest to Taeloc's gracefully spired skyline. It flickered in his mind, but the trip through the stone had made him weary, and Elidor struggled to focus his thoughts. "It's not your crown anymore, Defiler," Elidor snarled. "Leave us alone."

"The crown has always been mine. It will always be mine. Give it to me, or you will see her die."

"Don't do it, Elidor," Vael spat through gritted teeth. "Don't give in to him."

"You killed innocent people," Elidor snarled. "You destroyed Aerendor. I won't let you have Vael!" Elidor bared his dagger before his face, staring out over the gold-tinged blade into the lich's fiery eyes. "You can't do anything to me, Defiler. The Crown of Thieves prevents you."

Elidor saw the spirit of the crown suddenly standing in the clearing. The girl in white bowed down next to Vael, pressing her spectral arms around the baroness. Vael let out a shuddering breath as the pain eased for a second, the spirit protecting her from the Defiler's wrath.

"You dare defy me!" The defiler gestured, and the spirit screamed. She twisted, trying to hold on to Vael and offer some shelter from the Defiler's magic. *"You must obey!"*

She fell back from the onslaught. In a moment, she was gone, her body ripping away like paper in a strong wind.

Elidor felt the crown grow warm against his brow. "Get away from her," he yelled, racing forward toward his opponent.

"You cannot harm me. I am more than you can ever know," the Defiler roared.

"You are nothing but a memory." Elidor struggled, focusing his entire being within the crown, and fixed his thoughts on the image of an ivory arch. It flickered, twisted in his mind to black ash, and he fought it.

Elidor stumbled back as ash flowed around him. He grasped the trunk of a nearby tree, fighting to keep his footing. He struggled to breathe despite the ash that twisted around his body.

"Give me the crown." The Defiler slid along the ground, his movements leaving no mark on the mossy forest floor. "Or she dies a more horrible death than you can imagine."

The ash around the lich's hand swirled like a serpent, rushing down his arm into Vael's mouth. She choked.

"Vael!" Elidor screamed, lunging forward. For an instant, his mind was clear. The ivory arch swirled above him, the tree and the bubbling fountain close behind. The Defiler stood before him, not as the specter that held Vael, but as an elven king within an elven city.

He was tall and of noble bearing. Dark brown hair was pulled into a ponytail high on his head, the soft waves decorated with a thin cord of pearl and jade. He wore black, standing out against the pale white of the city wall and arches, long leather vest sweeping the ground as he turned to meet Elidor's attack. His hand clenched, and in the other world, Elidor half saw and half sensed that Vael was suffocating. He heard her choking, her throat filled with black ash, her lungs desperately trying to breathe.

Elidor thrust the dagger forward. At the last minute, the Defiler twisted aside as if recognizing the danger—but the dagger sank to its very hilt into his flesh.

"Give me the crown." The Defiler grasped the dagger's pommel, his fingers wrapping tightly around Elidor's own, and began to

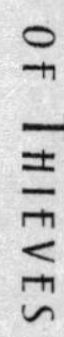

pull. Smoothly, he drew the blade from his flesh, forcing Elidor's hand away. The knife slid out, but Elidor was trapped, his knuckles crushed in the Defiler's iron grip. "Name your price, Elidor. Anything on Krynn, and it can be yours. Or keep the crown . . . and lose her." The Defiler tightened his hand, and Vael's eyes rolled back into her head, fighting a losing battle against unconsciousness.

The world shifted, flipping to the darkness of the cave, forest, and night. The Defiler's tattered robes fluttered, leathery skin covering an outstretched bony arm, clawed fingers tearing at the air. One hand was still tight in the Defiler's grip, but Elidor raised the other with a cat's quickness.

Elidor snaked his hand beneath the lip of the Defiler's hood. He tore it back, revealing a face of bone protruding from beneath stretched, worn skin. Ivory jawbones moved sickeningly under a face that was torn and yellowed like aged parchment.

"I have placed my greatest curse within her. Death is now a shadow in her soul. She has one year—only one year to the day—and she will die. You cannot save her. No one can help her. The crown has given you life, it is true, but you will purchase your life with hers. And when she dies, she will become one of my servants, a shell of herself. Perhaps, if I am pleased with her, I will even make her my queen."

The Defiler's voice sounded of sand scraping over glass, a sickly amused laugh rippling through the words. "Are you ready to pay the price for your life, Elidor?"

But at that moment, Solinari's light struck the distended flesh. It began to hiss and steam. The Defiler howled, releasing Vael from his magical grip. Still choking, she writhed at his feet, her hands clenched around her throat as if trying to force air into her lungs. Vael's pale face was greenish in the moonlight, her ice-blue eyes touched with a red rim of anguish.

The Defiler fought to get away from Elidor, reaching up to grasp the tattered leather hood and pull it back over his head. He released Elidor's hand, lunging backward into the shadow of the forest.

The world shifted, and Elidor's perspective changed between the shadow world of Taeloc and the solid reality of the mountain. Now, in Taeloc, Elidor could see the Defiler as the elven king. He scowled down at Elidor, his face pale and glowing in ages-dead moonlight. The elven king's noble features were a mockery of the pitted, decayed face that Elidor remembered behind the lich's robes. The Defiler, cruelty marking his every feature and motion, stood on the shadowy city road with blood streaming down his pale forehead.

"Not everything has a price." Elidor rammed the dagger forward once more, feeling it bite deep. "Especially not *me*."

Screaming from the touch of Solinari's light and the bite of the golden dagger, the lich fell back. "You cannot defy me forever, Elidor. Wherever you go, whatever you do, so long as the crown is upon your brow . . . "

His body changed, losing form and substance, ash pouring out of flapping leather sleeves. Black soot obscured Elidor's vision, but he kept pushing, driving the dagger deeper into the Defiler's flesh, feeling the tip scrape against the back of the leather robes.

" . . . I will be with you . . . "

Then the Defiler exploded into a cloud of ash and sulphur, his scream chasing the moonlight into the sky. Elidor thought he caught a glimpse of a spectral form darting up toward the clouds, abandoning the flesh before him. The leather robes collapsed, expelling ash across the forest floor. The torn remnants hung from Elidor's dagger, draping over his arm where he had stabbed the Defiler's chest. Elidor jumped, shaking his arm and dropping the dagger, robes and all, as if it were a snake that would bite him. More ash poured out as the robes fell to the ground, covering Elidor's boots in a light coating of black char.

"Is it over?" The voice was Kelenthe's. Pain laced her tone, but her voice was strong. "Is he gone?"

Elidor looked around the clearing. His fingers felt stiff and cold, as though he had plunged them into an icy mountain stream. The crown felt heavy on his brow.

Elidor turned to Kelenthe, opening his mouth to answer her, but no words came out. They were all moving now—Catriona, pushing herself up toward Rohawn; Kaja, renewing her prayers over the youth's fallen body; Kelenthe, Sindri, Rina, all of them opening their eyes and lifting themselves from the ground as the pain of the Defiler's spell left them.

Only Vael, lying silent and unmoving beneath a thick layer of ash, did not rise.

CHAPTER

21 A Cold, Still Dawn

Gerhalt stood in the doorway of the hearthstead, his face as gray as the foggy dawn. Elidor watched him, not wanting to say anything to break the silence, aware that Catriona still stood behind him against the bridge. She had not moved since they reached the village, standing cold and silent like a watchful statue at the river's edge.

Kaja and Elyana were inside with Vael.

There had been fog since long before the horizon was touched with light. It hung low over Tarrent, clinging to the river and the buildings, blocking Elidor's view of everything save the bridge and the hearthstead. Sindri kicked his feet off the edge of the bridge into the water, the splashing muffled in the morning mist.

"She'll be fine, for now. But there is a sickness in her lungs. I believe it will spread. Kaja says she's never seen anything like it." Kelenthe sat down on the steps of the hearthstead beside Elidor, brushing aside the coating of dirt that covered the stairs. There were boot prints on the ground all around them showing the signs of the battle two nights before. Occasionally, Elidor could hear the lilting shout of a villager returning home. Tarrent was safe. All of the undead soldiers that had not followed Gieden into the woods fell to ash when the Defiler left.

And just like that, there was nothing more to fight.

"Elidor?" Rohawn squatted down near Catriona's feet, wincing as he touched the bandages around his broad chest. "Kaja will help her. Don't worry about Vael."

But Elidor did worry. He remembered every step through the forest, carrying Vael in his arms. Kaja's magic glowed around Vael's pale skin, fighting the ash that slowly filled her lungs. When they reached Tarrent, Gerhalt took her from him. Elidor stood on the step of the hearthstead empty armed and watched them go inside.

Catriona said nothing, her eyes soft and sad. She understood. Elidor tried not to stare back and forth between the river and the door, but he couldn't help wondering when it would open and someone would come to tell him that Vael was dead.

The door to the hearthstead moved, swinging on its hinges with a creak that sounded like a mournful sigh. Elidor leaped to his feet, feeling the blood drain from his face.

Juggling a tray of food, Rina slipped out onto the steps. "My mother wants you all to eat." She handed them each a bowl of porridge, forcing the last one into Elidor's hands. "You better listen to her, or she'll have my hide."

Elidor sank down onto the stairs again, the bowl cooling in his hand. "I'm not hungry."

"I'm sure nobody is. But I don't particularly care." Rina sounded too much like her mother. Elidor grumbled and stuck his spoon into the bowl. Rina flopped down onto the stair between Elidor and Kelenthe, wriggling them apart.

Shoveling some of the food into her mouth, Rina mumbled, "I didn't think we'd ever be able to eat breakfast again."

"Me neither," Rohawn agreed. "I'm not sure I'll be able to sleep

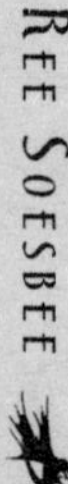

a whole night again. I just keep thinking that they're coming back."

"Not anytime soon," said Elidor. "The Defiler's injured. He's gone. His men are dead."

"But he still wants the crown," Kelenthe replied warily. "I don't care if he's injured, Elidor. He's also undead. He'll gather his power and return. No, that's not the last of the Defiler." The bard spooned her porridge disinterestedly. "We'll see him again."

"Oh boy," Rohawn muttered sarcastically, sinking lower into his meal.

"I have to go back to Aerendor and let them know that they're safe. I'm sure Fallerian is rebuilding the town. Someone has to be there to talk sense into them." Rina chewed thoughtfully. "Maybe I'll even go visit the Kagonesti. This whole thing has left me thinking that I've grown up with only one side of the story. I want to see the world—and make up my own mind."

Rohawn started to say something, but stopped. He sank lower on the step, toying with his food and not looking up at the elven girl.

"I'll miss you," he muttered shyly. Rina looked surprised, then smiled.

Suddenly the door to the hearthstead opened. Kaja stood just beyond, in the darkness of the hearthstead, her face drawn and wan. Elidor jumped to his feet again. His bowl of porridge tumbled to the ground, but he didn't care.

Kaja was drying her hands on a piece of linen, twisting it back and forth between her fingers.

"She wants to see you," Kaja said to Elidor at last, glancing around at everyone else. "But just you. Alone. Then she needs to rest."

Elidor followed her quickly, ignoring the worried stares of his companions. The door to the great building closed behind him with a solid thump, shutting him off from the world outside.

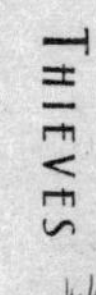

A fire roared in the tremendous hearth, crackling with a warmth and merriment that Elidor did not feel. He followed Kaja through the room toward a bed of furs that had been laid near the fire. His mother, Elyana, stood at her place by the fire as they approached. She met them halfway, taking Elidor's hand.

"Are you all right, my son?" she asked.

"How's Vael?" he countered.

Elyana and Kaja exchanged a concerned glance.

Elyana squeezed Elidor's hand. "I'm going to stay on as seneschal for a while. Gerhalt is trained to be a guard, not an administrator. Tarrent needs leadership, and in her condition, Vael can't do it by herself."

"What about Aerendor?"

"I think the Silvanesti can get along without me." Elyana forced slight humor into her tone. "Call it returning to my roots, my son. What I left undone among the Kagonesti, I'm going to make up for here. I once wanted to help people, share my knowledge and learn theirs. I can do that in Tarrent. This is where I am needed. Rina said she wanted to go home again. I'll let her explain to Fallerian why I've stayed."

"And Vael?" Elidor swallowed painfully, his throat tightening.

"She's waiting for you," Kaja interjected gently. "Go on."

The two women remained where they were as Elidor went on toward the fire. There, on a pile of furs arranged to be a bed, Vael rested. Her white hair spilled down over the covers, her back propped up on a pillow so that she could see him. When she smiled at him, Elidor felt his chest loosen and realized he had been holding his breath.

"Vael." He knelt down beside her. Her fingers interlaced with his, and he could see the blue veins on the back of her hand. Her skin was pale, as white as snow on the mountains, and her lips were stained with a strange blackish tinge.

"What did he do to you?" he choked out.

"Kaja says," Vael spoke softly, her voice cultured and even, "that I'm cursed."

Elidor whispered numbly, "But . . . there has to be an antidote."

Her face fell, and the baroness turned her head. She stared resignedly into the fire. "Maybe there was, before the Cataclysm, when Taeloc was a city and the Defiler learned his magic. But who would know such a thing now?"

"The Defiler said we had a year to find a cure. I'll go to Palanthas, to Solamnia, or Qualinost, or . . . " Elidor squeezed her hand. "Somewhere. Anywhere."

Vael coughed, her body shaking. For a moment, Elidor thought he could see a faint wisp of ash float up between her lips. She squeezed his fingers, her blue eyes meeting his. She coughed again, her body wracked with the effort of it. Her eyelids drooped lightly, and her head sank back into the pillows.

"I'm tired . . . " Vael whispered.

"Sleep." He placed her hand beside her body, slipping his fingers from Vael's soft grasp. For a moment, he stood over her, wanting to protect her from all dangers. His hands touched his daggers, but he felt useless, inept, powerless to stop the poison that raced through her veins.

Elidor turned on his heel, striding across the great meeting hall. He passed Kaja and Elyana without a word and threw open the oak doors at the far end of the chamber. The fog outside was fading, a victim of the first light of dawn. Below him, Elidor could see his other friends and the village of Tarrent drifting into focus as the mist receded and was gone. Closing his eyes, he felt the wetness of the morning, the cold, misty breeze touching his face. Kelenthe turned to face him, Rohawn and Rina staring up from the stairway below. Catriona's face was filled with concern, her hand falling

on Sindri's shoulder. The kender looked up from the water, his kicking feet falling still.

"What do we do now, Elidor?" Sindri asked, breaking the silence.

Elidor looked up at the rising sun. "We'll find a way to save her. Somehow . . . " He let the rest of his sentence die away, but the rest remained in his thoughts long after the morning mist faded.

I'll find a way to save her, he thought. *No matter what the cost.*

The story continues in . . .

THE CRYSTAL CHALICE

ELIDOR TRILOGY, VOLUME TWO

by Ree Soesbee

As the Defiler's curse holds Vael's health hostage, Elidor searches for a way to rescue her without succumbing to the evil wizard's demands.

Somewhere within the lost city of Taeloc, a crystal chalice may hold the answers to his prayers. A group of shady mercenaries offers to protect Elidor on the journey and give him the chalice, in exchange for his help in locating the city. Desperate to save his love, Elidor reluctantly agrees.

But nothing goes exactly as planned . . .

Available March 2006

THE NEW ADVENTURES

JOIN A GROUP OF FRIENDS AS THEY UNLOCK MYSTERIES OF THE DRAGONLANCE® WORLD!

TEMPLE OF THE DRAGONSLAYER
Tim Waggoner

Nearra has lost all memory of who she is. With newfound friends, she ventures to an ancient temple where she may uncover her past. Visions of magic haunt her thoughts. And someone is watching.

THE DYING KINGDOM
Stephen D. Sullivan

In a near-forgotten kingdom, an ancient evil lurks. As Nearra's dark visions grow stronger, her friends must fight for their lives.

THE DRAGON WELL
Dan Willis

Battling a group of bandits, the heroes unleash the mystic power of a dragon well. And none of them will ever be the same.

RETURN OF THE SORCERESS
Tim Waggoner

When Nearra and her friends confront the wizard who stole her memory, their faith in each other is put to the ultimate test.

For ages 10 and up

THE NEW ADVENTURES

THE DRAGON QUARTET

The companions continue their quest to save Nearra.

DRAGON SWORD

Ree Soesbee

It's a race against time as the companions seek to prevent Asvoria from reclaiming her most treacherous weapon.

DRAGON DAY

Stan Brown

As Dragon Day draws near, Catriona and Sindri stand as enemies, on opposing sides of a feud between the most powerful wizards and clerics in Solamnia.

DRAGON KNIGHT

Dan Willis

With old friends and new allies by his side, Davyn must enlist the help of the dreaded Dragon Knight.

DRAGON SPELL

Jeff Sampson

The companions reunite in their final battle with Asvoria to reclaim Nearra's soul.

Ask for Dragonlance: the New Adventures books at your favorite bookstore!

For ages ten and up.

For more information visit www.mirrorstonebooks.com

Knights of the Silver Dragon™

A young thief.

A wizard's apprentice.

A 12 year-old boy.

Meet the Knights of the Silver Dragon!

Secret of the Spiritkeeper

Matt Forbeck

Can Moyra, Kellach, and Driskoll unlock the secret of the spiritkeeper in time to rescue their beloved wizard friend?

Riddle in Stone

Ree Soesbee

Will the knights unravel the statue's riddle before more people turn to stone?

Sign of the Shapeshifter

Dale Donovan

Can Kellach and Driskoll find the shapeshifter before he ruins their father?

Eye of Fortune

Denise Graham

Does the fortuneteller's prophecy spell doom for the knights? Or unheard-of treasure?

For ages 8 to 12

More adventures for the

Figure in the Frost

A cold snap hits Curston and a mysterious stranger holds the key to the town's survival. But first he wants something...from Moyra. Will Moyra sacrifice her secret to save the town?

Dagger of Doom

When Kellach discovers a dagger of doom with his own name burned in the blade, it seems certain someone wants him dead. But who?

The Hidden Dragon

The Knights must find the silver dragon who gave their order its name. Can they make it to the dragon's lair alive?

EXPLORE THE MYSTERIES OF CURSTON WITH KELLACH, DRISKOLL AND MOYRA

THE SILVER SPELL

Kellach and Driskoll's mother, missing for five years, miraculously comes home. Is it a dream come true? Or is it a nightmare?

KEY TO THE GRIFFON'S LAIR

Will the Knights unlock the hidden crypt before Curston crumbles?

CURSE OF THE LOST GROVE

The Knights spend a night at the Lost Grove Inn. Can they discover the truth behind the inn's curse before it discovers them?

Ask for KNIGHTS OF THE SILVER DRAGON books at your favorite bookstore!

For ages eight to twelve

For more information visit www.mirrorstonebooks.com